Praise for Håkan Nesser

THE MIND'S EYE

'Veeteren is a terrific character, and the courtroom
scenes that begin this novel are cracking'
Daily Telegraph

'An Inspector Van Veeteren mystery which delivers an
ingenious plot, good characters and an excellent translation
from the original Swedish. Recommended'
Book Bag

'Håkan Nesser's Chief Inspector Van Veeteren has earned
his place among the great Swedish detectives with a series
of intriguing investigations . . . This is Van Veeteren at his
quirkiest and most engaging, revealing flashes of sardonic
humour as he pushes his reluctant staff to follow his hunch'
Seven magazine, *Sunday Telegraph*

THE RETURN

'Nesser made a strong impression with
Borkmann's Point, the first of his novels published
into English. *The Return* is just as tense and clever'
Marcel Berlins, *The Times*

'Nesser's insight into his main characters and
gently humorous narrative raise his otherwise
conventional police procedural to a higher level'
Sunday Telegraph

The Mind's Eye

Håkan Nesser was awarded the 1993 Swedish Crime Writers' Academy Prize for new authors for his novel *The Mind's Eye* (published in Sweden as *The Wide-Mesh Net*); he received the best novel award in 1994 for *Borkmann's Point* and in 1996 for *Woman with Birthmark*. In 1999 he was awarded the Crime Writers of Scandinavia's Glass Key Award for the best crime novel of the year for *Carambole*. His novels have been published to acclaim in nine countries. Nesser was born in Sweden, where he lives with his wife and two sons.

ALSO BY HÅKAN NESSER

Borkmann's Point
The Return
Woman with Birthmark

The Mind's Eye

AN INSPECTOR VAN VEETEREN MYSTERY

Håkan Nesser

Translated from the Swedish by Laurie Thompson

PAN BOOKS

First published in Sweden 1993 as *Det grovmaskiga nätet*
by Albert Bonniers Forlag, Stockholm

First published in English 2008 by Pantheon Books,
a division of Random House, Inc., New York

First published in Great Britain 2008 by Macmillan

This paperback edition first published 2009 by Pan Books
an imprint of Pan Macmillan, a division of Macmillan Publishers Limited
Pan Macmillan, 20 New Wharf Road, London N1 9RR
Basingstoke and Oxford
Associated companies throughout the world
www.panmacmillan.com

ISBN 978-0-330-49278-2

7 9 8

A CIP catalogue record for this book is available
from the British Library.

Printed and bound in the UK by
CPI Mackays, Chatham ME5 8TD

Visit **www.panmacmillan.com** to read more about all our books
and to buy them. You will also find features, author interviews and
news of any author events, and you can sign up for e-newsletters
so that you're always first to hear about our new releases.

When we finally find what we have been looking for in the darkness, we nearly always discover that it was exactly that.

Darkness.

— C.G. Reinhart, police officer

I

Saturday, 5 October–
Friday, 22 November

I

He woke up and was unable to remember his name.

His pains were legion. Shafts of fire whirled round in his head and throat, his stomach and chest. He tried to swallow, but it remained an attempt. His tongue was glued to his soft palate. Burning, smouldering.

His eyes were throbbing. Threatening to grow out of their sockets.

It's like being born, he thought. I'm not a person. Merely a mass of suffering.

The room was in darkness. He groped round with his free hand, the one that was not numb and tingling underneath him.

Yes, there was a bedside table. A telephone and a glass. A newspaper. An alarm clock.

He picked it up, but halfway it slipped through his fingers and fell onto the floor. He fumbled around, took hold of it again and held it up, close to his face.

The hands were slightly luminous. He recognized them.

Twenty past eight. Presumably in the morning.

He still had no idea who he was.

. . .

He didn't think this had happened before. He had certainly woken up and not known where he was. Or what day it was. But his name . . . Had he ever forgotten his name?

John? Janos?

No, but something like that.

It was there, somewhere in the background, not only his name, but everything . . . Life and lifestyle and extenuating circumstances. Lying there waiting for him. Behind a thin membrane that would have to be pierced, something that had not woken up yet. But he was not really worried. He would know soon enough.

Perhaps it was not something to look forward to.

The pain behind his eyes suddenly got worse. Possibly the strain of thinking had caused it; but it was there, whatever. White-hot and excruciating. A scream of flesh.

Nothing else mattered.

The kitchen was to the left and seemed familiar. He found the tube of tablets without difficulty; he was becoming increasingly sure that this was his home. No doubt everything would become clear at any moment.

He went back into the hall. Kicked against a bottle standing in the shadow cast by a bookcase. It rolled away over the parquet floor and ended up under the radiator. He shuffled to the bathroom. Pressed down the handle.

It was locked.

He leaned awkwardly forward. Put his hands on his knees to support himself, and checked the indicator.

Red. As he'd thought. It was occupied.

He could feel the bile rising.

'Open . . .' he tried to shout, but could produce no more than a croak. He leaned his forehead against the cool wood of the door.

'Open up!' he tried again, and this time managed to produce the right sounds, almost. To stress the seriousness of his situation, he banged several times with his clenched fists.

No response. Not a sound. Whoever was in there obviously had no intention of letting him in.

There was a sudden surge from his stomach. Or possibly from even lower down . . . It was obviously a matter of seconds now. He staggered back along the hall. Into the kitchen.

This time it seemed more familiar than ever.

This is definitely my home, he thought as he vomited into the sink.

With the aid of a screwdriver he succeeded in unlocking the bathroom door. He had a distinct feeling that it was not the first time he'd done this.

'I'm sorry, but I really had to . . .'

He entered the room and, just as he switched on the light, he became quite clear about who he was.

He could also identify the woman lying in the bath.

Her name was Eva Ringmar and she was his wife of three months.

Her body was strangely twisted. Her right arm hung over the edge at an unnatural angle. The well-manicured fingernails reached right down to the floor. Her dark hair was floating on the water. Her head was face-down, and as the bath was full to the brim there could be no doubt that she was dead.

His own name was Mitter. Janek Mattias Mitter. A teacher of history and philosophy at the Bunge High School in Maardam.

Known informally as JM.

After these insights he vomited again, this time into the lavatory. Whereupon he took two more tablets out of the tube and telephoned the police.

2

The cell was L-shaped and green. The same shade all over –
walls, floor and ceiling. A hint of daylight seeped in through a
small window high up on one wall. At night he could see
a star.

There was an ablutions corner with a handbasin and WC.
A bed fixed to the wall. A rickety table with two chairs. A ceiling light. A bedside lamp.

For the rest, noises and silence. The only smell was from
his own body.

The lawyer's name was Rüger. He was tall and lopsided, limping on his left leg. As far as Mitter could judge, he was in his
fifties; a few years older than himself. He might have come
across the man's son at school. He may even have taught him.
A pale youth with a spotty face, and not the brightest of pupils
academically, if he remembered correctly. Some eight or ten
years ago.

Rüger shook hands. Squeezed Mitter's proffered hand
tightly and lengthily, and looked serious, but also benevolently
disposed. It was obvious to Mitter that he had attended
courses on lawyer–client relations.

'Janek Mitter?'

Mitter nodded.

'A nasty business.'

He wriggled out of his overcoat. Shook water off it and hung it on the hook by the door. The warder double-locked it before going away down the corridor.

'It's raining out there. Much pleasanter in here, to be honest.'

'Have you got a cigarette?'

Rüger produced a pack from his jacket pocket.

'Take as many as you like. I don't understand why they won't even let you smoke.'

He sat down at the table. Put his thin leather briefcase in front of him. Mitter lit a cigarette, but remained standing.

'Aren't you going to sit down?'

'No, thank you.'

'Up to you.'

He opened a brown folder. Took out some typewritten pages and a notepad. Removed and replaced the cap of a ball-point pen a few times, resting his elbows on the table.

'A nasty business, as I said. I want to make it clear to you how things stand, right from the start.'

Mitter waited.

'There are a lot of things going against you. That's why it's important for you to be honest with me. If we don't have complete trust in each other, I won't be able to defend you as successfully as . . . well, are you with me?'

'Yes.'

'I assume you won't hesitate to make your views known . . .'

'Views?'

'On how we should go about things. Naturally, I shall work out the strategies, but you are the one at the sharp end. As far as I can make out, you are an intelligent man.'

'I understand.'

'Good. Would you like to tell me about it, or would you prefer me to ask questions?'

Mitter stubbed out his cigarette in the washbasin, and sat down at the table. The nicotine had made him a bit dizzy, and he was suddenly overcome by a feeling of weariness.

He felt tired of life. Of this hunchbacked lawyer, of the incredibly ugly cell, of the nasty taste in his mouth and of all the inevitable questions and answers in store for him.

Extreme weariness.

'I've already been through everything with the police. I've spent two days doing nothing else.'

'I know, but I have to ask you to do it again. It's an essential part of the game, as I'm sure you realize.'

Mitter shrugged. Shook another cigarette out of the pack.

'I think it would be best if you asked questions.'

The lawyer leaned back. Rocked back on his chair and adjusted the notepad on his knee.

'Most lawyers use a tape recorder, but I prefer to make notes,' he explained. 'I think it's less stressful for the client . . .'

Mitter nodded.

'Besides, I have access to the police tapes, if I should need them. Anyway, before we start going into details, I have to ask you the obligatory question. You will probably be charged with murder, or at the very least manslaughter, of your wife, Eva Maria Ringmar. How do you intend to plead? Guilty or not guilty?'

'Not guilty.'

'Good. There should be no doubt on that point. Neither on your side, nor mine.'

He paused and rolled the pen between his fingers.

'Is there any doubt?'

Mitter sighed.

'I have to ask you to answer my question. Are you absolutely certain that you didn't kill your wife?'

Mitter paused for a few seconds before answering. Tried to catch the lawyer's eye in an attempt to deduce what he really thought, but in vain. Rüger's face was as inscrutable as a potato.

'No, of course I'm not certain. You know that full well.'

The lawyer made a note.

'Mr Mitter, I must ask you to disregard the fact that I have read the transcript of your interrogation. You must try to pretend that you are now telling your story for the first time. Put yourself in that situation.'

'I don't remember.'

'No, I have grasped the fact that you don't remember what happened: that is precisely why we have to be meticulous about starting again from scratch. Your memory will not wake up if you don't try to go back to that night. Totally without prejudice. Don't you agree?'

'What do you think I spend my time doing? What do you imagine I think about in this cell?'

He was starting to get angry. The lawyer avoided looking him in the eye and made a note on his pad.

'What are you writing?'

'Sorry.'

He shook his head to indicate that was not something he was prepared to reveal. Took a handkerchief from his pocket and blew his nose loudly.

'Bloody awful weather,' he explained.

Mitter nodded.

'I just want you to understand,' said Rüger, 'what a precarious situation you find yourself in. You maintain that you are not guilty, but you don't remember. That is rather an insecure foundation on which to build a case for your defence, as I'm sure you realize.'

'It's the prosecutor's job to prove that I'm guilty. It's not up to me to prove the opposite, isn't that right?'

'Of course. That's the law, but . . .'

'But?'

'If you don't remember, you don't remember. But it could be rather difficult to convince a jury. Will you undertake to inform me the moment anything comes back to you?'

'Of course.'

'No matter what it is?'

'Naturally.'

'Let's go on. How long had you known Eva Ringmar?'

'Two years. Almost two years. Ever since she started working at our school.'

'Where you teach what?'

'History and philosophy. Mainly history. Most pupils don't choose to study philosophy.'

'How long have you been in post there?'

'Twenty years, roughly. Maybe nineteen.'

'And your wife?'

'Modern languages. For two years, as I said.'

'When did you start your relationship?'

'Six months ago. We got married last summer, at the beginning of July.'

'Was she pregnant?'

'No. Why . . .'

'Do you have any children, Mr Mitter?'

'Yes. A son and a daughter.'

'How old?'

'Twenty and sixteen. They live with their mother in Chadow.'

'When were you divorced from your former wife?'

'In 1980. Jürg lived with me until he started at university. I don't see what this has to do with . . .'

'Background. I need some kind of background. Even a lawyer has to solve puzzles, as I'm sure you'll agree. What kind of a relationship do you have with your ex-wife?'

'None at all.'

There was a pause. Rüger blew his nose again. He was obviously dissatisfied about something, but Mitter had no desire to pander to him. Irene had nothing to do with this. Nor did Jürg and Inga. He was grateful for the fact that all three had the good sense not to become involved. They'd been in touch, of course, but only that first day. Since then they'd been quiet. He'd received a letter from Inga that very morning, but only a couple of lines. To express support for him.

We are with you. Inga and Jürg.

He wondered if the same applied to Irene as well. Was she with him? Perhaps it didn't matter.

'What sort of a relationship did you have?'

'Excuse me?'

'Your marriage with Eva Ringmar. What was it like?'

'Like marriages are.'

'What does that mean?'

'...'

'Was it a happy marriage, or did you fight?'

'...'

'After all, you'd only been married for three months.'

'Yes, that's correct.'

'And then you found your wife dead in the bath. Surely you understand that we have to find an explanation?'

'Yes, of course.'

'Do you also understand that it's no good your not saying anything about this matter? Your silence would be taken as indicating that you were concealing something. It would be used against you.'

'I expect it would.'

'Did you love your wife?'

'Yes.'

'Did you fight?'

'Occasionally.'

Rüger made a note.

'The prosecutor will claim that she was killed. He will be supported by evidence from medical and technical specialists. We shan't be able to prove that she died a natural death. The question is whether she could have taken her own life.'

'Yes, I assume so.'

'You assume what?'

'That it depends on that. If she could have taken her own life.'

'Perhaps. Anyway, that evening – how much did you drink?'

'Quite a lot.'

'Meaning what?'

'I can't say for sure . . .'

'How much do you need to drink before losing your memory, Mr Mitter?'

He was obviously irritated now. Mitter pushed his chair back. Stood up and walked over to the door. Put his hands in his pockets and contemplated the lawyer's hunched back. Waited. But Rüger said nothing.

'I don't know,' Mitter said eventually. 'I've tried to work it out. Empty bottles and so on, you know. Presumably six or seven bottles.'

'Red wine?'

'Yes, red wine. Nothing else.'

'Six or seven bottles between two people? Were you alone all evening?'

'Yes, as far as I recall.'

'Do you have an alcohol problem, Mr Mitter?'

'No.'

'Would you be surprised if other people took a different view?'

'Yes.'

'What about your wife?'

'What do you mean?'

'Is it not true to say that she was admitted . . .' He pored over his papers and leafed through them. '. . . admitted to an institution for what is commonly known as drying out? In Rejmershus? I have the details here.'

'Why are you asking, then? It's six years ago. She lost a child, and her marriage broke down.'

'I know, I know. Forgive me, Mr Mitter, but I have to ask these questions, no matter how unpleasant they may seem. It will be much worse at your trial, I can assure you of that. You might as well get used to it.'

'Thank you, I'm already used to it.'

'Can we go on?'

'Of course.'

'What is your last clear memory from that night? That you can be absolutely certain about?'

'That casserole . . . We had a Mexican casserole. I've told the police about it.'

'Say it again!'

'We had this Mexican casserole. In the kitchen.'

'Yes?'

'We started to make love.'

'Did you tell the police that?'

'Yes.'

'Go on!'

'What do you want to know? The details?'

'Everything you can remember.'

Mitter returned to the table. Lit a cigarette and leaned

towards the lawyer. Might as well give him it good and proper, this hunchbacked pen-pusher.

'Eva was wearing a kimono. Nothing underneath. As we were eating, I started caressing her. We drank as well, of course, and she undressed me. Partly, at least. Eventually I lifted her up onto the table . . .'

He paused briefly. The lawyer had stopped making notes.

'I lifted her onto the table, pulled off her kimono and screwed her. I think she screamed – not because it hurt, but from sensual bliss, of course: she used to do that when we made love. I think we kept going for quite a long time. Continued eating and drinking as well. I know I poured wine over her pussy and then licked it off.'

'Wine on her pussy?'

Rüger's voice was suddenly muted.

'Yes. Was there anything else you'd like to know?'

'Is that the last thing you can remember?'

'I think so.'

Rüger cleared his throat. Took out his handkerchief and blew his nose again.

'What time do you think that would have been?'

'I've no idea.'

'Not even roughly?'

'No. It could have been any time between nine and two. I never looked at the clock.'

'I understand. Why should you?'

Rüger started gathering together his papers.

'Might I suggest that you refrain from going into too much detail of the, er, love-making, if the matter is raised in court. I think it could be misinterpreted.'

'No doubt.'

'Incidentally, there was no trace of sperm . . . Er, I expect you are aware that rather detailed examinations are made . . .'

'Yes, the chief inspector explained that. No, I never came. I suppose that's one of the effects of the wine. Or advantages perhaps, depending on how you look at it. Isn't that so, Mr Rüger?'

'Hmm. I take it you know that the time has been established?'

'What time?'

'The time of death. Not precisely, of course, that's virtually never possible. But some time between four and half past five.'

'I got up at twenty past eight.'

'We know that.'

He stood up. Adjusted his tie and buttoned up his jacket.

'I think that will be enough for today. Thank you very much. I'll be back tomorrow with some more questions. I hope you will be cooperative.'

'Haven't I been cooperative today?'

'Yes, very.'

'Can I keep the cigarettes?'

'Please do. May I ask one final question, which might be a little bit, er, uncomfortable?'

'Of course.'

'I think it's important. I don't want you to be casual about your answer.'

'No?'

'If you don't want to say anything, I shall understand completely, but I think it's important that you are honest with yourself. Anyway: are you quite sure that you really do want to remember what happened, or would you prefer not to know?'

Mitter did not answer. Rüger avoided looking at him.

'I'm shoulder to shoulder with you. I hope you realize that.'

Mitter nodded. Rüger rang the bell, and a few seconds later the warder appeared and let him out. Rüger hesitated in the doorway. Seemed to be unsure of himself.

'My son asked me to pass on greetings. Edwin. Edwin Rüger. You taught him history ten years ago, I don't know if you remember him. In any case, he liked you. You were an interesting teacher.'

'Interesting?'

'Yes, that's the word he used.'

Mitter nodded again.

'I remember him. Please pass on greetings, and thank him.'

They shook hands, and then he was alone.

3

An insect crawled up his bare right arm. A persistent little bug only a few millimetres long; he watched it, wondering where it was heading.

For the light, perhaps. He had left the bedside lamp on, even though it was the middle of the night. He found it difficult to cope with darkness, for whatever reason. This was not like him. Darkness had never been a threat as far as he was concerned, not even when he was a child. He could recall several occasions when he had attracted more admiration for daring and courage than he deserved, simply because he was not afraid of the dark. Mankel and Li had been especially impressed.

Mankel was dead now. He had no idea what had become of Li . . . It was odd that he should think of them now: he hadn't given them a thought for years and years. There were so many other things he ought to think of instead – but who can control the capricious mechanisms of memory?

He checked the clock. Half past three. Had he been dreaming?

He'd slept restlessly in any case. Perhaps something had come to him in his slumbers? In recent days he had become more and more convinced that everything would come back to him in his dreams. Nothing at all happened while he was awake; after more than a week, that night was just as much of a blank as it had been the morning after. The developer used in the darkroom was faulty, no images, not even a hint of an outline materialized on the paper. It was as if he hadn't even been there, as if nothing at all had happened after their wild love-making. The last images were clear enough: Eva's thighs opening and closing around his penis, her back arched extravagantly at the moment of ecstasy, her breasts bouncing and her nails digging into his skin . . . There was more to it than he had described to Rüger, but it was of no significance. After the embrace in the kitchen there was nothing. It was as blank as a mirror.

Like newly formed ice over dark water.

Had he simply fallen asleep? Passed out? He had been naked in bed when he woke up the next morning, dammit.

What in hell's name had happened?

Eva? He had heard her voice several times in his dreams, he was sure of that, but never any words. Never any message, just her voice. Deep, puckish, somehow alluring. He'd always been fascinated by her voice.

The flat had looked relatively tidy. Apart from the leftovers in the kitchen and the clothes on the floor, there had been no sign of untoward goings-on. A couple of full ashtrays, some half-empty glasses, the bottle in the hall. He'd cleared away what few things there were before the police arrived.

The same questions. Again and again. Over and over again. Reflecting themselves in the mirror. Bouncing like a fistful of gravel over the ice. But nothing came back to him. Nothing at all.

And even if anything had come back to him in his sleep, how the devil could he be expected to hang on to it? And not to lose track of it, as he always did?

His sleep was more irregular than ever. Never longer than an hour, often only fifteen or twenty minutes. He'd smoked the last of the cigarettes from Rüger at about two o'clock.

He'd have paid a fortune for a puff now: there was a tingling in his body that he couldn't get rid of, a sort of itch deep down under his skin that was inaccessible.

And weariness.

Weariness that came and went, and that might well have been a blessing in disguise, as it fended off other things that might have been even worse.

What was it that Rüger had wondered about?

Did he really want to know? Did he . . . ?

He felt a slight prick on his shoulder. The insect had bitten him. He hesitated for a moment before taking it between his finger and thumb and squashing it.

When he swallowed it, it felt like no more than an unchewed crumb of bread.

He turned over to face the wall. Lay there with his face pressed against the concrete, listening for sounds. All he could hear was the monotonous breathing of the air-conditioning system.

The whole of my world is going to collapse even more catastrophically, he thought. It's only a matter of time.

When the breakfast trolley arrived shortly after seven, he was still lying there in the same position. But he hadn't slept a wink.

4

Rüger's cold was no better.

'I ought to have a cognac and go to bed, but I must have a few words with you first. Have you slept well?'

Mitter shook his head.

'Have you slept at all?'

'Not a lot.'

'No, you look as if you haven't. Have you had any tablets? Some kind of tranquillizer?'

'No.'

'I'll fix that for you. We mustn't let them grind you down. I take it you don't believe that this long wait before the trial is a coincidence?'

He paused and blew his nose.

'Ah yes, the cigarettes.'

He tossed an unopened packet onto the table. Mitter tore off the cellophane and noticed that he wasn't in full control of his hands. The first puffs made everything go black before his eyes.

'Van Veeteren will come to interrogate you again this afternoon. I'd like to be present, but I'm afraid that won't be possible. But my advice is to say as little as possible. I take it you know you have a right to be silent from start to finish?'

'I thought you had advised me not to do that?'

'At the trial, yes. But not when the police question you. Just keep quiet, let them ask as many questions as they like. Or at least, just tell them that you don't remember. OK?'

Mitter nodded. He was starting to feel a degree of trust in Rüger, whether he liked it or not. He wondered if it was due to his lack of sleep, or the lawyer's increasingly bad cold.

'The stupidest thing you could possibly do is to jump to conclusions, guess things, speculate, and then be forced to retract. Every single word you utter during the interrogations will be used against you at the trial. If, for example, you suggest the chief inspector ought to kiss his own arse, you can bet your life he'll tell the jury – as an example of the kind of character you are. Would you like a cup of coffee?'

Mitter shook his head.

'OK. I'd like to talk to you about the morning.'

'The morning?'

'Yes, when you found her. There are several points that need clarification.'

'Such as?'

'Your . . . conduct after you'd phoned the police.'

'Oh?'

'You cleaned up the flat while your wife was lying dead in the bath, is that right?'

'I just tidied up a few things, that's all.'

'Don't you think that's rather odd?'

'No.'

'What exactly did you do?'

'I put some glasses away, emptied an ashtray, picked up some clothes . . .'

'Why?'

'I . . . I don't really know. I suppose I must have been a bit shocked. I didn't want to go back to the bathroom, that's for sure.'

'How long was it before the police arrived?'

'A quarter of an hour. Maybe twenty minutes.'

'Yes, that's about right. Your phone call was recorded at 08.27, and according to the report they arrived at 08.46. Nineteen minutes. What did you do with the clothes?'

'I put them in the washing machine.'

'All of them?'

'Yes. There weren't that many.'

'Where's the washing machine?'

'In the kitchen.'

'And you put everything into it?'

'Yes.'

'Did you switch it on as well?'

'Yes.'

'Do you usually take care of the laundry yourself?'

'I lived alone for ten years.'

'OK, but what about the different categories? Was the same programme really appropriate for all of them? Surely there must have been different colours and materials, and so on?'

'No, everything was dark colours.'

'So you used the colours programme?'

'Yes.'

'What temperature?'

'Forty degrees. Some should probably have had sixty, but it doesn't usually make much difference.'

There was a pause. Rüger blew his nose. Mitter lit another cigarette. His third so far. Rüger leaned back and looked up at the ceiling.

'Can't you see that all this is damned peculiar?'

'All what?'

'You doing the washing just after finding your wife dead in the bathroom.'

'I don't know. Maybe . . .'

'Or did you set the washing machine going before you called the police?'

'No, I rang right away.'

'Immediately?'

'Yes – well, I took a couple of tablets first. I had a blistering headache.'

'What else did you do while you were waiting for the police? Besides emptying the ashtray, rinsing some glasses, washing some clothes . . .?'

'I threw some leftover food into the bin. Tidied up a bit in the kitchen . . .'

'You didn't water the flowers?'

'No.'

'You didn't clean the windows?'

Mitter closed his eyes. That trust in Rüger was on hold now, he could feel that clearly. Perhaps it had only been due to the cigarettes. The one he was smoking now tasted anything but pleasant. He stubbed it out in annoyance.

'Have you ever found your wife dead in the bath, Mr Rüger? Even if not, perhaps you could inform me how one ought to behave while waiting for the police; it could be interesting to know . . .'

Rüger had fished out his handkerchief again, but paused.

'Can't you understand, for Christ's sake?'

'Understand what?'

'That your behaviour was highly suspicious, dammit. Surely you can understand how it will be interpreted. For God's sake! Washing up glasses, washing clothes! Talk about removing evidence . . .'

'You are assuming that I killed her, I gather.'

Rüger blew his nose.

'No, I'm assuming nothing. And thank God your behaviour was so idiotic that it will probably earn you more pluses than minuses.'

'What do you mean?'

'You drown your wife in the bath. Manage to lock the door from the outside. You get undressed and go to bed and forget all about it. The next morning you wake up, break into the bathroom and find her . . . You swallow a couple of pills to ease your headache, phone the police and start washing clothes . . .'

Mitter stood up and walked to his bed. He was suddenly overcome by exhaustion. He wanted nothing more than for Rüger to go away and leave him in peace.

'I didn't kill her . . .'

He stretched out on the bed.

'No; or at least, you don't think you did. You know, I think it's not impossible that the authorities might want to have you examined in order to assess your mental state. What would you have to say about that?'

'Are you saying they can't force me to do it?'

'Not unless there is sufficient reason.'

'And isn't there?'

Rüger had stood up and was putting on his overcoat.

'Hard to say . . . Hard to say. What do you think?'

'I have no idea.'

He closed his eyes and curled up facing the wall. He could hear Rüger saying something in the far distance, but his exhaustion was now a deep, swirling abyss and he allowed himself to sink down into it, offering no resistance.

5

Detective Chief Inspector Van Veeteren did not have a cold.

On the other hand, he did have a tendency to be depressed when the weather was poor, and as it had now been raining more or less non-stop for ten days, melancholy had made the most of the opportunity to sink deep roots into his mind.

He closed the door and started the car. Switched on the cassette player.

Vivaldi's mandolin concerto. As usual there was a gremlin in one of the loudspeakers. The sound came and went.

It wasn't just the rain. There were other things as well.

His wife, for instance. For the fourth or fifth time – he had lost count – she seemed to be on her way back to him. Eight months ago they had separated once and for all, but now she had started phoning again.

The point of return had not yet been reached, but it was clear which way the wind was blowing. He was pretty sure he could reckon on sharing household and bed by the run-up to Christmas, or thereabouts.

Again.

The only thing that could prevent it was for him to say no, but, needless to say, there was nothing to suggest such a development on this occasion, either.

He turned into Kloisterlaan and fished out a toothpick from his breast pocket. The rain was pounding down and the windscreen misting over again. As usual. He wiped it with the sleeve of his jacket, but for a few moments he could see nothing at all.

Death, here I come, he thought. But nothing happened. He jabbed at the air-conditioning buttons and adjusted the controls. The flow of hot air over his feet became more intense.

I ought to get a better car, he thought.

Not for the first time.

Bismarck was also ill.

Ever since his daughter Jess's twelfth birthday he had been saddled with the slow-witted Newfoundland bitch, but now all she did was lie in front of the refrigerator, sicking up foul-smelling yellowish-green lumps, and he was forced to drive home several times a day in order to clean them up.

The dog, that is. Not his daughter.

He hoped that Jess was in much better shape. She was twenty-four now, or possibly twenty-three; lived a long way away in Borges with new dogs, a husband who repaired teeth and a pair of twins who were busy learning to walk and to swear in a foreign language. He had last seen them at the beginning of the summer holidays, and felt no obligation to force himself upon them again before the New Year.

He also had a son. Erich.

Erich lived much closer. In the state prison in Linden, to be precise, where he was serving a two-year sentence for drug-smuggling. He was being well looked after, in other words. If Van Veeteren felt like it, he could visit him every day – it was just a matter of getting into the car and driving the fifteen miles or so alongside the canals, showing the warder his ID card and marching in. Erich was inside there; he had no possibility of avoiding his father, and as long as Van Veeteren took with him some cigarettes and newspapers, he generally seemed to be not entirely unwelcome.

But he sometimes wondered what was the point of sitting and staring at his long-haired crook of a son.

He wound down the window to let in a little fresh air. A shower of raindrops fell onto his thigh.

What else?

His right foot, of course.

He'd sprained it during yesterday's badminton match with Münster. 6–15, 3–15, abandoned due to injury with the score 0–6 in the third set . . . The figures told their own story, of course. This morning he'd had difficulty in getting a shoe onto that foot, and every step was agony. Oh, what joy to be alive!

He wiggled his toes tentatively, and wondered if he ought really to have gone to the X-ray department; but it was not a genuine thought, as he was well aware. He only needed to recall his father, that stoic who refused to go to hospital with double pneumonia on the grounds that it was unmanly.

He died two days later in his own bed, proud of the fact that he had not cost the health service a single penny and never allowed a drop of medicine to cross his lips.

He was fifty-two years old.

Didn't quite make his son's eighteenth birthday.

And now this high-school teacher.

Reluctantly, he turned his mind towards work. To be

honest, it wasn't just another humdrum case. On the contrary. If it hadn't been for all the rest of it, and the damned rain that never seemed to stop, he might have been forced to admit that there was a spark of excitement in it.

The fact is, he wasn't sure.

Nine times out of ten, he was. Well, even more often, if the truth be told. Van Veeteren was generally able to decide if he was looking the culprit in the eye in nineteen cases out of twenty, if not more.

No point in hiding his light under a bushel. There was always a mass of tiny little signs pointing in one direction or another, and over the years he had learned to identify and interpret these signs. Not that he was able to detect all of them, but that didn't matter. The important thing was that he could see the overall picture. The pattern.

He didn't find this difficult, and didn't need to overstretch himself.

Then finding proof, and building up a case that might hold water in court – that was another matter. But the knowledge, the certainty, always crept up on him.

Whether he liked it or not. He interpreted the signals emitted by the suspect; sometimes he found it as easy to do that as reading a book, just as a musician can pick out a tune from a mass of notes in a score, or a mathematics teacher can spot an inaccurate calculation. It was nothing special; but, of course, it was an art. Not something you could learn in the normal way, and not something it was possible to teach; just an ability that he had acquired after so many years in the force.

For Christ's sake, it was a gift, and in no way something that could be regarded as just deserts for work done.

He didn't even have the good sense to be duly grateful.

Of course he knew that he was the best interrogating officer in the district, possibly in the country; but he would have been delighted to abandon any such claim in return for being able to give Münster a sound thrashing at badminton.

Just once would be enough.

And needless to say, it was this ability of his that had motivated his promotion to detective chief inspector, despite the fact that there had been others much more interested in the post than he was, when old Mort retired.

And needless to say, that was why the chief of police kept tearing up his resignation letters and throwing them into the rubbish bin.

Van Veeteren needed to be at his post.

He had eventually reconciled himself to his fate. Perhaps that was just as well: as the years passed, he found it more and more difficult to imagine doing any other job in which he wouldn't immediately make himself impossible to work with.

Why be a depressed master gardener or bus driver when you can be a depressed detective chief inspector, as Reinhart had said in one of his more enlightened moments.

But how were things now?

In nineteen cases out of twenty he was certain.

It was the twentieth where the doubts surfaced.

What about the twenty-first?

An old rhyme came into his head.

Nineteen sweet young ladies . . .

He drummed his fingers on the steering wheel and tried to dig out the continuation from the dark recesses of his memory.

. . . aspired to be his wife?

That sounded a bit odd, but never mind. What next, then?

Nineteen sweet young ladies aspired to be his wife,
Number twenty spurned him . . .

Spurned, Van Veeteren thought? Why not?

Number twenty spurned him,
The next one took his life!

What a lot of rubbish! He spat out the toothpick and pulled up outside the police station. As usual he was forced to steel himself before getting out of the car – there was no doubt that this building was one of the three ugliest in town.

The other two were Bunge High School, from which establishment of learning he had once graduated and where Mitter was employed . . . And Klagenburg 4, the tenement building where Van Veeteren had been living for the past six years.

He opened the door and groped in the back seat for his umbrella, but then remembered that he'd left it to dry on the landing at home.

6

'Good afternoon.'

The door closed behind the chief inspector. Mitter looked away. If he excluded his former father-in-law and his colleague who taught chemistry and physics, Jean-Christophe Colmar, Van Veeteren must be the most unsympathetic person he had ever come across.

When the man sat down at the table and started chewing his ever-present toothpick, it struck Mitter that it might be an idea to admit everything. Just to get rid of him.

Just to be left in peace.

But presumably it was not as easy as that. Van Veeteren wouldn't be fooled. He sat with his bulky body crouched over the cassette recorder, looking like a threatening and malicious trough of low pressure. His face was criss-crossed by small blue veins, many of them burst, and his expression was reminiscent of a petrified bloodhound. The only thing that moved was the toothpick, which wandered slowly from one side of his mouth to the other. He could talk without moving his lips, read without moving his eyes, yawn without opening his mouth. He was much more of a mummy than a person made up of flesh and blood.

But beyond doubt a very efficient police officer.

It seemed not at all improbable that the chief inspector

would know the extent of Mitter's guilt long before Mitter himself did. Van Veeteren's voice modulated between two quarter-tones below bottom C. The higher one denoted a question, doubt or scorn. The lower one stated facts.

'So, you have not achieved any more insight,' he stated. 'Would you kindly extinguish that cigarette! I have not come here to be poisoned.'

He switched on the cassette player. Mitter stubbed out his cigarette in the washbasin. Returned to his bed and stretched out on his back.

'My lawyer has advised me not to answer any of your questions.'

'Really? Do whatever you like, I shall unmask you anyway. Six hours or twenty minutes, it makes no difference to me. I have plenty of time.'

He fell silent. Mitter listened to the air conditioning and waited. Van Veeteren did not move a muscle.

'Do you miss your wife?' he asked after several minutes.

'Of course.'

'I don't believe you.'

'I couldn't care less what you think.'

'You're lying again. If you don't care what I think, why are you telling me such idiotic lies? Use your brains, for God's sake!'

Mitter made no reply. Van Veeteren reverted to the lower quarter-tone.

'You know I'm right. You want to talk me into believing that you miss your wife. But you don't, and you know I know you don't. If you tell the truth, at least you don't have to be ashamed of yourself.'

It was not a criticism. Merely a statement of fact. Mitter said nothing. Stared up at the ceiling. Closed his eyes. Perhaps it would be as well to follow his lawyer's advice to the letter. If he didn't say a word and avoided all eye contact, no doubt it would . . .

But behind closed eyelids something different became clear.

Something different came instead and pinned him against the wall. There was always something.

Wasn't Van Veeteren right after all?

The question nagged at him.

You don't miss her, do you?

He was damned if he knew. She had entered his life. Smashed down an open door, charged forward like a dark princess and taken him into her power. Completely, totally.

Taken him, held on to him . . . and then gone away.

Is that how it was?

No doubt it could be described like that, and once he'd started putting things into words, there was no going back. Eva Ringmar turned up in the fourteenth chapter of his life. Between pages 275 and 300, roughly, she played the role that overshadowed all others: the priestess of love, the goddess of passion . . . And then she went away, would probably continue for a while to live a sort of life between the lines, but soon she would be forgotten. It had all been so intense that it was pre-ordained to come to an end. An episode to add to the plot? A sonnet? A will-o'-the-wisp?

Finished. Dead, but not mourned.

End of valediction. End of contradiction.

The chief inspector's chair scraped. Mitter gave a start. No doubt this was . . . no doubt this must be the state of shock, the paralysis, the state of shock that was driving his thoughts into such channels. That had crushed and demolished everything, made it impossible for him to grasp what had happened. To grasp what was happening to him . . . ?

'I'm right, am I not?'

Van Veeteren spat out a toothpick and took a new one from his breast pocket.

'Yes, of course. I grew tired of her and drowned her in the bath. Why should I miss her?'

'Good. Exactly what I thought. Now we'll move on to something else. She had rather a beautiful body, did she not?'

'Why do you ask that?'

'I shall ask whatever questions I like. Was she strong?'

'Strong?'

'Was she strong? Will it be easier for you if I ask each question several times?'

'Why do you want to know if she was strong?'

'In order to exclude the possibility of her having been drowned by a child or an invalid.'

'She was not especially strong.'

'How do you know? Did you fight?'

'Only when we were bored.'

'Do you have a tendency to be violent, Mr Mitter?'

'No, you don't need to be afraid.'

'Can you give me six candidates?'

'Eh?'

'Six candidates who might have murdered her, if it wasn't you who did it.'

'I've already named several possibilities.'

'I want to know if you remember the persons you mentioned.'

'I don't understand why.'

'That's irrelevant. I have no exaggerated ideas about your intelligence.'

'Thank you.'

'Don't mention it. Now I'll explain. Tell me if I'm going too fast for you. In seven out of ten cases it's the husband who kills his wife. In two out of ten it's somebody else in the circle of acquaintances.'

'And in the tenth?'

'It's an outsider. A madman or some kind of sex killer.'

'So you don't regard sex murderers as madmen?'

'Not necessarily. Well?'

'Our mutual enemies, you mean?'

'Or hers.'

'We didn't have much of a social life. I've already talked about this.'

'I know. You stopped meeting most of your so-called friends when you got together. Well? If you give me six names, you can have a cigarette! Isn't that how you do things at school?'

'Marcus Greijer.'

'Your former brother-in-law?'

'Yes.'

'Who you hate. Go on!'

'Joanna Kemp and Gert Weiss.'

'Colleagues. Languages and . . . social studies?'

'Klaus Bendiksen.'

'Status?'

'Close friend. Andreas Berger.'

'Who's he?'

'Her former husband. One more?'

Van Veeteren nodded.

'Uwe Borgmann.'

'Your neighbour?'

'Yes.'

'Greijer, Kemp, Weiss . . . Bendiksen, Berger and . . . Borgmann. Five men and a woman. Why these particular people?'

'I don't know.'

'Yesterday you gave me a list of . . .' He picked up a sheet of paper and added up rapidly. '. . . twenty-eight names. Andreas Berger is not on that list, but all the rest are. Why did you pick out this particular six?'

'Because you asked me to.'

Mitter lit a cigarette. The chief inspector's advantage was not as great now, that could be felt clearly. Although he might have slackened off a little in the hope that Mitter would give something away.

But what?

Van Veeteren glared sullenly at the cigarette and switched off the cassette recorder.

'I shall tell you how things stand. I have received the final medical report today, and it is completely out of the question that she could have killed herself. That leaves three possibilities: One! You killed her. Two! One of the people on your list did it, either one of the six whose names you have just given me, or one of the others. Three! She was the victim of an unknown murderer.'

He paused briefly, took the toothpick out of his mouth and contemplated it. Evidently it was not quite completely chewed up, so he put it back between his front teeth.

'Personally, I think it was you who did it, but I admit that I'm not quite certain.'

'Thank you very much.'

'On the other hand, I'm pretty sure that the court will find you guilty. I want you to be aware of that, and when it comes to verdicts passed in court, I am hardly ever wrong.'

He stood up. Put the cassette recorder into his briefcase and rang for the warder.

'If this lawyer of yours tries to fool you into thinking anything different, it's only because he's trying to do his job. You shouldn't be under any illusion. I don't intend to disturb you any more. I'll see you in court.'

For a moment Mitter thought Van Veeteren was going to shake hands, but of course that would not have been possible. Instead the chief inspector turned his back on Mitter, and although it was nearly two minutes before the warder appeared, he remained motionless, staring at the door.

As if he were in a lift. Or as if Mitter had ceased to exist the moment the conversation was over.

7

Elmer Suurna wiped an imaginary speck of dust from his desk with the sleeve of his jacket. Glanced out of the window as he did so and wished it were the summer holidays.

Or at least the Christmas holidays.

But it was October. He sighed. Ever since taking up his post as headmaster of Bunge High School fifteen years ago, he had cherished an ambition. One only.

To keep his handsome red-oak desk top clean and shiny.

In his younger days, when he had been a temporary assistant master, his aim had been different: no matter what they do, they will not disturb my equanimity! It was after being forced to admit that this credo was being shaken to the core, day after day, hour after hour, that Suurna decided to set his sights on a career as a school administrator instead. To become a headmaster, in fact.

It had taken its toll: a few friends, some invitations, several years; but by the time he celebrated his fortieth birthday he had achieved his aim. He sat down at his desk and looked forward to a quarter of a century of undisturbed equanimity. Should there be any matters that needed dealing with – student demonstrations, budget deficits or timetables that needed adjusting – there would always be a deputy head to whom the problems could be delegated. He would be too busy taking care of the red oak.

And then, after fifteen years of devoted polishing, this damned business had come about.

Days had passed. Evenings. Even nights, but there seemed to be no end to it. Just now a snivelling lawyer was sitting slumped on the visitor's chair, reminding him uncannily of a starving vulture he had once seen while on summer holiday in the Serengeti.

The only person I would allow him to defend, Suurna thought, is my mother-in-law.

'You must understand, Mr Rütter—'

'Rüger.'

'I'm sorry, Mr Rüger, you must understand that this has been a difficult time for us all, difficult and exhausting. One teacher is dead, another is in prison. The police are running around here every day. Surely you can see that our school has to be spared any further stress.'

'Of course. You don't need to worry.'

'Perhaps it's not necessary for me to point out that our pupils have been affected in most undesirable ways, Mr Rüger. They are young people, and easily thrust into a state of confusion. What we now need to do as a matter of urgency is pull ourselves together and move on. I bear the ultimate pedagogical responsibility, and can't just stand by and watch . . .'

The door opened tentatively and a woman with mauve-coloured hair and mauve-coloured spectacles put her head round it.

'Would you like me to serve coffee now, Mr Suurna?'

Her voice was soft and meticulously articulated.

As if her words were made of bone china, Rüger thought. It seemed clear that she was a former primary-school teacher.

'Of course, Miss Bellevue. Bring it right in.'

Rüger was quick to make the most of his opportunity.

'Of course I understand your difficulties. I have a son who graduated from this school ten years ago.'

'Really? I didn't think . . .'

'Rüger, his name was. Edwin Rüger. Obviously, I can see that this must have been a particularly difficult time for you, but even so, Mr Suurna, we must ensure that justice takes its course, don't you agree?'

'Of course, Mr Rüger. Surely you don't think for a moment that I would want anything different?'

He glanced after Miss Bellevue, who was just leaving the room, and Rüger wondered if there really was an ounce of unrest in the man, or if he was just imagining it.

'Not for a moment, no. You merely want a degree of . . . discretion. Is that what you're saying?'

'Precisely. But if you'll allow me to say so, that hasn't exactly been the strongest side of our police authorities. Or perhaps I should say: let's hope they have stronger sides.'

He peered over his spectacles and tried to smile, as if to suggest they were singing from the same hymn sheet. Rüger blew his nose.

'However, you represent . . .?' wondered Suurna, dropping three lumps of sugar into his plastic mug.

'I'm Mr Mitter's lawyer. You must surely agree that it's in the best interests of the school for him to be found not guilty?'

Suurna gave a start.

'Naturally, without a shadow of doubt, but . . .'

'But what?'

'Don't get me wrong . . . But what do you think yourself?'

'I'm the one who ought to be asking that question. Of you, that is.'

The headmaster stirred his coffee. Adjusted his tie. Looked out of the window and moved the pens in his desk tidy around.

'Mitter has always been a loyal member of staff, a much-admired teacher. He's been at the school almost as long as I have myself. Very knowledgeable and . . . independent. I have difficulty in believing . . . Real difficulty.'

'And Eva Ringmar?'

The pens were slowly starting to return to their original positions.

'I don't really have much of an idea about her, I'm afraid. She's only been with us for a short time, two years, or thereabouts. But of course she was a very well-qualified teacher. May I ask you something? What kind of a stand is Mitter making?'

'What do you mean?'

Suurna shuffled in his chair.

'Well, er, what kind of a stand is he making?'

'Not guilty.'

'I see . . . Yes, of course. He's not pleading without premeditation, nothing like that?'

'No. Nothing like that.'

Suurna nodded.

'And what you are looking for now is . . .?'

'I'm looking for two or three witnesses.'

'Witnesses? But surely that's impossible?'

'Character witnesses, Mr Suurna, people who are willing to stand up in court and speak in support of Mitter. People who know him, as a person and as a colleague, who can give a positive picture of him. And a true one, of course.'

'I'm with you. The man behind the name?'

'Something like that. Perhaps a pupil as well. And preferably you yourself, Mr Suurna.'

'Oh, I don't really think . . .'

'Or somebody you can suggest. If you give me four or five names, I can choose from among them.'

'Who would he prefer to have? Wouldn't it be more appropriate for him to say who he'd like to have?'

'Hmm, that's the tricky thing . . .' Rüger took a sip of coffee. It was weak and had a faint taste of disinfectant. He gave thanks for his bad cold. 'Mitter has, er, how should I put it? On principle he declines to speak in his own favour. It goes against the grain for him to . . . proselytize. I must say that I can sympathize with him. Sigurdsen and Weiss seem to have been the members of staff closest to him, but I don't know . . .?'

'Weiss and Sigurdsen? Yes, that's probably correct. Yes, I've nothing against them.'

'Even so, it might also be good to have somebody who wasn't all that close to him. Good friends naturally only have good things to say about one another. Nobody expects anything different.'

'I understand.'

Rüger closed his eyes and forced down the rest of the coffee.

'To be precise, what I am asking you to provide is a colleague, one of his pupils, and, er, shall we say a representative of the school management – you yourself, or somebody you think would be suitable.'

'I'll have a word with Eger, he's our deputy head. I've no doubt he'll be happy to oblige. As for the pupils, I have no idea. I must ask you to be extremely discreet. Perhaps you could get some help from Sigurdsen and Weiss, if you speak to them.'

'I'm most grateful.'

'You ought to know that I'm . . . er, we all are, of course . . . very upset about what has happened. Some have taken it harder than others, and it's obvious that everybody on the staff has been on edge. But even so, we have managed to carry on working. I'd like you to bear that in mind. It has been . . . and still is . . . a very difficult time for all of us at this school. However, I think we've succeeded in showing the pupils that we don't let them down, even when we're under this kind of pressure.'

'I understand, Headmaster. I'm very well aware of what you must have been going through. When do you think I'll be able to meet my witnesses?'

'When would suit you? You must give me a little time, and obviously it must take place after school is finished for the day. We must not disrupt teaching any more than has happened already.'

'The trial starts on Thursday. Witnesses for the defence are unlikely to be called before Tuesday or Wednesday next week.'

'I shall make appropriate arrangements, Mr Rüger. Tomorrow afternoon, perhaps?'

'Excellent.'

'I'll be in touch.'

He slid back his desk chair. Rüger handed him his business card and started wriggling his way up from the armchair.

'Edwin Rüger . . . Yes, I do believe I recall him. A promising young man. What's he doing now?'

'Unemployed.'

'Ah, I see . . . So, goodbye, Mr Rüger. Is there anything else I can do for you?'

Hardly, Rüger thought. He shook his head and wiped his nose. Headmaster Suurna leaned over his intercom and summoned the mauve woman.

'Haven't you got an umbrella?' she asked as she guided him through the corridors.

'No,' said Rüger, 'but I've been thinking about buying one.'

He couldn't be bothered to explain that in fact he owned two: one was at home, the other was in his car. As he hastened over the wet school playground, he wondered who on earth it was the headmaster reminded him of. Some politician or other involved in a scandal many years ago, he suspected. Surely they couldn't be one and the same person?

For Mitter's sake, he hoped that Suurna would not change his mind and volunteer to be a witness himself. Nobody but the opposition would relish the prospect of evidence given by a witness like that, so much was obvious. And he doubted if he would have the courage to put a muzzle on the man.

Speaking of which, how many witnesses had the prosecution managed to winkle out of these walls? He had the distinct impression that there were two or three to be found, if anybody made the effort.

But as he sat in his car again and watched the gloomy outline of the Bunge High School fade away in his rear-view mirror, what filled his mind above all else was a hot bath and an extra-large and well-deserved cognac.

It was true that his wife maintained that nobody cured a cold with hot baths and cognac nowadays, but he had decided to pay no more attention to her. For three whole days his breakfast had comprised a nasty-tasting little vitamin pill, and that had failed to shift him even an inch closer to good health.

8

Why didn't they come?

That question cropped up the day after, but not until nearly evening. The day had passed, hour after hour, in a sort of glassy trance, a state of utter confusion; but as soon as thoughts had succeeded in breaking through, that was the question that registered first.

Why had he heard nothing from them?

Another night passed. And another day.

Nothing happened. He went to work, did what he had to do, went back home in the evening. His strength was returning fast and problem-free, and he knew that a confrontation wouldn't cause him any bother at all.

But nothing happened.

After a week the ridiculous question was still nagging him. He thought there must be some kind of mistake – perhaps they had come looking for him, but failed to find him.

Neither at home nor at work.

This was just as ridiculous, of course, but nevertheless he stayed at home for a few days during the second week. Told his employers that he had a stomach upset, and stayed in all the time.

To make certain that they could find him.

In any case, he needed the rest. He sat in his flat day after day, and let all the circumstances tick over in his mind. And suddenly, everything fell into place. He realized how the whole of his life had been leading up to exactly this. Realized that he ought to have caught on much sooner. It would have saved him a lot of trouble. He realized that this was his escape route, and that there was no other possibility. It was now so obvious that he was forced to give his head a good shaking to make up for his blindness.

She was dead. Now he could live.

And nothing happened.

No unknown voice telephoned and asked him to answer some questions. No stern-looking men in damp trenchcoats knocked on his door. Nothing.

What were they waiting for?

He occasionally stood behind the curtains and peered down at the street, looking for mysterious parked cars. He listened for the telltale little click confirming that his phone was being tapped. He read all the newspapers he could get hold of, but nowhere . . . nowhere could he find even a hint of an explanation.

It was incomprehensible.

After three weeks it was still just as incomprehensible, but he had grown used to it. The situation wasn't entirely unpleasant. The uncertainty brought with it a little tingling feeling.

That tingling.

The morning the trial was due to start he got up early. Stood for ages in front of the bathroom mirror, smiling at his own reflection. Toyed with the idea of going there. Sitting in the public gallery, gaping at all the goings-on.

But he knew that would be going too far. Tempting fate. Why tempt something that had treated him so favourably?

In the car, on the way to work, he suddenly found himself singing.

It wasn't yesterday. He looked at his eyes in the rear-view mirror. There was a sparkle in them.

And as he waited at a red light, he saw out of the corner of his eye the woman in the Volvo alongside him turning her head to smile at him.

He swallowed, and felt his passions rising.

9

The dream came in the early hours of the morning; when the first grey light slowly started to squeeze out the darkness in his cell. The breakfast trolleys might even have started to rattle in the corridors.

And he remembered it in detail; it might have happened just as he was waking up, and perhaps a lot of things might have been explained if only he'd been granted a few more minutes' sleep. Even a few more seconds might have been enough.

At first he was out walking. A dreary march over a never-ending, barren plain. A desolate landscape with no villages, no trees, no water courses. Nothing but this dried-out, cracked earth. Apart from the greenish-black little lizards darting back and forth between stones and fissures, he was the only living being. He was alone, lugging a shapeless rucksack, its straps chafing against his shoulders and digging into his waist. He had little idea of his destination or purpose; only knew that it was important. Perhaps he'd known more at the beginning, but it had fallen by the wayside.

But he must not give up, must not pause, must not sit down; only keep plodding on, yard after yard, step after step. And the wind was getting stronger, forcing him to lean forward into it; it was blowing more and more strongly at him, hurling sand and dry twigs into his face, and he leaned further and further forward, closing his eyes in order to protect them.

And then he was there, in front of that house, large and battered, so alien and yet at the same time so familiar. And people were standing in long rows to welcome him, pressed against the walls in the corridors; all kinds of people imaginable, but he knew them all and nobody escaped his memory. Many of his friends, Bendiksen and Weiss and Jürg, his own son, but others as well; people from the great wide world, and from history: the Dalai Lama and Winston Churchill and Mikhail Gorbachev. Gorbachev read a poem in fluent Latin about the transience of all things, and shook him by the hand. Everybody shook him by the hand and passed him on to the next one; led him gently but firmly further into the house, up winding staircases and through long, dimly lit corridors.

He finally came to a room, darker than any of the others, and he realized he had reached his destination. The man sitting on the other side of the low table – he recognized the table, it was his own – and it was definitely a man, it was . . . it must have been . . . it was surely?

The light hanging down from the ceiling had a flat shade made of tinplate, and it was hanging at such a ridiculously low level that all he could see was lower arms and hands resting on the table, but he thought he recognized them. They were, they were . . . were they?

And on the table was Eva's kimono; his first impulse was to grab hold of it and put it in the washing machine, but something held him back; he didn't know what it was, because the man in there, in the darkness, was more scared than he was himself; that was why he couldn't show his face, but it was surely . . . And then he felt a sudden aversion, an irresistible urge, a horrific force compelling him to get out of that room before it was too late, and he woke up.

He woke up.

Yes, now that he looked back, he was certain that it wasn't anything external that had dragged him out of his dream. It was the room itself that had thrown him out. Nothing else.

He was awake. Wide awake. His breath was heavy with the sleeping tablets Rüger had made him take. Perhaps he would have had the strength to remain in that room just a little longer, but for the effect of those tablets. Long enough to get an inkling, at least?

The kimono on the table was not just a dream, he knew that; it was a memory, a fragment of that night. It wasn't a real kimono, of course. Only an imitation. She had found it in one of the narrow alleys in Levkes last summer, and he'd bought it for her. One of those evenings when they'd sat outside the tavernas until closing time and then wandered back to their lodgings along the beach. Made love in the sand in the warm, black darkness, and then walked the rest of the way naked, and there had been people here and there, quite close to them, but the darkness had been so incredibly dense, they needed no other covering. Even so, the sky had teemed with stars, myriads of stars, and shooting star after shooting star after shooting star. They had stopped counting once they had wished for everything they could possibly want . . .

This was, he reckoned, less than three months ago. It could just as well have been three million years ago. The irrevocable nature of the passage of time struck him with full force; the irrevocable and unalterable sequence of every second, every moment. The desperate inevitability of it all. We are closer to the end of the world than to that minute that has just passed by, because that is lost forever. There is no way Levkes will ever come back; nor will the retsina and the beggar with the blue eyes; they will never come back.

But there again, nor will all the rest.

Did it really matter?

Did life really matter?

Difficult to find the right balance now.

You will find out who you are when the difficult moment comes.

I am nobody, he thought. So I am nobody.

I find it more meaningful to lie here on my bed and observe a small patch of wall. Observe it and scrutinize it close up, pick out a stain, as big as a postage stamp, or a fingernail. Concentrate on it with all my senses, smell it, feel it with my tongue, with my fingers, over and over again, listen to it, until I know it inside out . . . more meaningful than to go back and remember what was, and what happened.

Those were his thoughts as he woke up out of that dream, and it was not a new thought or a thought he could banish.

Now the breakfast trolleys were getting closer. The hatch in his door opened and the breakfast tray was slid inside. The hatch closed again. It was seven o'clock; he had slept for nearly eight hours; for the first time in three weeks he had slept for a whole night. And today . . .

What day was it today?

It took him several seconds to work it out.

His trial would begin today.

He took a bite of bread and contemplated his thoughts. What were his feelings?

A sort of apathetic expectation?

Get it over with?

Or perhaps simply . . . nothing at all.

10

The courtroom was almost Gothic. A high, vertical style of architecture that reminded him of the anatomy lecture theatre in Oosterbrügge. Steep galleries of seats on three sides; on the fourth side perched the judge and other court officials behind brownish-black bars. The small amount of natural light allowed in came from a circle of stained-glass windows high up in the pointed roof, and without doubt reinforced the impression of a vertical, descending hierarchy, a vision of the world order that must have hovered in the mind's eye of the building's creator in the middle of the previous century.

This courtroom was crammed full, with not a single seat vacant.

The majority, getting on for 200 people, was naturally seated in the public gallery. And the majority of those were pupils of Bunge High School. Mitter gathered that he was the direct cause of this year's top-of-the-league score for truancy.

There were also journalists in the public gallery. They sat without exception on the front row, their legs crossed and with notebooks on their knees. Or sketchbooks – taking photographs was not permitted in court, he now remembered. He was surprised by the large number, there must have been a dozen of them. That surely had to indicate that this case was of national interest, not just a provincial happening.

Mitter's place was below the gallery, in the arena itself; also Rüger, whose cold seemed to be getting better, Havel, the judge, prosecuting attorney Ferrati and his assistants, and a small number of other lawyers and ushers.

Plus a jury. This comprised four men and two women, sitting behind a partition to the right of the judge, all of them looking sympathetic. Apart from the second from the right, who was an erect gentleman with an artificial arm and a furrowed brow.

Also present was a large bluebottle. It spent most of its time on the ceiling, directly above the prosecuting attorney's desk; but occasionally it undertook tours of the room and almost always homed in on one of the two female members of the jury; sitting on the right of the furrowed brow. The fly launched an attack on her nose over and over again, and despite the fact that she brushed it aside every time, it kept on coming back with renewed energy and unfailing persistence. These raids were accompanied by a low humming noise, which made a pleasant contrast to the rather shrill voice of the prosecuting attorney. A bit like a duet featuring a cello and a cembalo, and especially noticeable in the pauses, while he was recovering his breath.

Apart from that, the day's events were quite boring.

To start with, everybody kept having to stand up and sit down again as the judge and jury took their places. Then the judge outlined the charge, and Rüger explained that his client was not guilty. Next the prosecuting attorney started to present the case for the prosecution, an exercise that lasted for an hour and forty minutes and concluded with the accused, Janek Mattias Mitter, forty-six years old, born in Rheinau, resident in Maardam for the past twenty-six years, appointed as a teacher of history and philosophy at Bunge High School in 1973, being accused of murdering (or alternatively unlawfully killing) his wife Eva Maria Ringmar, thirty-eight years of age, born in Leuwen, resident in Maardam since 1990 and until her death employed as a teacher of English and French at the previously mentioned high school, by drowning her in the bath at the flat they shared in Kloisterlaan 24, at some point early on the morning of 5 October. The crime had been committed under the influence of intoxicating alcoholic beverages, but there was nothing, and he repeated that there was nothing at all, to suggest that Mitter had been so intoxicated that he was not responsible for his actions. These accusations would be supported by an overwhelming mass of technical proof, expert analysis and statements taken from witnesses, and when this process was completed it would be clear to members of the jury and everyone else present that the accused was obviously guilty as charged and there could only be one verdict: guilty.

Of murder.

Or, at the very least, manslaughter.

Then it was Rüger's turn. He blew his nose and spent the next hour and twelve minutes asserting that nothing at all had happened as described by the prosecuting attorney, that his client had nothing at all to do with his wife's death, and this would be proved without a shadow of doubt.

Then came a two-hour break for lunch. The bluebottle left the jury benches and made its way to the ceiling in order to sleep, while everybody else murmured their way out of the courtroom, duly observing the proprieties of the occasion. One of the girls in the gallery was bold enough to wave to Mitter, who gave her an encouraging nod in response.

It took him just over ten minutes to consume his pasta dish in his cell in the basement of the courthouse. He spent the rest of the lunch break lying on his back on the bed and observing a damp patch on the ceiling, while he waited for the afternoon's proceedings to commence.

These proceedings were devoted exclusively to so-called technical evidence. A number of police officers of various kinds took to the stand, including Van Veeteren; also a pathologist, a physician, a forensic specialist and somebody called Wilkerson. He stuttered, and called himself a toxicologist.

The public gallery was somewhat less full – presumably headmaster Suurna had got wind of what was going on. But the journalists were still present in force, leaning back in relaxed postures in order to assist the digestive process. If any of them dozed off, at least they refrained from snoring.

It was not easy to determine what was achieved during the afternoon. Ferrati and Rüger exchanged hair-splitting sophistries, Judge Havel occasionally intervened to restore order, and a member of the jury asked a question about the possible presence of fragments of skin under fingernails.

At no point did Mitter himself need to speak, and when the court adjourned shortly after 4 p.m., he had long since ceased to pay any attention. Instead, he yearned for three things: solitude, silence and darkness.

As for who had taken the life of Eva Ringmar, it could be said that, generally speaking, nobody knew anything more than the bluebottle.

II

Rüger arrived while he was having breakfast.

'I'd like to have a little chat with you.'

'OK.'

'I don't suppose there's a cup for me?'

Mitter called the warder and was passed another mug of coffee through the hatch.

'Have you remembered anything more?'

'No.'

'I see.'

Rüger leaned over the table, rested his weight on his elbows and blew at the coffee.

'I'd like you to . . . consider your testimony.'

Mitter chewed his sandwich and looked intently at Rüger.

'What do you mean?'

'Whether you are going to say anything or not.'

Mitter thought for a moment. Perhaps the implication was not all that surprising, all things considered . . .

'As I explained,' said Rüger, 'it's not necessary for the defendant to allow himself to be interrogated.'

'You said it was unusual for a defendant to . . .'

Rüger nodded.

'That may well be, but even so, I'd like you to think about it. The way things look, in my judgement your chances would be just as good if you don't go into the witness box.'

'Why?'

'Because there's nothing you can add. You can't even make a case for yourself. The bottom line is that you can't provide any proof to show that it wasn't you who killed her. The only thing you can say is that you don't remember, and that really isn't a convincing argument, as you must be able to see yourself. We would have nothing to gain in that respect, and the fact is, that is the key to everything.'

He paused and took a sip of coffee.

'And in other respects?'

'Ugh, this coffee is poisonous. I don't understand why they can't learn how to . . . Anyway: another thing is whether or not you make a good impression on the court.'

Mitter lit a cigarette and fingered his stubble. Rüger continued:

'Making a good impression is vital. Nobody will know if you drowned her, so they'll have to guess. Ferrati will do everything he can to make you lose your composure, and Havel will allow him free rein. If Ferrati succeeds in that, everything could be lost. He can be extremely difficult. If he were to carve you to pieces, it's not at all sure that I could patch you up afterwards.'

Mitter shrugged.

'Don't you have to give a reason?'

'In theory no, but it is usual, it gives a better impression. We could say that you don't feel up to it, the stress would be too great. Severe psychological pressure, state of shock, and similar things. I have a doctor who could write out a certificate for you right away. It would be accepted, and it wouldn't harm your case, I can promise you. What do you say?'

'What do you think yourself?'

Rüger thought it over. Or pretended to do so. There was no doubt it would be very strange if he had hastened to

Mitter's cell at this time in the morning if he hadn't already made up his mind. He didn't want to see Mitter in the dock, it was as simple as that.

'I want you to decline to give evidence,' he said eventually.

Mitter went to the washbasin and stubbed out his cigarette. Stretched out on the bed and closed his eyes.

'I'm not going to refuse, Mr Rüger. You can forget about any such possibility. You can go home and wash your hands.'

Rüger sat in silence for a few seconds before responding.

'As you wish, Mr Mitter. As you wish. No matter what you think, I shall do the best I can for you. I'll see you in court.'

He rang for the warder and was escorted out. Mitter didn't open his eyes until the cell door had closed.

Ferrati was wearing glasses today. Large, round goggles with light-coloured metal frames, which made him look like a newly woken lemur. Or possibly a hypnotist.

'Janek Mattias Mitter,' he began by saying.

Mitter nodded.

'Will you please answer the attorney's questions loudly and clearly,' interrupted Judge Havel.

'I didn't hear a question,' said Mitter.

Havel turned to Ferrati:

'Please repeat the question!'

'Are you Janek Mattias Mitter?' asked Ferrati.

'Yes,' replied Mitter.

Something that could have been interpreted as a titter was audible from the public gallery and Havel hammered loudly on his desk.

He was already annoyed. That was not a good start. Rüger blew his nose and contemplated his ballpoint pen.

'Would you kindly tell us when you first met Eva Ringmar?'

'That would be . . . in September 1990. At the start of term.'

'What was your first impression of her?'

'Nothing at all.'

'Nothing at all? Didn't you think she was an attractive woman?'

'Yes, I suppose so.'

'But you can't really remember?'

'No.'

'When did you start your relationship with her?'

'In April.'

'What year?'

'This year.'

'Can you tell us how it happened?'

'We had both been on the same study course one weekend, and had talked quite a bit. I took her to the cinema, and we had a few drinks afterwards.'

'And then you started your affair?'

'Yes.'

'You were both . . . single?'

'Yes.'

'Can I ask why you started going out together?'

'I think that is an idiotic question.'

'All right, I'll take it back. When did you decide to get married?'

'In June. We moved in together at the beginning of July and got married on the tenth.'

'Shortly before you went to Greece?'

'Yes.'

'A sort of honeymoon, then?'

'If you want to call it that, yes.'

'Why did you get married? I hope you don't find that question idiotic as well, because I'd like an answer.'

Mitter paused. Momentarily looked away from Ferrati and eyed the jury instead.

'I put the question, and she said yes,' he stated.

'Can you elaborate a little?'

'No.'

There was a faint murmur in the public gallery, but Havel didn't need to intervene.

'You have both been married before,' the prosecutor affirmed. 'You meet and begin a relationship. Three months later you get married. Don't you think that seems a little . . . hasty?'

'No.'

'You weren't in a hurry for some specific reason?'

'No.'

'She wasn't pregnant?'

'Is that a sufficient reason nowadays?'

'Would you please answer my question!'

'No, Eva was not pregnant.'

'Thank you.'

There was a short pause while Ferrati went back to his desk and consulted some notes.

'Mr Mitter, how would you describe your relationship with, and your marriage to, Eva Ringmar?'

'What do you want to know?'

'Were you happy together? Did you regret it?'

'No, I didn't regret it, and neither did Eva. We had a good relationship.'

'You were happy?'

'Yes.'

'You loved your wife?'

'Yes.'

'And she loved you?'

'Yes.'

'I have some information about an incident on 22 September, fourteen days before the murder. You were together at the Mephisto restaurant. After the meal you had a fierce argument, and your wife stormed out of the building. We shall call witnesses later to confirm this. Is that what happened, Mr Mitter?'

'Yes.'

'What was the quarrel about?'

'I don't want to go into details.'

'Mr Mitter, you are accused of murder. I want to know what the quarrel was about.'

'It was nothing of relevance to these proceedings.'

'Don't you think that's something for the jury to decide?'

Mitter didn't answer. Ferrati allowed several seconds to pass before continuing.

'Might I request that it is recorded in the proceedings that the accused declined to answer my question about the reason for the quarrel at the Mephisto restaurant on 22 September. You remained in the restaurant after your wife had left, Mr Mitter. May I ask how long you stayed there?'

'I don't know. A few hours.'

'We have evidence from a neighbour of yours . . .' He went to check his notes again. '. . . a Mr Kurczak, who says that he was woken up by loud noises coming from your flat later that night, at about half past two. Was that about the time you got home, do you think?'

'That's possible.'

'And what was the row about?'

'I don't remember. I was a bit drunk.'

'You don't remember?'

'No.'

'You don't know what the row was about?'

'No.'

'But you know what the row in the restaurant was about?'

'Yes.'

'But you do admit that you quarrelled with your wife when you came home in the middle of the night?'

'Yes.'

'Did you hit her?'

'No.'

'Are you sure, or don't you remember?'

'I'm sure.'

'Your neighbour heard some noises that could have been made by blows.'

'Really?'

'Did you threaten your wife?'

'No.'

'Are you sure?'

'Yes.'

'Kurczak maintains that he heard you yell, and I quote: "If you don't tell me about it, I won't be responsible for what happens!" What have you to say to that?'

'It's a lie.'

'It's a lie? Why would your neighbour lie?'

'He misheard. I never threatened her.'

'What did you do next?'

Rüger interrupted at this point.

'My lord, my client has already explained that he doesn't remember. There are no grounds for the prosecutor forcing him to speculate.'

'Agreed!' Havel thundered. 'Would my learned friend please restrict himself to questions that the accused is able to answer.

'By all means,' said Ferrati with a smile. 'But it's not always easy to know what he remembers and doesn't remember. Mr Mitter, are you aware that your wife was afraid?'

'Nonsense.'

'A few days before her death, she confided in a female colleague that she was scared that something was going to happen.'

'I don't believe that. What could she be scared of?'

'Might I ask you to try and answer the question instead?'

'I've no idea. Why don't you ask . . . whoever the hell it could have been?'

'Because she doesn't know. It was only a brief meeting, but nevertheless she had the impression that it was you your wife was scared of.'

'Rubbish.'

'I think we can leave it to the jury to decide what is rubbish and what isn't. Your colleague will present her testimony next week . . . Anyway, you have no explanation for why your wife was frightened?'

'None at all.'

'How were things with your former wife, Irene Beck? Were you in the habit of beating her?'

'What the hell . . .'

But Rüger was quicker. He leaped up from his chair.

'My learned friend is making insinuations!'

'Sit down!' Havel roared. 'What do you mean, Mr Ferrati?'

'Irene Beck has testified that her former husband, the defendant, hit her on at least two occasions.'

'That was when we were separating. She hit me and I hit her back. For Christ's sake, surely she's not suggesting that . . .'

'Are you admitting, or are you not admitting, that you beat your former wife?'

Mitter made no reply. Rüger was on his feet again.

'My lord, why are you allowing the prosecuting attorney to insinuate things that are completely irrelevant to the case?'

Havel's face was now puce in colour.

'I must insist that my learned friend sits down and refrains from interrupting! And that the prosecuting attorney kindly explains where he hopes his questions will lead.'

Ferrati smiled again. It seemed that he always smiled when he looked at the judge.

'I am merely trying to establish the extent of the defendant's tendency to resort to violence.'

Havel appeared to be thinking.

'Might I request the defendant to answer the question?' he said eventually.

'What question?'

'If you did or did not beat your former wife.'

Mitter waited for several seconds before answering.

'I slapped her twice in thirteen years. Evidently that wasn't often enough.'

His response triggered mutterings in the public gallery, but a look from Havel was enough to restore order. Meanwhile an assistant had stepped forward to whisper something in Ferrati's ear. The latter nodded, and stepped forward in turn to whisper something to the judge that Mitter was unable to hear. Havel seemed to hesitate, but then nodded.

Ferrati continued:

'Have you ever been violent towards your pupils, Mr Mitter?'

'Objection!' yelled Rüger, who was beginning to look indignant.

'Overruled!' bellowed Havel. 'Answer the question!'

'Never,' said Mitter.

'Is it not a fact that you were reported for striking a pupil? In March 1983, according to the information at my disposal?'

Ferrati looked pleased with himself. Mitter said nothing.

'Do you intend to reply, or don't you remember?'

'I was reported, yes.'

'But nevertheless you claim that you have never been violent towards your pupils?'

'I was falsely accused. Declared wrongfully convicted, just as I shall be again now.'

More reaction from the gallery. This time it was so loud that Havel was forced to resort to his hammer.

'I must ask the public to remain silent during court proceedings . . . and request the defendant to answer the questions put to him! Nothing else!'

Rüger obviously felt that this was the time to make a decisive intervention.

'My lord, I really must insist that we must call a halt to this line of questioning. My learned friend the prosecuting attorney has been asking irrelevant questions for far too long. His intention is clear: he is intent on maligning my client, because he has no solid evidence to support the prosecution case. If he is going to be allowed to continue, I must insist that he asks questions that are relevant to the case!'

For a moment it looked as if Havel was intent on aiming his hammer at Rüger's skull, but in fact he turned to Ferrati:

'May I ask that my learned friend comes to the point!'

'By all means.'

Ferrati produced his friendly smile once more, this time directed at the jury. The two lady members were only too keen to smile back.

'Mr Mitter, did you drown your wife?'

'No.'

'How do you know?'

'Because . . . because I didn't do it.'

'You mean that you didn't kill her because you didn't kill her?'

Mitter allowed himself a couple of extra seconds thinking time before replying. Then he said, calm and restrained:

'No, I *know* I didn't kill her, because I didn't kill her. Just as I'm sure that you *know* you are not wearing frilly knickers today, because you aren't. Not today.'

The gallery exploded. Ferrati sat down. Havel hammered away at his desk. Rüger shook his head, while Mitter stood upright in the dock and then bowed modestly to acknowledge the applause.

Now he was in an excellent mood, albeit dying for a cigarette. Nevertheless, his next comment came as a surprise to himself, not to mention everybody else.

'I admit everything!' he yelled. 'Provided somebody gives me a cigarette!'

When Judge Havel was eventually able to make himself heard, he announced:

'The court will adjourn for twenty minutes! The prosecuting and defending attorneys will report to my room immediately!'

And with a resounding blow of his hammer, he concluded the proceedings for the time being.

12

'Excuse me.'

Van Veeteren elbowed aside two reporters and forced his way into the telephone kiosk. Slammed the door shut so as not to hear the curses and protests . . . Who did they think they were? Surely the police took precedence over the press?

While he was waiting for a reply he observed the grotesque face glaring at him from the shiny surface above the telephone. It was a few seconds before it dawned on him that he was looking at his own reflection. There was something unusual about it, evidently, and it took him a few more seconds to realize what it was.

He was smiling.

The corners of his mouth were raised to form a generous curve and gave his face an expression suggesting a touch of lunacy.

Like a posturing male gorilla, he thought glumly, but that didn't help much. The smile stayed in place, and deep down inside himself he began to feel vibrations, a sort of muffled purring, and he realized that all this must combine to form an expression of satisfaction. Warm and grateful satisfaction.

He couldn't recall having experienced anything funnier; not since the former chief of police ran over his wife on a pedestrian crossing, in any case. The image of the prosecuting attorney, Ferrati, in frilly knickers was something he could hide in the innermost recesses of his mind, to be dug out whenever it suited him for the rest of his life. Ponder over it, and enjoy it.

Not to mention the sheer pleasure to be derived from entering Ferrati's office on Monday mornings and saying:

'Hi there! What colour are your knickers today, then?'

It was priceless. As he stood there glowering at the gorilla, it struck him that his present state was something reminiscent of a kind of happiness.

Measured by his own standards, at least.

It didn't last long, more's the pity; but at least it was real.

However, the problem at the moment was Münster. The badminton match scheduled for noon would have to be postponed. Van Veeteren would have to blame his foot.

'It's this damned awful weather. I don't think it feels stable enough yet. I'm sorry, but it's just not on.'

Münster understood. No problem. He could take on PC Nelde instead. The chief inspector didn't need to worry.

Worry? Van Veeteren thought. Why the hell should I worry? Who does he think he is?

But then he turned his mind to the real reason.

The fact was that he had no desire to leave the courtroom for the sports hall. Not yet.

Mitter.

This damned Mitter.

Those vibrations were starting up again, but he suppressed them. Anyway, this case. He had come here this morning because he didn't feel like starting on anything new. An arsonist was lying in wait on his desk, he knew that; and if there was anything he hated, it was arsonists.

He thought he would hang around for an hour or so. Just to see how the schoolteacher coped with being in the dock, and with Ferrati. Not very long, he could fill in an hour or two before it was time for badminton and lunch.

But now he was hooked. Couldn't bring himself to leave. Not yet. It wasn't the line about Ferrati's knickers that compelled him to stay, despite the fact that on grounds of pure politeness he'd have been prepared to hang around for hours simply to have had the privilege of being there at that moment. No, it was something else. Even before the palaver and the adjournment, it had become clear to him that he would have to stay on and see how the trial developed – not because he thought that Mitter had a cat in hell's chance in the long run: that wasn't the point. He had no doubt that Mitter would be found guilty in the end.

But had he done it?

Had this crazy schoolteacher really pressed his wife's head down under the water and held it there until she was dead?

Two minutes? No, that wouldn't have been long enough. Three, three and a half?

Van Veeteren doubted it. And he didn't like doubts.

And was Mitter in his right mind?

He certainly had been at the time of the murder.

But now?

You're not wearing frilly knickers. Not today!

I'll admit everything if somebody gives me a cigarette!

In court. That was brilliant.

And then, when all was said and done: if Mitter hadn't killed his wife, who had?

He recalled Reinhart once saying that no two professions were more similar than those of teachers and actors.

If he was wrong, the winners would have to be police officers and mud wrestlers, Van Veeteren thought as he elbowed his way back to his seat in the public gallery.

13

'Would you please tell us as much as you can remember about the evening and night between 4 and 5 October.'

Havel had opened the session by warning all concerned: there would be new adjournments and proceedings behind locked doors if there were any further interruptions or indiscipline. Nevertheless, there was a murmur from the gallery in anticipation of Mitter's answer.

'Where would you like me to begin?'

'From when you left school.'

'By all means.' Mitter cleared his throat. 'I finished at 15.30. Eva only had lessons in the morning, so we didn't go home together. I had the car. Called in at Keen's and bought a drop of wine.'

'How much wine?'

'How much? A case. Twelve bottles.'

'Thank you. Please go on.'

'I got home at half past four, or thereabouts. Eva had started preparing the evening meal, a stew we were going to eat later on. She paused when I arrived, and we had a glass of wine and a cigarette on the balcony instead. It was very pleasant weather, and I suppose we sat outside for an hour or more.'

'What did you talk about?'

'Nothing special. School, books . . .'

'You didn't have any visitors?'

'No.'

'Any telephone calls?'

'Just the one, Bendiksen.'

'Who's Bendiksen?'

'A good friend of mine. We'd planned a fishing trip for the Sunday. He rang about some detail or other.'

'What, precisely?'

'I can't really remember. What time we should leave, I think.'

'No other telephone calls?'

'No.'

'Or visits?'

'No.'

'As far as you can remember?'

Ferrati smiled.

'Yes. As far as I can remember.'

'OK, so you sat out on the balcony until about . . . half past five, is that right?'

'Roughly.'

'How much did you drink?'

'I don't know. A bottle, perhaps.'

'Each?'

'No, between us.'

'Not more?'

'Well, possibly.'

'And then? Please go on.'

'We went indoors and finished preparing the stew. Then we had a shower.'

'Separately, or . . . ?'

'No, together.'

'Go on!'

'We watched television for a while.'

'What programme?'

'The news, and then a film.'

'What was the film?'

'I don't remember. French, from the Sixties, I think. We switched it off.'

'And then?'

'We went to the kitchen and started eating.'

'What time was it by now?'

'I don't know. Presumably about half past eight . . . nine o'clock . . . something like that.'

'Why are you guessing that time?'

'The police showed me the TV programme for that evening. A French film started at eight o'clock.'

'But you don't remember yourself?'

'No.'

'Thank you. Let's assume that it's correct even so. You and your wife are sitting in the kitchen, eating, round about nine o'clock. What happens next?'

'I don't know.'

'You don't know?'

'No. I have no memory of what happens after that.'

'You remember nothing more from the whole evening?'

'No.'

'But you have told the police that you had sexual intercourse with your wife as well . . .'

'Yes.'

'Is that correct?'

'Yes, but it was the same time.'

'What do you mean?'

'It was at the same time as we were eating dinner.'

'You had intercourse while you were eating dinner?'

Somebody sighed in the gallery. Ferrati turned his head.

'Yes. More or less the same time.'

More muttering, and Havel picked up his hammer. But this time he didn't even need to raise it. It was clear that he had the situation under control.

'What else do you remember from that evening?' Ferrati asked.

'Nothing, as I've already said.'

'Nothing?'

'No.'

'You don't remember getting undressed and going to bed? Or that your wife took a bath?'

'No. Would you kindly refrain from asking the same question over and over again!'

'Now let's get this straight, Mr Mitter: you are accused of murder. I think it's in your best interests for us to be a bit more precise. Just one more thing, before we move on to the next morning. How much did you drink during the course of the evening?'

'I don't know. Six or seven bottles, perhaps. Between us, that is.'

'Wine?'

'Yes.'

'But surely you hadn't managed to get through six bottles of wine when you were having your, er, intercourse dinner?'

Somebody giggled again, and Rüger protested.

'Overruled!' Havel roared. 'Answer the question!'

'No . . . I don't think so.'

'So I can draw the conclusion that you didn't go to bed at about nine o'clock?'

'Yes, I suppose so.'

'In any case, you must have been pretty drunk – or what do you think, Mr Mitter?'

'Yes.'

'I can't hear you!' Havel bellowed.

'Yes, I was drunk.'

'Were you also drunk when you slapped your former wife a couple of times?'

'Why are you asking that?'

'Surely you must understand why?' said Ferrati with a smile.

'Objection!' shouted Rüger, but it was in vain.

'Yes, I was drunk then as well,' admitted Mitter. 'Being drunk is not a crime, I hope.'

'Certainly not,' said Ferrati amiably. 'And your wife – Eva Ringmar, that is – was she also drunk?'

'Yes.'

'Was it usual for you to drink such amounts, Mr Mitter? Your wife had a blood alcohol count of over three hundred.'

'It happened.'

'Is it true to say that your wife had a drink problem?'

'Objection!' shouted Rüger once more.

'Rephrase the question, please!' said Havel.

'Has your wife received clinical treatment for an alcohol problem?' asked Ferrati.

'Yes. That was six years ago. She received treatment at her own request. It was in connection with some very tragic incidents . . . I think . . .'

'Thank you, that will do. We know the details. What is your next memory?'

'Excuse me?'

'What's the next thing you remember after the stew and the sexual intercourse?'

'Waking up.'

'What time?'

'Twenty minutes past eight. The next morning.'

'Tell me what you did!'

'I got up . . . and found Eva in the bathroom.'

'What about the state of the door – the bathroom door, that is?'

'It was locked. I opened it with a screwdriver.'

'Was it difficult to open?'

'No, not at all.'

'So you opened the locked door from the outside, no problem. Would you have been able to lock it from the outside as well?'

'Objection! My learned friend is forcing my cli—'

'Overruled! Answer the question!'

'I . . . I suppose so.'

'You could have drowned your wife in the bath and then locked the door from the outside, is that right?'

Rüger started to stand up, but Havel raised a warning finger.

'Will the accused please answer the attorney's question!'

Mitter moistened his lips.

'Of course,' he said calmly. 'But I didn't.'

Ferrati stood for a few seconds without saying anything. Then he turned his back on Mitter, as if he could no longer bear to set eyes on him. When he started speaking again, he had sunk his voice half an octave, and spoke slowly, as if addressing a child. Trying to make it see reason.

'Mr Mitter, you have no memories at all from that night, but nevertheless you maintain that you didn't kill your wife. You have had a month to think about it, and I have to say that I'd expected rather more logic from a teacher of philosophy. Why can't you at least admit that you can't remember if you killed her or not?'

'I wouldn't forget something like that.'

'I beg your pardon?'

'I wouldn't forget having drowned my wife. I don't remember having killed her . . . ergo, I didn't kill her.'

Rüger blew his nose. It might have been an attempt to divert attention from Mitter's last words. If so, it failed because Ferrati repeated them, albeit somewhat distorted. Standing in front of the jury, only an arm's length away, he intoned:

'I don't remember, therefore I'm not guilty! Might I request, members of the jury, that you consider these words carefully, and weigh their significance. What do you conclude? I can see that you know the answer already – they weigh less than air! And that is characteristic of the whole case for the defence! Air, nothing but hot air!'

He turned to look at Mitter again.

'Mr Mitter, for the last time . . . Why don't you confess to killing your wife, Eva Ringmar, by drowning her in the bath? Why persist in being so stubborn?'

'May I point out that I've admitted it already, before the adjournment,' said Mitter. 'Who's being stubborn?'

The reply aroused considerable enthusiasm in the public gallery, and Havel was forced to resort to his hammer. Ferrati took the opportunity of consulting his assistant before confronting Mitter once again.

'Tell us what you did while waiting for the police!'

'I . . . tidied up a bit.'

'What did you do with the clothes that you and your wife had been wearing the previous evening?'

'I washed them.'

'Where?'

'In the washing machine.'

Ferrati took off his glasses and put them into his inside pocket.

'While your wife was lying dead in the bath and you were waiting for the police to arrive, you took advantage of the opportunity to wash clothes?'

'Yes.'

New pause.

'Why, Mr Mitter? Why?'

'I don't know.'

Ferrati shrugged. Walked back and stood behind his chair. Stretched both arms out wide.

'Your honour, I have no more questions to ask the defendant.'

Havel looked at the clock.

'We have half an hour until lunch. How long does my learned friend require?'

Rüger stood up and took the floor.

'It's enough. My client is under intense psychological strain, and I shall be very brief. Mr Mitter, what about the door to your flat? Was it locked or unlocked that evening and the subsequent night?'

'Unlocked. We never lock – er, we never used to lock the door when we were at home.'

'Not even at night?'

'No, never.'

'What about the entrance door to the block of flats, the street door?'

'It's suppose to be locked, but I can't remember it being locked for as long as I've lived there.'

Rüger turned to Havel and held up a sheet of paper.

'I have a signed statement from the landlord confirming that the outside door was not locked on the night in question. Mr Mitter, isn't it true to say that anybody at all could have entered your flat and murdered your wife during the night of 4 October?'

'Yes, I assume so.'

'If we take it that you fell asleep at, let's say, ten o'clock or thereabouts, is it not possible that your wife might have left the flat . . .'

'Pure speculation!' protested Ferrati, but Havel merely gave him a look.

'. . . left the flat without your knowledge?' Rüger asked.

'I don't think she did,' said Mitter.

'No, but it's not impossible, is it?'

'No.'

'What other men friends did your wife have?'

'What do you mean?'

'Well, she must surely have had other men as well as you – I mean, you'd only been together for six months. She separated from her former husband, Andreas Berger, six years ago. Do you know anything about relationships she had in the meantime?'

'None at all,' said Mitter abruptly.

Rüger looked surprised.

'How do you know that?'

'Because she said so.'

'Do I understand this rightly? Are you saying that your wife had no relationship at all with another man for six years?'

'Yes.'

'She was a beautiful woman, Mr Mitter. How is that possible? Six years!'

'She didn't have any other men. Have you got that into your head? I thought you were supposed to be my lawyer. My lord, do I have the right to terminate this line of questioning?'

The judge looked somewhat confused, but before he had time to reach a decision, Rüger was speaking again.

'I apologize, Mr Mitter. I merely want the matter to be clear to the jury as well. Allow me to take another approach. Everyone agreed that your wife, Eva Ringmar, was a beautiful and attractive woman. Even if she didn't want to enter into a relationship, surely there must have been other men who, er, expressed an interest?'

Mitter said nothing.

'Before you came into the picture, at least. What about the situation at your school, for example?'

But Mitter had no desire to answer, that was obvious. He leaned back and folded his arms.

'You'll have to ask somebody else about that, my learned friend. I have nothing to add.'

Rüger hesitated a moment before putting his next question.

'Your quarrel at the Mephisto restaurant, referred to by the prosecuting attorney – it didn't have anything to do with another man, by any chance?'

'No.'

'You're certain?'

'Of course.'

Ferrati suddenly intervened.

'Are you jealous, Mr Mitter?'

'Stop!' bellowed Havel. 'Erase that question! You have no right to intervene at this stage, that was . . .'

'I can answer it even so,' insisted Mitter, and Havel fell silent. 'No, I'm no more inclined to jealousy than anybody else. Nor was Eva. And besides, neither of us had any need. I don't understand what my lawyer is getting at.'

Havel sighed and looked at the clock.

'If you have anything else to ask, please keep it short,' he said, turning to Rüger.

Rüger nodded.

'Of course. Just one more question, Mr Mitter: are you quite certain that your wife wasn't lying to you?'

Mitter appeared to be pausing for effect before answering.

'One hundred per cent certain,' he said.

Rüger shrugged.

'Thank you. No more questions.'

He's lying, Van Veeteren thought. The man is sitting there and lying his way into jail.

Or . . . Or is he extending the premise of telling the truth *in absurdum*?

God only knows. But why? If he doesn't miss her, why defend her as if she were an abbess?

And as he elbowed his way out through the crowd of reporters, he decided to leave the pyromaniac lying in peace for another half day.

14

Why the mother?

He didn't know the answer to that himself. Perhaps it was a question of geography. Mrs Ringmar lived in Leuwen, one of the old fishing ports on the coast. It meant an hour in the car through the polders, and perhaps that was what he needed right now. A lot of sky, not much earth.

He arrived at the precise moment the clock in the little town hall struck three. He parked in the square and asked his way to Mrs Ringmar's house.

The air was full of sea.

Sea and wind and salt. If he wanted, he could allow it to remind him of his childhood summers: but there was no reason why he should.

The house was small and white. Wedged in a confusion of shacks, sheds, fences and net racks. He wondered if there could be any room for integrity in a place like this. People lived in each other's kitchens, and every bedroom must be surrounded by listening ears.

The higher the sky, the lower the people, he thought as he rang the doorbell. Why did there have to be people in every kind of landscape?

The woman who peered at him through the barely open door was small and thin. Her hair was short and straight and completely white, and her face seemed to be somehow introverted. Van Veeteren recognized the expression from lots of other old people. Perhaps it had something to do with their false teeth . . . As if they had bitten into something thirty years ago, and stubbornly refused to let go ever since, he thought.

Or was there more than that to this woman?

'Yes?'

'Mrs Ringmar?'

'Yes.'

'My name's Van Veeteren. It was me who phoned.'

'Please come in.'

She opened the door, but only wide enough for him to be able to squeeze through.

She ushered him into the drawing room. Indicated the sofa in the corner. Van Veeteren sat down.

'I've put the coffee on. I suppose you'd like some coffee?'

Van Veeteren nodded.

'Yes, please. If it's not too much trouble.'

She left the room. Van Veeteren looked round. A neat, attractive room. A low ceiling and a degree of timelessness. He liked it. Apart from the television set, there was not much about it later than the Fifties. The sofa, table and armchairs all in teak, a display case, a little bookcase. The windowsill tightly packed with potted plants – to prevent people from seeing in, presumably. A few paintings of seascapes, family photographs. A newly married couple. Two children, at various stages. A boy and a girl. They looked to be similar in age. The girl must be Eva.

She returned with a coffee tray.

'Please accept my condolences, Mrs Ringmar.'

She nodded and clenched her teeth even more tightly. She made Van Veeteren think of a stunted pine tree.

'There's been a police officer here already.'

'I know. My colleague, Inspector Münster. I don't want to inconvenience you, but there are a few questions I'd like to ask you, just to complete the picture.'

'Fire away. I'm used to it.'

She poured out the coffee and slid the plate of biscuits towards Van Veeteren.

'What do you want to know?'

'A bit about . . . the background, as it were.'

'Why?'

'You never know, Mrs Ringmar.'

For some reason she seemed happy with this answer and, without his needing to prompt her, she set off talking.

'I'm on my own now, you know – are you a chief inspector?'

Van Veeteren nodded.

'I don't know if you can understand, but it's something I always seemed to know would happen. I've always sort of known I'd be the last one left.'

'Your husband?'

'Died in 1969. It was better that way. He wasn't . . . wasn't himself those final years. He drank a lot, but it was the cancer that got him.'

Van Veeteren slipped a small, pale-coloured biscuit into his mouth.

'The children didn't miss him, but he meant well. It's just that he didn't have the strength to do what he should have done. Some people are like that, aren't they, Chief Inspector?'

'How old were the children then? Am I right in thinking there was Eva and a son?'

'Fifteen. They are twins . . . were twins, or however I should put it.'

She took a handkerchief from her apron pocket and blew her nose.

'Rolf and Eva. Ah well, it was a good job they had each other.'

'Why was that?'

She hesitated.

'Walter had what you might call old-fashioned ideas about bringing up children.'

'I see. You mean, he beat them?'

She nodded. Van Veeteren looked out of the window. He didn't need to ask any more questions. He knew the implications; he only needed to think back to his own childhood.

Locked in the attic. Heavy footsteps on the stairs. That dry cough.

'What happened to your son? Rolf?'

'He emigrated. Signed on with a ship when he was only nineteen. It must have been a girl, but he never said anything about it. He was introverted, a bit like his father. I hope he grew out of it.'

There was something in her tone of voice that suggested . . . well, what did it suggest? Van Veeteren wondered. That she had already given up on everything, but nevertheless was determined to live life through to the end?

'Do you go to church, Mrs Ringmar?'

'Never. Why do you ask?'

'It doesn't matter. What happened to Rolf?'

'He settled down in Canada. I have . . . I've never seen him since that evening he left.'

Even though she had been living with that fact for a long time, she found it difficult to say so, that much was obvious.

'He wrote letters, presumably?'

'Two. One came in 1973, the year he left. The other came two years later. I think . . .'

'Yes?'

'I think he was ashamed. It's possible he wrote to Eva, she claimed he did in any case, but she never showed me anything. Perhaps she made it up, to make me feel better.'

They sat in silence for a while. Van Veeteren sipped at his coffee, she slid the biscuit plate in his direction.

'When did Eva leave home?'

'Six months after Rolf. She did well in her school-leaving exams and won a place at the University of Karpatz. She was the bright one, I don't know where she got it from. She read modern languages, and became a teacher, French and English – but you know that, of course.'

Van Veeteren nodded.

'And then she married that man Berger. Maybe it would have turned out all right, despite everything. After a few years they had a child. Willie. Those were happy years, I think, but then came the accident. He drowned. Our family is jinxed, Mr Van Veeteren, I think I've been aware of that the whole of my life. That's the way it is for some people . . . There's nothing you can do about it . . . Don't you think so too?'

Van Veeteren drank the rest of his coffee. Thought fleetingly of his own son.

'Yes, indeed, Mrs Ringmar,' he said. 'I think you're absolutely right.'

She smiled wanly. Van Veeteren realized that she was one of those people who have learned to find a certain grim satisfaction in the midst of all the misery.

A sort of: what did I tell you, God! I knew You had led me up the garden path from the very start! . . .

'I gather they divorced after the accident?'

'Yes, it wore Eva down, and Andreas couldn't cope with it all.'

'What do you mean?'

'Well, the loss of Willie, and Eva turning to drink and carrying on . . . She was in a home . . . for six months – I suppose you know about that?'

Van Veeteren nodded.

'Ah well, that's the way it went.'

She sighed. But there again, it was not total dejection. Only resignation, a sort of stoic calm in the face of the repugnant realities of life. Van Veeteren found himself feeling something that must have been sympathy for this long-suffering little woman. Warm sympathy. It was not an emotion he was normally prone to feel, and totally unexpected. He sat in silence for a while before asking his next question.

'But she got back on her feet again, your daughter?'

'Oh yes. You could certainly say that. I thought her husband could have helped her a bit more, but she pulled through. Oh yes.'

'Did you have a lot of contact with your daughter, Mrs Ringmar?'

'No, we were never close. I don't know why, but she had a life of her own. She didn't turn to me for help, not even then. I think . . .'

She fell silent. Chewed at a biscuit and appeared to be searching through her memory.

'What do you think, Mrs Ringmar?'

'I think she thought I had let her down. And Rolf as well.'

'In what way?'

'That I could have protected them more from Walter.'

'Didn't you do that?'

'I tried to, I suppose, but perhaps it wasn't enough. I don't know, Chief Inspector. It's hard to know things like that.'

There followed a short pause. Van Veeteren carefully brushed a few crumbs onto the floor. He had only two questions left, the ones he had actually come here to ask.

'Do you know if Eva met a new man? Before Janek Mitter, I mean?'

Mrs Ringmar shook her head.

'I don't know. I don't think so. She didn't mention anything of the sort, but then she never did. She lived in Gimsen for a few years, she had a post at a Catholic school for girls. I used to phone her once a week, but we never met.'

'Why did she move to Maardam?'

'I don't know. The job, perhaps: I don't think she liked teaching only girls. The atmosphere became a bit like a nunnery, I should imagine.'

'I can understand that. And Janek Mitter – what do you think about him?'

'Nothing. I've never met him. My daughter sent me a postcard from Greece saying that she'd remarried.'

'Were you surprised?'

'Yes, I think I was. I was pleased as well. But then things went the way they did . . .'

She shrugged again.

As if life was nothing to do with her, Van Veeteren thought. Maybe that wasn't such a silly approach.

'So you don't know anything about their relationship? Eva didn't tell you anything?'

'No. I think I only spoke to her twice on the telephone since she came back from Greece. Oh, Mitter answered the phone one of those times. I thought he sounded nice.'

When he emerged into the square it had started raining again. A few of the stall-holders were busy pulling plastic covers over their wares: vegetables, an array of fish, some glass jars with what looked like home-made confectionery. They nodded as he passed by, but that was the limit of their contact.

He pulled up his collar and sunk his hands into his pockets. Stood beside his car for a while, wondering what to do next. The rain was merely drizzle, not really falling, just floating around in the wind like a damp veil. Like a caring and sensitive hand stroking the low roofs, the modest, whitewashed town hall, caressing the lonely church spire – the only thing that dared to stand up and challenge the all-powerful sky.

The meeting with Mrs Ringmar had not really gone according to expectations. It was not easy to say exactly what he'd expected, but he had certainly had expectations . . .

He let go of the car keys. Glanced at the clock and set off towards the sea. Walked out to the end of one of the jetties, stood at the extreme edge and watched the choppy waves thudding apathetically against the concrete foundations. The air was a trinity of dampness, salt and seagull cries. He suddenly noticed that he was freezing cold.

There's something, he thought. Something compelling me to stay here.

Then he dug his hands even deeper into his pockets and started walking back towards land.

He'd asked for some paper and been given a whole ream.

Right at the top, her name; and then a single line. Nothing else. One line. He stared at it.

How do I not miss her?

It was a peculiar formulation. He underlined *how*. *How* do I not miss her?

Underlined *not* as well.

How do I *not* miss her?

Even more peculiar. The longer he stared at the question, the more telling the implications became; not the opposite, which would have been more reasonable. He smiled, concentrated, and did not let go for even a second, neither with his eyes nor his thoughts. Way back in his unconscious, the answers had already begun to form.

In the same way as I don't miss the past.

In the same way as I don't want things that happened in the past to happen now.

When I am found not guilty, or let out on parole, he thought, I shall go to her grave and sit there. Sit there with cigarettes and wine.

Guilt, punishment, mercy. Guilt, punishment, mercy. What did it matter if you were punished for something else?

Sentence me! Sentence me harshly, but be quick about it!

He threw the pen away. Curled up on the bed again, with his knees drawn up and his hands tucked away, just like a little child. He closed his eyes and the images came floating into his head.

29 June, a Thursday.

'Do you know what happened to me today, Janek?' she'd said. 'I had a proposal.'

His blood had stood still. His smile was in cement.

'Yes, a man I didn't know came up to me while I was waiting for the bus and asked me to marry him. Some people certainly know how to seize the moment.'

'What did you say?'

'That I'd think it over.'

She had also smiled, but he knew that her womb was wide open and there was blood between her teeth.

'Let's get married, Eva.'

And that was that.

He pressed his forehead against the wall. It felt good. At any moment he could choose to be completely normal, it was an act of the will, nothing else – to choose the thinnest and most durable and greyest of all the lines of thought and cling onto it like a blind priest.

How did he not miss her?

In the same way as you don't miss the unbearable.

As a young tiger doesn't miss its own death.

This man.

Who existed. Who didn't exist.

Who kept phoning, but replaced the receiver when Mitter answered. Time after time.

Whom she spoke to when Mitter was not at home.

Who didn't exist, and about whom she used to have nightmares. Who made her say:

'If I die soon, please forgive me, Janek! Forgive me, forgive me!'

Whom she renounced over and over again.

'There is no man. There *is* no man. There's only you and me, Janek. Believe me, believe me, believe me!'

It was so damned theatrical that it must be true. For it had to be the blood and the pain and her death that was the truth . . . not the lie. And when she welcomed him between her legs, that could be nothing but the truth. There were no questions. It must be strength, not weakness. Guilt and punishment and mercy had no place and no name in all this.

Forget me! Let us forget each other when we've gone! Could we ever make love if there were no such thing as death?

What was your quarrel about?

What did you talk about out there on the balcony?

He thumped his head against the wall. Roared with laughter and wept.

16

'What is your full name, please?'

'Gudrun Elisabeth Traut.'

'Occupation?'

'Teacher of German and English at Bunge High School.'

'You are a colleague of Janek Mitter and Eva Ringmar, is that correct?'

'Well . . . I am a colleague of Mitter's. I was a colleague of Eva Ringmar's.'

'Of course. Are you . . . were you . . . closely acquainted with either of them?'

'No, I wouldn't say that. I've been working at the school for about as long as Mitter, but we teach different subjects. We've never had much to do with each other.'

'And Eva Ringmar?'

'She joined the staff two years ago, when Mr Monsen retired. We both worked in the modern languages department.'

'Were you close?'

'No, certainly not. We attended the same planning meetings, shared some examinations, stood in for one another when one of us was sick, the usual kind of thing in the languages department.'

'But you didn't socialize in your spare time?'

'With Eva Ringmar?'

'Yes.'

'No, never.'

'Do you know if Eva Ringmar used to meet any of the other teachers – outside working hours, that is?'

'No, I don't think anybody did – apart from Mitter, of course.'

'Naturally. Miss Traut, I'd like you to inform us about an incident you told the police about, which happened on 30 September, five days before Eva Ringmar was murdered.'

'You mean the episode in the staff workroom?'

'Yes.'

'By all means. It was after the last lesson of the day. I'd set a test in German for year two, and we'd overrun our time slightly. It was probably around a quarter past four when I got to the languages room, where we have our desks. I thought I'd be the last one there, but to my surprise I saw Eva Ringmar sitting at her desk. It's not usual for either of us to stay on after the last lesson. You feel so tired after six or seven lessons that you simply don't have the energy to do any work; it's better to take home whatever needs marking and spend half the night on it. That's the way it is for teachers . . .'

'I understand. But on that particular day, Eva Ringmar was still there?'

'Yes, but she wasn't working. She was just sitting with her head in her hands, gazing out of the window.'

'Did you speak to her?'

'Yes. I asked her if she wasn't thinking of going home, of course.'

'What did she say?'

'At first she gave a start, as if she hadn't noticed me coming into the room. Then she said . . . without looking at me . . . she just kept on staring out of the window . . . she said that she was scared.'

'Scared?'

'Yes.'

'Can you recall her exact words?'

'Of course. She said: "Oh, it's just you, is it, Miss Traut? Thank goodness. I'm so scared today, you see."'

'You're sure those were the very words she used?'

'Yes.'

'Did you say anything else?'

'Yes, I asked her if she was afraid to go home.'

'And how did she answer that?'

'She didn't. She simply said: "No, it's nothing." Then she took her bag and left.'

'Miss Traut, what conclusions did you draw from what she said? What was your first impression?'

'I don't know . . . Perhaps that she sounded more resigned than scared, in fact.'

'Did she seem to have been expecting to see somebody else rather than you? The way she expressed herself seems to have suggested that.'

'Yes, I think that's right.'

'You interpreted it as meaning that she was pleased to see it was you, rather than one of her other colleagues?'

'Yes, it sounded like that.'

'Who might that have been?'

'Is there more than one possibility?'

'You are referring to the accused?'

'Yes.'

It was only now that Rüger made his objection.

'I insist that the last five questions and answers be erased from the proceedings! My learned friend is encouraging the witness to guess! To speculate on things she hasn't the slightest idea about . . .'

'Objection overruled!' said Havel. 'But members of the jury should bear in mind that the witness drew her own conclusions on the basis of meagre observations. Does my learned friend have any more questions for this witness?'

'Two, my lord. Do you know, Miss Traut, if Eva Ringmar had any relationship, apart from a purely professional one, with any of your male colleagues? With the exception of Janek Mitter, of course.'

'No.'

'Did you see, or hear about any other man, apart from Mitter, in connection with Eva Ringmar, during the two years she was working alongside you?'

'No.'

'Thank you, Miss Traut. No more questions.'

Rüger didn't even bother to stand up.

'Miss Traut, do you know anything at all about Eva Ringmar's private life?'

'No, there was no . . .'

'Thank you. Do you know anything about the relationship between Ringmar and Mitter?'

'No.'

'If there were any other men in Eva Ringmar's life, then, there is no reason, no reason at all, why you should know anything about it?'

'Er, no.'

'Thank you. No more questions.'

'Full name and occupation?'

'Beate Kristine Lingen. I work as a beautician at the Institut Mètre in Krowitz, but I live here in Maardam.'

'What was your relationship with the deceased, Eva Ringmar?'

'I suppose you could say I was a friend of hers, although we didn't meet very often.'

'How did you get to know Eva Ringmar.'

'We were in the same class at high school. In Mühlboden. We graduated at the same time. Saw a bit of each other afterwards as well.'

'And then?'

'Then we lost contact. We moved to different towns, got married, and so forth.'

'Are you married now?'

'No, I've been divorced for five years.'

'I see. When did you catch up with Eva Ringmar again?'

'Just after she moved here. That was two years ago, more or less. We bumped into each other in the street, and arranged to meet – we hadn't seen each other for over fifteen years. Well, we met occasionally after that, but not all that much.'

'How often?'

'Well, I suppose we saw each other about once a month, perhaps. No, maybe not as often as that. Probably about ten or twelve times in all over the last two years.'

'What did you do?'

'When we met? Er, it varied. Sometimes we just sat together at her place or mine, sometimes we went out, to the cinema or to a restaurant.'

'Did you go dancing?'

'No, never.'

'Were you, shall we say, on intimate terms?'

'Yes, I suppose you could say that. Maybe not completely, though.'

'Do you know if Eva Ringmar had any other women friends, or even one other woman friend, with whom she was on intimate terms?'

'No, I'm quite sure she didn't. She liked to be on her own.'

'Why?'

'I think it had to do with what she'd been through. The accident involving her son – I suppose you know about that?'

'Yes. You mean that she chose to live a rather solitary life?'

'Maybe not solitary, but she didn't seem to need to be together with other people. Er, she used to say something along those lines, in so many words.'

'What about her relations with men?'

'I don't think she had any. Not before Mitter, that is.'

'You think?'

'I'm pretty sure.'

'She never mentioned anybody?'

'No.'

'But you did talk about men?'

'Sometimes – there are more interesting topics, you know.'

'Really? Anyway . . . During the time you used to meet, those ten to twelve occasions, did you ever notice anything to suggest that she was having a relationship with a man?'

'No.'

'Do you think you would have noticed, if that had been the case?'

'Yes. And she'd have told me as well.'

'Really?'

'Yes. She told me about Mitter, after all.'

'When was that?'

'In May. Around the tenth, if I remember rightly. I rang her to ask if she wanted to go to the cinema, but she said she didn't have time. She'd met a man, she said.'

'Did she say who it was?'

'Yes, of course.'

'Did you speak to her, or meet her, again after that?'

'Yes. She phoned in the middle of September. Said she'd got married, and wondered if we could meet.'

'What did you decide?'

'I was about to leave for Linz, I was going on a course for two weeks, but I said I'd be in touch when I got back.'

'But it was too late by then?'

'Yes.'

'How did you think she sounded, when you spoke to her in September?'

'How she sounded?'

'Yes, did you notice anything special? Did she seem happy, or worried, or anything else?'

'No. I didn't notice anything unusual.'

'Were you surprised that she'd got married?'

'Yes, I suppose I was.'

A brief pause. Ferrati leafed through his papers. The bluebottle woke up after having slept for four days. Buzzed around the courtroom, but found nothing of interest and retired once more to the ceiling. The judge watched it for a while, as he wiped the back of his neck with a colourful handkerchief.

'Miss Lingen,' said Ferrati eventually. 'During the two years you associated with Eva Ringmar, did you ever have any reason to suspect that she might be having a relationship with a man, other than Janek Mitter?'

'No.'

'Did she have any . . . enemies?'

'Enemies? No, why on earth should she?'

'Thank you, Miss Lingen. No more questions.'

Rüger remained seated this time as well.

'Miss Lingen, does the name Eduard Caen mean anything to you?'

'No.'

'Nothing?'

'No, nothing at all.'

'You're sure?'

'Yes.'

Rüger stood up. Took a folded sheet of paper from out of his inside pocket and handed it to Havel.

'My lord, may I present the court with this list of dates on which Eva Ringmar met Eduard Caen from 15 October 1990 to 20 February 1992. Fourteen meetings in all. The dates are in chronological order and confirmed by Mr Caen himself. I have no further questions.'

17

He woke up at twenty past five.

Stayed in bed for a while and tried to go back to sleep, but that was impossible. Old images and memories of every possible occasion flooded into his consciousness, and after half an hour he got up. Put on a jumper and trousers over his pyjamas and went to the kitchen. Looked out of the window, saw that the news-stand in the square below hadn't opened yet, and sat down at the table to wait.

When the shutters were removed, he was standing there, ready. There was no risk. The woman who ran the stand recognized him, but it wasn't the first time he'd been there so early.

With *Neuwe Blatt* under his arm, he rushed up the stairs in a series of long leaps. Locked the door behind him and spread the newspaper out on the kitchen table. Started looking.

The report covered a whole page, and he read it twice. Folded the paper up, rested his head on his hands and pondered.

Loss of memory?

Of all the possibilities he'd considered over the last few weeks, that was something that had never occurred to him.

Loss of memory?

After a while, he concluded that this was the only answer.

The only one, and the right one. Mitter had forgotten him. He'd been so drunk that he quite simply didn't remember.

There was a twitching at the corners of his mouth, he could feel it. He felt drowsy now, after getting up so early. But surely this was an omen. Another sign that he was on the right path. He was free now, and strong. He only needed to look ahead. No need to fear anything. A lion.

Something was nagging deep down in his stomach.

Fear?

Was it possible that Mitter might remember?

He belched. A sour taste filled his mouth.

He took two tablets to calm down his stomach. Washed them down with soda water. Went back to bed.

The thought was already in his mind. He didn't bother to examine it more closely. It wasn't necessary yet. There was no hurry. He would surely be well advised to wait and see how things developed. The itch was there again, but he suppressed it. He had the strength and the determination, no doubt about that; but it was too soon. For the moment he could devote himself to other things. Other itches.

Liz. He stuck his hand down behind the waistband of his trousers. This is what he had to look forward to. The sick goings-on of the past were behind him now. On Wednesday, it would be Liz. His woman.

She was going to seduce him, he'd seen it in her eyes. And he would let her have her way. He'd let her do whatever she wanted until the very last moment, then he would force his way inside her and make her squeal in ecstasy. From behind and from in front and from the side.

Eva was gone. Now it was Liz. On Wednesday.

18

'Why the hell did we know nothing about this Caen?'

Van Veeteren started before Münster had time even to close the door. Münster flopped down on his usual chair between the filing cabinets and popped two throat tablets into his mouth.

'Well?'

'We were told we didn't need to trawl through the whole of her past. I don't understand why you are still persisting with this case. I've just been chatting to the chief of police downstairs in the canteen, and he said we must get down to serious work on those arson attacks now.'

'Münster, I couldn't give a shit what Hiller thinks we ought to be doing. If it's of any interest to you, your pyromaniac is called Garanin. He's Russian, and it'll be enough if we put a man on him from the twelfth onwards.'

'Why?'

'He's moonstruck. He only lights fires when there's a full moon. I had a look at the material this morning. I've got his address as well, but it'll be best to catch him in the act. Just now we're concentrating on Caen. What have you found out?'

Münster cleared his throat.

'I haven't spoken to him personally: I sent a fax this morning. We'll presumably get a reply tonight – they don't have the same time as we do down there.'

'Really?'

'Yes. And I also went to see Rüger. He didn't want to say anything, of course, so I gave him a few tips in connection with the Henderson case.'

'Bravo, Münster! Go on!'

'Well, Caen was her therapist. He looked after her when she was in Rejmershus, and they stayed in contact after she'd been let out. Rüger doesn't have much more than the dates of their meetings, in fact. His main intention was to clamp down on that witness, who claimed she knew all there was to know about Eva Ringmar, he said.'

'Is that all?'

'He's spoken to Caen on the telephone a couple of times, but he didn't think it was relevant to the case. I'm inclined to agree with him.'

'Leave me to decide what's important and what isn't, Münster! What else do you know?'

'He moved to Australia in March this year. That was why they stopped meeting. He has a private clinic in Melbourne. His wife comes from there, so presumably that's why . . .'

'What did he have to say about Eva Ringmar?'

'Not much, apparently; but I don't think Rüger pressed him very hard.'

Van Veeteren scratched the back of his neck with a pencil and pondered.

'Rüger? No, probably not. What did you write in the fax?'

Münster fidgeted.

He's gone and done something silly again, Van Veeteren thought. I'll have his guts for garters if he's made a mess of things!

'Er, I asked him to confirm the dates, and to be available for telephone contact – I said you would be speaking to him. If he answers the fax, you can call him tomorrow morning.'

Van Veeteren took out his toothpick and considered it for a few moments.

'Well done, Münster!' he said eventually.

Münster blushed.

A man who's turned forty ought to have stopped blushing, Van Veeteren thought. Especially as he's a police officer.

But never mind. Van Veeteren stood up.

'Let's go and play badminton now!'

He practised a couple of smashes.

'I have the feeling I'm going to wipe the floor with you today, Inspector!'

'But . . .'

'No buts! Stick your snout round Hiller's door and tell him we're working our butts off with the arson case. Oh yes, we'll have to pay a quick visit to my place first. I have to sort out that damned dog . . .'

Münster sighed discreetly. When the chief inspector was in the mood to make jokes, it could mean almost anything – but one thing was certain: he didn't want to be contradicted.

'What impression did you get of Andreas Berger?' Van Veeteren asked as Münster was trying to find his way out of the labyrinth that was the garage of police headquarters.

'Innocent, no doubt about it.'

'Why?'

'He has an alibi for the whole night. He lives right up in Karpatz, with a new wife and a couple of kids, and a third on the way. Very pleasant, and his wife as well. He tried to help Eva get back on track after the tragedy, wanted them to try again to make a go of it. She was the one who asked for a divorce.'

'Yes, I'm aware of all that. So there wasn't anything rotten?'

'Rotten?'

'Yes, in the State of Denmark. He wasn't trying to pull the wool over your eyes, I hope?'

Münster paused for a few seconds.

'Haven't you listened to the recording?'

'Yes . . . Yes, of course I have. I just wanted to make sure I'd got the right end of the stick . . .'

'So you can't fill me in on why we're still rooting around in this case? I thought you'd decided that Mitter had done it ages ago?'

'It's only cows who never change their opinions, Münster. It's running on rails, the whole of this case; that's the problem. I don't like trials that run on rails. For Christ's sake, even the defence's own witnesses managed to cast a shadow over him. Weiss and . . . what's his name?'

'Sigurdsen.'

'Yes, Sigurdsen. And that pale-faced deputy head. They've been colleagues of his for fifteen years, and the best they can come up with is that they haven't noticed any violent tendencies! What? We haven't seen anything! With friends like that, who needs enemies? I'll be damned if the teachers aren't just as bad as the drips we had when we were at the same school. Some of them are still there, of course.'

'What about Bendiksen, though?'

'A bit better, but even he doesn't seem to exclude the possibility that Mitter did it. That's the key, Münster. Every bastard – including Mitter himself, come to that – thinks that he did it. But there's barely a blemish on his record. A couple of slaps for his former wife, which she no doubt deserved, and some shitty little scapegoat fabrication from a schoolkids' party. I'll put money on your own history of criminal activity being ten times as bad, Münster!'

'Don't say that, sir. At least I've never been arrested.'

Van Veeteren snorted.

'I should damn well think not! You're a police officer after all. Police officers don't get arrested.'

He sat quietly for a while, busy with his toothpick.

'Anyway,' he said eventually, 'there's not a scrap of evidence to suggest that Mitter did it, and that means he'll be found guilty. Then they can sit there and go on about the burden of proof here and the burden of proof there until mould comes creeping out of their mouths. It's all irrelevant in this case. The prosecuting counsel hasn't proved a thing. But Mitter will be found guilty even so.'

'Of murder?'

'I wouldn't be surprised. Yes, I reckon that's what the verdict will be. But even if they send him to the loony bin, it makes no difference. The poor devil has probably lost the plot for good. A pity – he seems to be an amusing bastard, in fact – stop! Why aren't you driving straight ahead, Münster? We're stopping off at my place first!'

'One-way street, sir.'

'Oh my God!' Van Veeteren groaned. 'Your catalogue of sins isn't much to boast about, I regret to say.'

Münster sighed and increased speed. The chief inspector was lost in thought. When they came to Keymer Church he produced a slim cigarillo from an inside pocket and glanced sideways at Münster. He wasn't really a smoker, but he knew that the acrid fumes from this black beauty would have more of an adverse effect on his opponent's fitness than it would on his own. Especially if he avoided inhaling. If nothing else, it was an important tactical move in the psychological warfare prior to the coming match.

Münster pulled up outside Klagenburg 4. Van Veeteren carefully balanced the smouldering cigarillo on the ashtray and clambered out of the car.

'You can wait here. I'll be back in five minutes.'

Münster switched off the engine and wound down the window. Watched the chief inspector jogging up the steps.

He'll retire in ten years, he thought. Ten years . . . How long can anybody keep on summoning up enough strength to carry on playing badminton?

He recalled seeing old men who must have been well over seventy strutting around in the sports hall. He preferred to think about other things instead.

About Synn, for instance. His beautiful wife who wanted them to take the kids with them on a real winter holiday this year. Two weeks in December, when prices were at rock bottom – that's what she had in mind, if he'd understood her correctly. To some island or other, far away in a blue sea, with rustling palm trees and a bar on the beach.

And about the best way of pleading for leave with Hiller. He had plenty of overtime in the bank – but two weeks?

'Two weeks?' Hiller would gasp, looking as if he'd been asked to pose naked in the police journal. 'Two weeks?'

And now he was going to play badminton in working hours yet again.

19

Somebody had sent him a priest.

He didn't know who. Rüger, or the chief of police, or that senile judge: hard to say. Perhaps he'd come of his own accord; as Mitter understood the situation, there didn't need to be an intermediary. Just God the Father.

The vicar smiled a watery smile. Needed to keep wiping his eyes. Blamed the dry air and the air conditioning.

'I spend a lot of time listening to the air conditioning,' said Mitter. 'I think it might be the voice of God.'

The vicar nodded, and seemed interested.

'Really?'

'You are familiar with the voice of God, I take it?'

'Yes . . .'

'It's quite monotonous, don't you think?'

'I suppose the voice of God sounds different in different people's ears.'

'What kind of bloody relativism do you call that?' wondered Mitter.

'Oh . . . I was only . . .'

'Are you suggesting that the Good Lord is nothing more than a phenomenological manifestation? I think I'd better take a look at your ID, if you don't mind.'

The vicar smiled wanly. But a doubtful frown made an effort to establish itself on his shiny brow.

'If you are unable to present me with an ontological proof of the existence of God, I'll have you thrown out without more ado!'

The vicar wiped his eyes.

'Perhaps I'd better come back some other time. I see that my presence annoys you.'

Mitter rang for the warder, and two minutes later he was alone again.

He was also sent a social worker.

It was a woman in her thirties, and the warder stood on guard outside the door the whole time.

'Are you Danish?' Mitter asked.

She had blonde hair and a long neck, and so it was a reasonable question. She shook her head.

'My name's Diotima,' she said. 'Will you allow me to talk to you for a while?'

'That's a beautiful and unusual name,' said Mitter. 'You may stay as long as you like.'

'You are going to have to undergo a mental examination,' said Diotima. 'Irrespective of the verdict.'

'I'm glad to hear that,' said Mitter. 'Mind you, I hadn't intended to start teaching again right away.'

Diotima nodded. She had her hair in a ponytail, which swayed back and forth slightly whenever she moved her head. Mitter would have loved to step forward and put his hand on the back of her neck, but he didn't feel clean enough. Diotima had an air of virginal purity that was unmistakable; he concealed his hands between his knees and tried to think about something else.

'How do you feel?' she asked.

He thought it over, but failed to come up with a good answer.

'It's been very trying . . .'

She lowered her voice at the end, and so he couldn't decide if what she said was a question or a statement. If it referred to him, or to herself.

'This isn't exactly a place to be if you want to get healthy again,' she said.

He smiled.

'Do you know how long you've been in here?'

He nodded.

'What day is it today?'

'Wednesday.'

'Yes. Your verdict will be announced this afternoon. Why have you chosen not to be present?'

He shrugged.

'Would you like a cigarette?'

'Yes, please.'

She produced a pack from her briefcase. Placed it on the table between them. He released his right hand. Took a cigarette and lit it. It was a weak menthol thing, typical woman's tobacco, but he was grateful for the opportunity to smoke it right down to the filter.

Somehow or other, smoking a cigarette like that required greater concentration than usual, and he wasn't at all clear about what questions she asked him while he was busy with it. In any case, he made no replies.

When he stubbed out the cigarette in the washbasin, she stood up and he realized she was about to leave. He had a lump in his throat; it blended most unpleasantly with the vapid taste of cold smoke. Perhaps she noticed his discomfort, for she took two steps towards him and put her hand on his arm for a moment.

'I'll be back, Mr Mitter,' she said. 'And no matter what happens, you won't need to stay locked up in here.'

'Janek,' he said. 'My name's Janek. I don't want you to call me Mr Mitter.'

'Thank you. My name's Diotima.'

'I know. You've already told me.'

She smiled. Her teeth were pure white, and immaculate. He sighed.

'Are you sure you're not Danish?'

'My grandmother came from Copenhagen.'

'There you are, you see! I could tell!'

'Farewell, Janek.'

'Farewell, Diotima.'

Rüger turned up an hour after dinner to inform Mitter about the verdict. He seemed to be even more hunched than usual, and blew his nose twice before speaking.

'We didn't make it,' he said.

'Really?' said Mitter. 'We didn't make it.'

'No. But they settled for manslaughter. The jury was unanimous. Six years.'

'Six years?'

'Yes. With good conduct you could be out after five.'

'I'd have nothing against that,' said Mitter.

Rüger paused.

Then he said: 'You'll have to undergo a little mental examination. Unfortunately, it's all to do with your present state of mental health. Perhaps we should have taken another line, but nobody thinks you were not responsible for your actions at the time of the crime.'

'I see,' said Mitter. He was beginning to feel really tired now. 'Please say what you have to say as briefly as possible. I think I need to catch up on some sleep.'

'If you pass the test, it will be the state prison. If not, it will be the secure institution in Greifen or Majorna.'

'Majorna?'

'Yes, in Willemsburg. Do you know the place? It's an old lunatic asylum from the nineteenth century. Perhaps Greifen would be better.'

'Hmm, I don't think it makes any difference to me.'

'If you recover your mental health while in the institution, you will be transferred immediately to a prison – but your time spent in an institution will count towards the length of your sentence. Anyway, that's the way it looks. Are you tired?'

Mitter nodded.

'You'll be moved from here tomorrow. I hope you get a good night's sleep in any case.'

He held out his hand. Mitter shook it.

'I'm sorry we didn't make it. Really sorry . . .'

'It doesn't matter,' said Mitter. 'Please leave me alone now. No doubt we'll have an opportunity to talk some other time.'

'I'm sure we shall,' said Rüger, blowing his nose one final time. 'Farewell, and good luck tomorrow, Mr Mitter.'

'Farewell.'

The man has verbal diarrhoea, he thought as the door closed behind his lawyer. I must make sure I can keep him brief and to the point another time.

20

'Well,' said Münster, 'so that's that, then.'

'Really?' said Van Veeteren.

'Where have they sent him?'

Van Veeteren snorted.

'Majorna. Hasn't Caen answered yet?'

'No, but we have lots of other things to see to.'

'Oh yes? What, for example?'

'This, to start with,' said Münster, passing him the newspaper.

The case of the black street girl who was discovered nailed to a cross in the fashionable suburb of Dikken kept Van Veeteren and Münster busy for thirty-six hours without a break. Then a neo-Nazi organization claimed responsibility and the whole business was handed over to the national anti-terrorist squad.

Münster went home and slept for sixteen hours, and Van Veeteren would have done the same, had it not been for Bismarck. The dog was now in such a bad way that the only option left was to have it put down. He phoned Jess and explained the situation, whereupon his daughter was suddenly afflicted by an attack of sentimentality and begged him to keep the dog alive for two more days, so that she could be present at the end.

It was her dog, after all.

Van Veeteren spent those two days half crazy with exhaustion, shovelling gruel into one end of the bitch, and wiping it clean at the other end with a wet towel. By the time Jess finally turned up, he was so purple with anger and fatigue that she felt obliged to remind him of the fifth Commandment.

'Oh, Daddy,' she said, giving him a kiss. 'Might it not be just as well to take you as well, while we're at it?'

This induced from Van Veeteren a bellow so loud that Mrs Loewe, a widow who lived in the flat below, felt it incumbent upon her to ring the police. The duty officer, a young and promising constable by the name of Widmar Krause, recognized the address and had a fair idea of the circumstances. On his own authority, he cancelled the police response that he had promised the complainant.

Jess took over Bismarck, drove her to the vet's, and a few hours later the dog breathed its last in her lap.

Van Veeteren took a shower, then chased up Münster on the telephone with unusual enthusiasm.

'Has Caen replied?' he roared into the receiver.

'No,' said Münster.

'Why the hell not?'

'How's Bismarck?' enquired Münster, refreshed after his rest.

'Hold your tongue!' yelled Van Veeteren. 'Answer my question!'

'I've no idea. What do you believe the reason might be?'

'Belief is something you have in church, and God is dead! Give me his telephone number this instant, and shove the fax up Hiller's arse!'

Münster looked up the number, and half an hour later Van Veeteren got through to Caen.

'Caen.'

'Eduard Caen?'

'Yes.'

'My name is Detective Chief Inspector Van Veeteren. I'm phoning from Maardam, in the Old World.'

'Yes?'

'I'd like to ask you a few questions. I'm sorry we're so far apart.'

'What's it about?'

'Eva Ringmar. I assume you are familiar with that name.'

There was silence for a few seconds.

'Well?'

'May I remind you of my oath of professional secrecy . . .'

'The same here. May I also remind you that I have the authority to summon you to Europe for interrogation, if I want to.'

'I understand. Let's hear it, then. What do you want to know?'

'A few minor details. In the first place, did you have an affair with her?'

'Of course not. I never had an affair with any of my clients.'

'So that's not the reason why you emigrated to Australia?'

'Don't be silly, Inspector! I really have no intention of answering that kind of . . .'

At that point the connection was lost. Van Veeteren thumped the receiver on his desk a few times, and after a short intermezzo in Japanese, Caen was back on the line.

'That kind of what?' asked Van Veeteren.

'Insinuation,' said Caen.

'I'm looking for a murderer,' said Van Veeteren, unmoved. 'A man. Can you give me any suggestions?'

There was a pause.

'No . . .' Caen said hesitantly. 'No, I don't think I can. To tell you the truth – can I rely on you, Inspector?'

'Of course.'

'To tell you the truth, I didn't get anywhere with her. But she got better even so. The reason I was brought in was the problems caused by the death of her son . . . but there was something . . .'

It sounds as if he's weighing every single word, Van Veeteren thought. Does he have any idea of what it costs to phone halfway across the world?

'What?'

'I don't know. There was something hidden. She didn't bother to pretend – that there wasn't anything, I mean. Perhaps it wasn't possible to hide it. There was something she didn't tell me about, and she was quite open about that fact. Are you with me? It's not easy to explain this over the telephone.'

'She had a secret?'

'To put it simply, yes.'

'A man?'

'I have no idea, Inspector. No idea at all.'

'Give me a clue!'

'There's nothing else I can say. I promise you!'

'What the hell did you talk about?'

'Willie. Her son. Yes, we talked almost exclusively about him. She used me as a means of remembering him. I have a son myself, about the same age as hers, and she liked to compare . . . We often pretended that Willie was still alive, we talked about our sons and discussed their futures. That kind of thing.'

'I see . . . And she got better?'

'Yes, she did. Those meetings in Maardam were not justified at all from a therapeutic point of view, but she was insistent. I liked her, and she paid my fee. Why should I turn her away?'

'Why indeed, Mr Caen? What was your impression of her husband, Andreas Berger?'

'Not much at all. We never met, and she didn't say much about him. She was the one who wanted a divorce . . . It was due to the accident, no doubt about that; but don't ask me how. I think he wanted to keep her, even when she was at her worst.'

Van Veeteren pondered that.

'I thought you had arrested a suspect?' Caen said.

'He's been tried and sentenced,' said Van Veeteren.

'Sentenced? Has he admitted it? Then why are you still . . .'

'Because he didn't do it,' interrupted Van Veeteren. 'Can I ask you to do something for me?'

'Of course.'

'If anything occurs to you, no matter how insignificant it might seem, would you please get in touch with me and tell me. You have my number, I take it?'

'No, I don't think I have.'

'Didn't you receive our fax?'

'Your fax? I'm afraid I haven't checked the fax machine for a week or more. I'm on holiday, you see.'

'On holiday in November?'

'Yes, it's early summer here. Twenty-five degrees, the lemon trees are in blossom . . .'

'I'll bet they are,' said Van Veeteren.

21

When Lotte Kretschmer woke up on Sunday 17 November, she decided almost immediately to put an end to her affair with her boyfriend, a twenty-one-year-old electrician from Süsslingen by the name of Weigand. The decision had been maturing inside her for several weeks, but now the time had come. As usual, Weigand was lying asleep beside her, his mouth wide open, and as she didn't want him to stagger through the next few days in ignorance of such an important decision, she gave him a good shaking, woke him up and explained the facts.

They had been together for eight months, it's true; but even so, she hadn't reckoned with the argument, the tears and the accusations taking up the whole day.

When she eventually set off for work at about seven o'clock that evening, she felt that what she needed more than anything else was twelve hours of sound sleep. Instead, she was faced with twelve hours of night duty.

This is mentioned as an explanation, not as an excuse.

However, when the evening round of medication took place at nine o'clock, Janek Mitter – along with several other patients – was not given the usual mild, sedative anti-depressants, but instead was required to swallow two multi-vitamin tablets enhanced with ten vital minerals plus selenium.

Both types of pill were pale yellow in colour, round in shape and coated with sugar, and were stored in the same cupboard.

This is not mentioned as an excuse, either.

There was no lack of repercussions. Instead of a deep and dreamless sleep, Mitter was surprised to find himself lying wide awake in his tubular steel bed, gazing out through the window at a starry sky almost as dense as that night in Levkes. He remembered that November was the ideal month for astronomers, and that his birthday must have been and gone – because it was on the occasion of his fourteenth birthday that he had been given the telescope by his father.

Where was it now?

It took a while to work that one out. But he managed it. It was with Jürg, of course. Jürg had kept it in his room when he was staying with Mitter, but he'd taken it with him when he moved to Chadow.

So, he could still remember some things.

Various other details cropped up, then faded away again as he lay there; some from long ago . . . memories of his childhood, and his youth; some more recent . . . Irene and the children, goings-on at school and trips with Bendiksen; but it was well into the early hours before that night cropped up in his mind's eye . . .

He was sitting on the corner sofa. He had got dressed and there were candles burning here and there. Eva was wandering round in her kimono and singing something, he had some difficulty in keeping his eyes on her. He had a glass in his hand, and remembered that it was absolutely essential . . . absolutely vital that he didn't drink another single drop. He turned his head, the room was swaying to and fro . . . Not another single drop.

He took a swig. It was a good wine, he could taste that despite all the cigarettes: dry and full-bodied. And the doorbell rang. Who the hell . . .?

Eva shouted something and disappeared. He realized that she had gone to open the door for the visitor, but he couldn't see the hall from where he was sitting. He grinned.

Yes, he remembered grinning at the fact that he was so drunk, he daren't even try to look back over his shoulder. Then Eva came back into the room with the visitor, the visitor first. He couldn't see the man's face, it was too high up; a move like the one required to see it was impossible. The visitor remained standing for quite some time before sitting down, and Eva was somewhere else, she'd shouted something, but now the man was sitting there in any case; Mitter could see his torso and his arms, only the lower part of his arms, his rolled-up shirt sleeves . . . He was smoking, and Mitter also took a cigarette and the nicotine made him feel dizzy. The smoke was hot and nauseating in his throat, and it wasn't long before they started talking. And then the visitor leaned forward and flicked the ash off his cigarette, and Mitter saw who it was.

He opened his eyes and the myriad stars came meandering into his consciousness, making him feel dizzy.

I shall forget this again, he thought. It came to me for just a moment, but tomorrow it will have gone.

He fumbled for the pencil lying on the bedside table. Heard it fall on the floor. Leaned tentatively over the side of the bed and groped around in the dark over the cold stone flagstones, and eventually found it.

Where? he thought. Where?

Then he took the Bible out of the drawer in the bedside table. Thumbed through as far as Mark or thereabouts, and wrote down the visitor's name.

Closed the Bible. Put it back in its place and closed the drawer. Fell back exhausted on his pillows, and felt . . . felt something starting to tremble inside him.

It was a flame. A pitifully small candle flame that somebody had lit, and was no doubt well worth looking after. Keeping alight.

He was mad, but at least he understood the implications of this memory.

And thanks to the power of that pale candlelight, he gave himself the task of coming to terms with it all when dawn came.

Writing a letter to the visitor.

Just a line.

He fell asleep. But woke up again.

Perhaps he should also make a phone call.

To that unpleasant person . . . whose name escaped him for the moment.

As long as the flame doesn't go out.

22

The telephone call was put through from the switchboard to the duty officer only minutes before he was due to be relieved.

In fact, he ought to have been relieved several hours previously, but Widmar Krause's young wife had started to feel labour pains in the early hours of the morning, and it was her first pregnancy. Erich Klempje had no alternative but to stay on duty. He'd started his shift as early as 9 p.m. the previous night, but isn't that what colleagues are for . . .?

He was only staying on until the emergency was over.

There was no question of her giving birth already, but getting to the hospital and waiting, and then the examination followed by getting back home again, all took time.

He noted it down automatically in the black folder.

11.56 Incoming call from Majorna.

'Police. Sergeant Klempje. How can I help you?'

At that very moment the doors were flung open and in marched two constables, Joensuu and Kellerman, dragging with them a whore from V-Square high on drugs.

'You can only have me one at a time!' she yelled. 'And it's double price for bleeding police bastards!'

Although the whore was only small, and the combined weight of Joensuu and Kellerman must have been upwards of 32 stone, they were obviously having trouble in propelling her to the cells. Blood was pouring from scratches on one of Kellerman's cheeks, and Klempje suspected that the whore would not be totally unmarked if only they could get her into a dark corner.

'Kiss my arse! But brush your teeth first!' she screeched, landing a well-directed knee between Joensuu's legs.

Joensuu cursed and bent double. Klempje sighed and put his hand over the receiver.

Two probationers who had been writing reports came to assist, and before long the whole group was out of earshot.

For Christ's sake, Klempje thought. If I don't get some sleep soon I shall start crying.

He returned to the telephone call.

'Yes, what do you want?'

'This is JM from Majorna. This is JM from Majorna.'

Oh no! Klempje thought.

'Yes, I've made a note of that. What's it about?'

'I'd like to speak to . . . I'd like to speak to . . .'

Silence. Klempje shook his head. The voice was monotonous, but tense. It sounded as if he was reading out something he'd learned off by heart.

'Yes?'

'I'd like to speak to . . .'

'Who do you want to speak to? This is the police here.'

'I know that,' said the voice. 'I want to talk to the unpleasant one.'

'The unpleasant one?'

'Yes.'

'Who is the unpleasant one? This place is teeming with unpleasant police officers,' said Klempje, suffering from an attack of disloyalty to his colleagues.

'The worst of them all . . . He's big and his face is purple and he swears. I want to speak to him.'

'OK, I'll make a note of that.'

'Is he there now?'

'No.'

'Thank you.'

The caller hung up. Klempje sat for a few seconds with the receiver in his hand. Then he also hung up and went back to his crossword.

Two minutes later Krause appeared.

'Thank God for that,' groaned Klempje. 'Well?'

'Nothing,' said Krause. 'False alarm.'

'If it hurts, it hurts, I suppose.'

'Klempje, when it comes to pregnant women you are a greenhorn.'

'You can call me a buffalo if you like, as long as I can get some sleep now.'

'Anything special?'

Klempje thought for a moment.

'No. Some madman or other rang from Majorna just a couple of minutes ago and wanted to talk to what he called the unpleasant one. Funny, eh? Who do you think he could have meant?'

'VV?'

'Who else?'

'What was it about?'

'No idea. He hung up. And Joensuu and Kellerman are down in the cells wrestling with a whore on cloud nine. Holy shit, but what a glamorous life we lead!'

Klempje staggered out and Krause took his place in the glass booth.

The unpleasant one? he thought. Majorna?

He thought for a moment, then called the fourth floor.

No answer.

He tried Münster.

No answer there, either.

Oh, what the hell? he thought and took a paperback out of his inside pocket. *Parenting*.

23

The letter arrived in the afternoon post.

Without giving it a second thought he put it in his pocket; he had a number of things to do that couldn't wait, and he might just as well read it when he got home. He might have wondered in passing what it could be: he didn't often receive post at work, and this letter seemed to be private.

He then forgot all about it, of course, and it wasn't until he was feeling around in his jacket pockets for laundry tokens that he discovered it. He used a propelling pencil to split it open and took out a sheet of paper folded twice.

It was only one single line. But it was clear enough.

The first few seconds, his mind was a complete blank. He stood there motionless, leaning over the desk, his eyes nailed to the words.

Then his brain started working. Slowly and methodically. Yet again he was surprised by how he could be so worked up and yet so calm at the same time. How he could simultaneously feel his blood seething and also let his thoughts coldly and objectively glean the reality behind this letter.

He examined the postmark. Yesterday's date.

Looked more closely. A few letters were illegible, but it must be Willemsburg.

That fitted. That's where he was incarcerated. Everybody knew that. A few had even been to visit him.

He stretched out on the bed and switched off the light. Felt the prickling sensation in his gut, but was able to keep it under control without difficulty. The question was . . .?

The question was so easy to formulate that it was almost embarrassing.

Were there any more letters?

Were there any more letters?

He went to the kitchen and opened a beer. Sat by the window. Drank a few long swigs and blinked away the tears caused by its kick.

With the certainty of a sleepwalker he produced the answer.

No, there were no more letters.

He had been at home for three hours. Nobody had phoned. A delay of that length would have been inconceivable: no, there were no other letters.

He drummed his fingers on the bottle.

There was just one other possibility . . . His brain was working lightning fast now . . . the possibility that it took longer for letters to be delivered to police headquarters. They might receive a letter tomorrow. That was a possibility. It had to be faced up to.

He took another swig. Jackdaws were cawing outside the window. His mind wandered to Hitchcock and *The Birds*, and there was something attractive about that memory, something that appealed to him – but perhaps now wasn't the right time to be thinking about that.

But if . . . If there was another letter, already written and posted . . . irrevocably . . . it must arrive by tomorrow. Tomorrow at the latest.

Tomorrow. If he hadn't heard anything by noon tomorrow, he was safe.

That was the answer. He raised the bottle to his mouth and emptied it. Looked up at the sky over the rooftops. Darkness was falling fast; no doubt there would be another star-filled sky tonight. He wondered vaguely if that would be an advantage or a disadvantage.

But the final answer was still in the offing even so. He had waited and been patient. Bided his time.

He took a deep breath. The prickling sensation in his gut was strong and pleasant now. Almost erotic.

It was time.

24

He woke up and couldn't remember his name.

That had happened before, he was sure. He had a memory of another morning.

But now it was night. A shaft of pale moonlight enveloped the foot end of his bed, and draped a figure standing there.

It was a woman, no doubt about it. Her silhouette was outlined clearly against the window, but her face was in darkness.

'Diotima?' he whispered out of the blue, he didn't know why. It was just a name that floated up to the surface of the well of forgetfulness. Somebody he missed.

But no, surely it wasn't her?

She came closer. Walked slowly round the head of the bed, came round to his right side. Raised her arm, and something glinted in her hand . . .

Mitter . . . Janek Mattias Mitter . . . He remembered just as the pain cut him in two.

And before the scream had time to leave his mouth, a pillow had been pressed down over his face. He groped around with his hands, tried in vain to grasp his visitor's wrists . . . But he lacked the strength, and pain pumped white-hot glowing waves out of his chest and stomach.

I am nobody, he thought. Nothing but a colossal pain.

The last thing to come to him was an image.

An old picture, something he might have drawn himself once. Or taken from a book.

It was an image of death, and it was a very personal truth.

An ox.

And a swamp.

This was his life. An ox that had fallen into a swamp.

Sinking slowly down into the mud. Sinking slowly into death.

When night came, a calm and starry night, only his head was still above ground, and the last thing . . . the very last thing to disappear, was the ox's surprised eye, staring up at the millions of stars.

That was the final image.

And when night closed in over the eye, everything became nothing.

II

Friday, 22 November–
Sunday, 1 December

25

'Rooth, would you mind asking Miss Katz to bring us a few bottles of soda water, please!'

Hiller removed a strand of hair from his jacket collar and eyed the assembled police officers.

'Where's Van Veeteren? Didn't I say that everybody was to be here at five o'clock? It's three minutes past. The press conference is at six on the dot, and we need to know exactly where we are by then. This is a shitty situation if ever I saw one!'

Reinhart stood up.

'I'll go and fetch him. He's busy scaring the life out of a psychiatrist.'

Münster leaned back and tried to see out of the window. The chief of police's office was on the fifth floor, and was generally called either 'the fifth column' or 'the greenhouse'. The former connotation referred to the enemy in our midst, the latter to the occupier's partiality for potted plants. The picture window looking out over the southern part of the town allowed in such a generous intake of warm light that a wide array of azaleas, bougainvillea and all manner of palms were able to flourish. So successfully that the intended panoramic view had long since been replaced by an almost impenetrable wall of greenery.

Münster sighed and observed the chief of police instead. He was rotating back and forth on his swivel chair. Moving papers, adjusting his tie, brushing dust from his midnight-blue suit . . . These were all telltale signs: press conference! And it wouldn't be just newspaper reporters and photographers eager for details, but radio and television news hounds as well. Münster had seen an outside-broadcast van park in the court-yard down below half an hour or so previously. Presumably they were busy with cables and light meters in the conference room. Hiller was no doubt right.

This really was a shitty situation.

'Van Veeteren, can you fill us in on the current situation,' said Hiller when everybody had finally turned up. 'I have to meet the press in forty-five minutes . . .'

'No,' said Van Veeteren. 'I have a headache. Münster can do it.'

'Oh, OK,' said Münster, taking out his notebook. 'From the beginning, or . . .?'

The chief of police nodded. Münster cleared his throat.

'Well, it was 7.10 a.m. when we received an emergency call from Majorna, the psychiatric hospital out at Willemsburg.'

'We know that,' said Hiller.

'Reinhart and I arrived there at 7.35, together with Jung and deBries. The victim was lying in his bed in ward 26B. We cordoned it off, of course. The other patient had already been moved to another room.'

'Very sensible,' muttered Van Veeteren.

'Anyway, the dead man was Janek Mitter – we both recognized him, and it was obvious what had happened. The whole bed was full of blood, and there was a lot on the floor as well.'

He leafed through his notebook.

'According to Meusse, who arrived ten minutes later, the cause of death was internal injuries and loss of blood caused by three deep stab wounds, one of which had sliced right through the aorta. Death appeared to have been more or less instantaneous, a few seconds at most; and Meusse estimated the time of death at somewhere between three and half past three.'

'The hour of the wolf,' said Van Veeteren. 'The time of nightmares and death.'

'How come the press got to the scene before we did?' Hiller asked. 'Yet again,' he added.

'Tip-off from the staff,' said Reinhart. 'One of the nurses had a girl staying the night with him – a hack with *Neuwe Blatt*. They'd spent the night screwing in his flat in the staff quarters, so she was only a three-minute walk away. Pretty, incidentally . . .'

'Hm,' said Hiller. 'Go on!'

'Rooth and Van Veeteren arrived half an hour later,' said Münster. 'Along with the forensic team. They ran a fine-tooth comb over the place, of course, but there wasn't much to find.'

'Really?'

'Apart from what was obvious, that is. The murderer had entered the room, killed the victim – a scary sort of knife, apparently, double-edged, some kind of hunting knife; there are so many variations of that type of thing nowadays. Anyway, the murderer left through the window and down the drainpipe . . .'

'I thought all the patients were locked up,' said Hiller.

'Not necessary,' said Rooth. 'Not with the sophisticated drugs they have nowadays – although they have bars on the first- and second-floor windows. The drainpipe held on this occasion, but the next one to try it will probably fall to his death: three of the anchor brackets have come loose.'

'We'd better inform the murderer,' said Reinhart. 'We can't have him falling and hurting himself.'

'Any fingerprints?' Hiller asked.

'Not a trace, and no marks where he landed, either. There was a paved path at that particular point.'

'Are we allowed to smoke?' Reinhart wondered.

'Sit next to the window,' said Hiller.

Reinhart and Rooth changed places. Reinhart scraped out the spent contents of his pipe into a flower pot. Van Veeteren gave him an approving nod.

'Carry on!' said Hiller.

Münster closed his notebook again.

'There were four people on night duty – on ward 26, that is. Four rooms make up that ward. It's the same on the first and second floors.'

'Wards 24, 25 and 26, each on a different floor,' explained Rooth. 'A, B, C and D in each of them. Twelve rooms in all in that building. Two beds per room, eight in each ward; but some were empty. That happens occasionally, every other year or so – somebody is cured, or dies, and so there's a vacancy.'

'But there are plenty of loonies waiting in the queue,' said Reinhart, finally getting his pipe to burn.

'So twelve staff on night duty?' Hiller wondered.

'Yes,' said Münster. 'Two awake and two asleep on every ward. We've interrogated all twelve, especially the ones on ward 26, of course. And . . . well, it seems pretty clear what happened.'

'Really?' said Hiller, and stopped rotating his watch round his wrist at last.

'It was some time before we realized, of course. We had to check with the day staff as well, but everybody seems to agree. There was a visitor who stayed behind.'

'Stayed behind?' said Hiller.

'Yes, she arrived at about five o'clock – visiting hours last until half past six. But that woman stayed behind, and everybody forgot about her.'

'A woman?' Hiller asked.

'Yes, that's what they say,' said Reinhart, blowing a smoke ring that slowly sailed in the direction of the chief of police. 'But it could have been a man, of course.'

'Huh, what the hell are their routines?' Hiller asked, wafting away the smoke ring. 'Do we have a description?'

'Eight,' said Münster. 'They are more or less in agreement. Quite a tall woman with thick, dark hair and glasses. Duffel coat and jeans. Only three of them spoke to her, but another five saw her. Including a patient. He's prepared to swear on oath that it was a man dressed up as a woman. The rest are not sure.'

'Van Veeteren, what do you think?' Hiller asked.

'I agree with the loony,' said Van Veeteren. 'But he'll have to look after the oath himself.'

Hiller clasped his hands in front of him on his desk.

'So this . . . person . . . remained hidden inside the building until . . . three o'clock, half past three in the morning. Then murdered Mitter, and climbed out through the window? It sounds a little on the cold-blooded side, don't you agree, gentlemen?'

'You can say that again,' said Reinhart.

'As callous as it comes,' said Rooth. 'It's like a damn B-film more than anything else . . .'

'The other patient,' interrupted Hiller. 'The one sharing the same room. What did he have to say?'

'Nothing,' said Münster. 'He slept like a log, I don't think he even woke up when they carried him out.'

'Very fancy drugs they have nowadays,' said Rooth.

'Remember *One Flew Over the Cuckoo's Nest*?' asked Reinhart.

Hiller looked at the clock.

'A quarter of an hour to go,' he informed everybody.

'Can't you keep the hacks waiting for a while?' asked Reinhart.

'Even if we can't do anything else, at least we can make a point of being punctual,' said Hiller, glaring at Reinhart's pipe. 'Besides, I gather it's a live broadcast.'

'Well, I'll be damned,' said Rooth.

'OK,' said Hiller. 'Van Veeteren, what clues do we have? What theories are you working on? I couldn't care less about your headache.'

Van Veeteren removed his toothpick from between his lower teeth, broke it in two and laid it on the shiny table in front of him.

'Do you want to know what you ought to say, or what I think?'

'Both. But perhaps we can take your private thoughts afterwards. Give me some pearls to cast before the swine.'

'As you wish,' said Van Veeteren. 'An unknown person has entered Majorna and killed Janek Mattias Mitter, who was found guilty of the manslaughter of his wife a few weeks ago. He was being looked after in Majorna because of his frail mental condition. There is nothing to suggest that the two deaths are connected in any way.'

'I can't say that, for Christ's sake!' roared Hiller nervously, wiping his brow.

'Say that there is a connection then,' Van Veeteren suggested. 'It makes no difference to me.'

There followed a few seconds of silence. The only sounds came from Reinhart's pipe and the chief of police's rotating wristwatch.

'Was Mitter innocent then?' asked Rooth.

Nobody answered.

'So it's the same person that committed both the murders?' Rooth continued.

Van Veeteren leaned back and stared up at the ceiling.

'He was an amusing devil, I must say,' he said eventually. 'There's only one thing that surprises me: that he didn't try to contact us instead, if he'd remembered something.'

'What do you mean?' said Hiller.

'You mean . . .' said Reinhart.

Van Veeteren nodded slowly.

'. . . that Mitter tipped off the murderer?' said Münster. 'But not us?'

Van Veeteren said nothing.

'How could anybody be so damned stupid?' Reinhart wondered.

'You try spending some time in the loony bin and let them fill you up with drugs, and see how smart you feel after a week of that,' said Rooth. 'If it's as VV says and Mitter managed to beat a hole through his memory loss, what the hell did he think he was playing at? I have to say I have my doubts.'

'No, it's as I say,' said Van Veeteren with a yawn. 'But we don't need to quarrel over it. You'll see in the end.'

Hiller stood up.

'It's time. Van Veeteren, I want a word with you afterwards.'

'By all means. You'll find me in the canteen. There's a programme on the box that I don't want to miss . . .'

Hiller adjusted his tie and hurried out through the door.

'A shitty situation if ever I saw one,' he muttered.

26

Münster knocked on the door and came in.

'Take a seat,' said Van Veeteren, pointing at the chair between the filing cabinets. Münster sat down and slumped back against the wall.

'It's eleven o'clock,' he said. 'Why can't we go home and get some sleep, and continue tomorrow instead?'

Van Veeteren clasped his hands on the desk in front of him.

'People think better at night. You'll get fat if you sleep too much. You're already starting to get slow when you come forward to the net. A murderer is on the loose. Do you need any more explanations?'

Oh shut up, Münster thought; but he didn't say it.

'Coffee?' Van Veeteren asked in a friendly tone.

'Yes, please,' said Münster. 'That would be appreciated. I've only drunk eleven cups so far today.'

Van Veeteren poured out something evil-smelling and brown from a grimy Thermos flask. Handed Münster a paper mug.

'Now listen carefully, Inspector. You had better concentrate hard, otherwise you could find yourself sitting here all night. The hard work starts tomorrow, so it would be as well if we had some idea of what the hell we should do. Do you want to call your wife?'

Münster shook his head.

'I've already done so. She saw on the television that . . .'

'Good. Well, who's our culprit? Our murderer?'

Münster sipped the lukewarm coffee. Pulled a face as he swallowed, and guessed that it must have been brewed between twelve and eighteen hours previously.

'Does that mean that you don't know?' Van Veeteren asked. Münster nodded.

'That means: no, I don't know,' he confirmed.

'Same here,' said Van Veeteren. 'And I have to admit that I haven't the slightest trace of a suspicion, either. That's why you have to pull your socks up. Let's start with number two!'

'Eh?'

'With the second murder, the murder of Mitter. What is the most important question?'

'Why!' said Münster.

'Correct! We can ignore for the moment when and how and if the victim emptied his bowels during the last eight hours. What we need to concentrate on is why. Why was Mitter murdered?'

'We're assuming that it was the same killer?'

'Yes,' said Van Veeteren. 'If it isn't the same one, it will be a different matter altogether. A case we won't solve for a very long time, not using the methods we use in any case. No, dammit, it is the same person, I know it is. But why? And why just now?'

'He was warned?'

'Do you really think so?'

'But, sir, you said yourself . . .'

'You can drop the sir after ten o'clock.'

'You said yourself that the murderer must have been warned by Mitter himself. That Mitter must have remembered something to do with the first murder.'

'Let us assume that I'm certain of that. Mitter informed the murderer that he remembered who he was.'

'Or she.'

'Is that likely?'

'No.'

'We'll assume it's a man. Next question, Münster!'

Münster scratched the back of his neck.

'How?' he said. 'How did he inform the murderer?'

'Correct again! You're on top form, Münster!'

'And why did he say nothing to the police?'

'We'll take that later,' said Van Veeteren. 'First things first. How? What do you think?'

'I . . . he phoned, or wrote a letter. I don't think he sent a fax.'

Van Veeteren's baggy cheeks twitched to form something that might have been a smile. But it was so brief that Münster was unable to decide for certain.

'He wrote,' Van Veeteren confirmed.

'How do you know?'

'Because I checked. Listen carefully, and I'll explain. Mitter wrote a letter last Monday . . . the eighteenth . . . and it was posted the same day. He was given an envelope, paper and a pen by the staff. They evidently have everything locked up, and hand it out to the patients on request. If they've been behaving themselves, that is. Everything seems to be locked up at that place – apart from the patients, but they get pills instead, of course. Anyway, it's clear that he sent a letter last Monday. If we assume that the murderer lives here in Maardam, or in the district at least, he should have received it on Tuesday. He spends Wednesday waiting, and then he strikes on Thursday evening. He gets dressed up, finds a way of entering the ward, waits calmly. Hides himself for eight or nine hours – just imagine that, Münster. That bastard stays in there for eight or nine hours until it's time, that's what's so impressive about this whole business. It's not just anybody we're dealing with, I think we ought to be clear about that.'

Münster nodded. His tiredness was fading away now, thinning out and being penetrated by concentration. He looked out of the window. The silhouettes of the cathedral and the skyscrapers at Karlsplatsen were outlined against the night sky, and that feeling came slowly creeping up on him, the feeling that always turned up sooner or later in an investigation, that could keep him lying wide awake in his bed, despite being so exhausted that he was on the point of collapse. This was the challenge, this was the core of their work. The murderer was somewhere out there. One of this town's 300,000 inhabitants had taken it upon himself to kill two of his fellow human beings, and it was the duty of him, and Van Veeteren and all the rest of them, to nail the man – or the woman. It was going to be one hell of a job in fact. They would work for thousands of hours before the case was closed, and when they eventually had all the answers, it would become clear to them that nearly everything they had done had been a complete waste of time. They would realize that if only they'd done this or that right away, they would have cracked it in two days instead of two months.

But this was only the beginning. So far they knew virtually nothing. There was only Van Veeteren and himself shut up in this messy office, hemmed in by questions and answers and guesses, in a slow but inexorable search for the right track. If they didn't find it, if they took a wrong turning at the very beginning – well, it could be that two months from now they would be sitting around in this very same room with their thousands of wasted hours and no murderer. This was the millstone round their necks: finding themselves at the far end of a cul-de-sac, knowing that they would have to walk all the way back. And it was always the first turning that was the most important one.

'We made a mistake,' said Van Veeteren, as if he'd been able to read Münster's thoughts. 'We jailed Mitter, and now he's dead. The least we can do for him is to get the right man this time.'

'One thing has struck me,' said Münster. 'They're so different, these two murders. Assuming it is the same killer, that is. This second one is so much more . . . professional than the first one. Perhaps Mitter was even a witness to the first one. That seemed to be unplanned . . . random. This second one is so much more . . . ice-cold.'

Van Veeteren nodded.

'Yes, I know. He's acquired a taste for blood, he's learned a thing or two. But let's go back to that letter. Are you with me?'

'Of course.'

'Mitter writes a letter to the murderer, to the person he suspects has had something to do with the death of his wife . . .'

'Stop!' said Münster. 'How do you know that he really did write to the murderer? Why couldn't it have been an ordinary letter to . . . to a friend?'

'We've started checking,' said Van Veeteren, inserting another toothpick into his mouth. 'But the investigation isn't quite finished yet. None of those close to him has received a letter – his ex-wife, his children or his good friends. There are a few we haven't managed to get hold of yet: Petersén and Stauff are working on that. But I don't think they'll find anybody.'

'But couldn't that indicate . . .'

'Yes, of course it's very possible that the murderer is one of those; but I don't think it will do any harm if he is made aware that we are not a bunch of idiots. If we then pin him down a week or two from now, all we have to do is nail him. There's nothing like a murderer who's been kept on tenterhooks for a while.'

Münster nodded.

'Back to that letter,' said Van Veeteren. 'Let's assume it is in fact a letter to inform the murderer about something. Questions, Münster!'

'Well, the address, of course. Could somebody have checked the address? But I don't suppose so . . .'

'Absolutely right! Those blind idiots who run Majorna haven't seen a thing! Not a single letter! Even though somebody was standing over Mitter as he wrote, watching him.'

'Why?'

'I don't know. Either they keep a check on letters written for reasons of security, or there's some weirdo writing a dissertation – the link between schizophrenia and left-handedness, who cares! The important thing – and listen carefully to this, Inspector, because it's crucial – Mitter is given paper, pen, envelope and stamp by a nurse, he sits down in the assembly hall – yes, that's what they call it – and writes his letter, it takes no more than ten minutes, he hands it to the nurse who posts it in the box outside the entrance when he goes home two hours later. Until then, he's been carrying it around in the pocket of his working jacket. Is that all clear?'

'Of course.'

'What strikes you about it?'

Münster closed his eyes. Leaned his head against the wall and thought about it.

'I don't know . . .'

'The address.'

'What do you mean?'

'Think, Münster, for Christ's sake! If you can't work this one out, I'll never support your application for promotion!'

'Of course: how did he know the address?'

'Of the murderer, yes.'

'Address book?'

'No. He didn't have one with him. Not anywhere in the hospital.'

'Telephone directory?'

'There isn't one in the assembly hall.'

'And he stayed in there all the time?'

'The nurse was standing outside, keeping an eye on him. Never let Mitter out of his sight – don't ask me why. There are glass doors between the rooms, he smoked two cigarettes, he said. Evidently a five-minute brand . . .'

'If the nurse was being that careful, surely he could have taken a look at the letter as well.'

Van Veeteren grunted.

'Do you think I haven't explained that to him? Mind you, it's by no means sure that would have helped us: he didn't seem all that good at reading. He's the sort of he-man who can overturn a locomotive, but doesn't know which end of a pen to hold downwards.'

Münster smiled dutifully.

'Enough of that,' said Van Veeteren. 'Nobody has seen what Mitter wrote on the envelope. He had no help from an address book or a telephone directory or anything else. So that means . . .'

'That he knew the address off by heart. Oh, shit . . .'

'I'm coming to the same point, though I have to say I get there a bit faster. How many addresses do you know off by heart, Munster?'

Münster pondered that one.

'Count them!' said Van Veeteren.

'My own,' said Münster.

'Bravo,' said Van Veeteren.

'My parents' . . .'

'And?'

'My childhood address in Willby . . .'

'Too old.'

Münster hesitated.

'My sister's in Hessen – I think.'

He paused.

'Oh, and police HQ, of course,' said Münster eventually.

Van Veeteren felt for a new toothpick, but he'd evidently run out.

'Finished?' he asked.

Münster nodded.

'You're forty-two years old and have learned four addresses off by heart. Well done, Inspector. I could only manage three. What conclusion do you draw from that?'

'He wrote to somebody . . . very close to him.'

'Or?'

'To himself?'

'Idiot,' said Van Veeteren. 'Or?'

'Or to his workplace.'

Van Veeteren clasped his hands behind his head and stretched himself out on his desk chair.

'Bunge High School,' he said. 'Fancy a beer?'

Münster nodded again. Van Veeteren looked at the clock.

'If you give me a lift home, you can buy me a glass of beer on the way. I think Kraus will be best.'

Münster wriggled into his jacket.

I suppose he's doing me a favour, he thought.

'It's Friday already, dammit!' Van Veeteren announced as they elbowed their way through to the bar.

Carrying two foaming tankards, he wriggled into an almost non-existent space between two young women on a bench. He lit a cigarillo, and after a couple of minutes there was room for Münster as well.

'Bunge or a good friend,' said Van Veeteren. 'And we can no doubt forget about the good friends. Any snags?'

'Yes,' said Münster. 'At least one. An unusual name.'

'What do you mean?'

'If you have an unusual name, letters get through to you no matter what. Dalmatinenwinckel, or something like that . . .'

'What the hell are you on about?'

'Dalmatinenwinckel. I once had a girlfriend called that. It was enough to write her name and the town, a street address wasn't necessary.'

'A good job you didn't marry her,' said Van Veeteren. 'But I expect you're right. We'd better send somebody to check at the post office.'

He drank deeply and smacked his lips in appreciation.

'How are we going to go about it?' Münster asked. He suddenly felt exhausted again. He was slumped down in a corner of the bench, and the smoke was making his eyes hurt. It was turned half past one. If he added up the time it would take them to drink the beer, then to drive VV home, drive out to his own suburb, get undressed and take a shower, he concluded that it would be three o'clock at the earliest before he could snuggle down beside Synn . . .

He sighed. The thought of Synn was much more persistent than the murder chase just now: still, no doubt that was a healthy sign, when all was said and done.

'You can take Bunge,' said Van Veeteren. 'You and Reinhart. I suppose you won't be able to get started before Monday.'

Münster nodded gratefully.

'The letter is the first thing, of course. It's possible that we won't be able to track it down at all, obviously, but if we have an amazing stroke of luck . . . Well, if somebody remembers it, we'll know. We'll have him, Münster, and it'll be all over there and then!'

Münster said nothing.

'But I don't think we're going to have an amazing stroke of luck, I can feel it in my bones. Check the postal procedures at the school in any case – who sorts out incoming post, if they put stuff in different pigeonholes, that kind of thing. You'll get an envelope from Majorna to take with you, of course, but there's nothing special about it, unfortunately. It looks like any other bloody envelope. And be careful – it's not necessary for all and sundry to know about this letter.'

'How many teachers are there?' asked Münster.

Van Veeteren pulled a face.

'Seventy, I think. And the bastards get half a ton of post every week.'

Münster wasn't sure if Van Veeteren was exaggerating or not.

'What about the pupils?'

'Seven hundred of them,' sighed Van Veeteren. 'I don't suppose they get many letters sent to them at school, but still: seven hundred. Bloody hell!'

'I read a detective story once, about a pupil who started executing his teachers. He disposed of nine of them before they nailed him.'

'I know the feeling,' said Van Veeteren. 'I was tempted to do the same when I was a pupil there.'

'What do we do next? Alibis?'

'Yes. Interrogate every single one of the bastards. Tell Reinhart to be hard on them. The time involved is nice and clear: Thursday afternoon to Friday morning. This morning. Anybody who can't account for that period will be locked up anyway.'

'Eva Ringmar as well? Or have we enough to be going on with?'

'Have another go at the Ringmar alibis, it won't do any harm. And, Münster, if we find anybody who might have had an opportunity both times, lie low: I'd like to be in on what happens next.'

He raised his tankard and drained it completely.

'That was good,' he said. 'Fancy another one?'

Münster shook his head.

'Really? Ah well, I suppose it's starting to get a bit late. Anyway, Rooth and deBries can spend a bit longer out at Majorna, and then they can do the rounds of the neighbours. Plus Bendiksen, I think. Sooner or later we have to find out what happened to Eva Ringmar.'

'And what are you going to do yourself, sir?'

Without thinking about it, he'd slipped back into the usual formal politeness. Van Veeteren sat for a while without answering.

'First of all I shall talk to the wig-makers,' he said eventually. 'Did you know that in this town you can buy or hire wigs from eleven different places?'

'I had no idea,' said Münster. 'Just think.'

'Yes; and there are a few more loose ends I'm intending to tie up,' Van Veeteren said as he dropped his cigarillo into his tankard. 'Do you know what I think, Münster?'

'No.'

'I think this is a nasty business. A very nasty business indeed, dammit.'

27

He took the route over the moors. It would doubtless add an hour to his journey time, but that was what he wanted today.

Alone behind the wheel with Julian Bream and Francisco Tárrega echoing in his ears, and the barren landscape acting as a barrier and a filter between himself and all-too-importunate reality; that was more or less what he had reckoned on. He also chose a car from the police pool with considerable care: an almost-new, red Toyota with tinted windows and some decent loudspeakers at front and back.

He was on his way by eight or so; a dark, foggy morning that improved as time wore on, but the damp, grey clouds never really went away. When he stopped for lunch at an inn in Moines, the whole village was still shrouded in a heavy mist that seemed to come rolling in from the moors. He realized that it was one of those days when the light would never really break through. Darkness would never be totally conquered.

He ate a fish stew with a lot of onion and wine in it, and allowed his thoughts to wander over the previous day and the paltry results it had produced. He had spent more than eight hours interviewing the staff of various wig boutiques, a thankless and monotonous exercise that he could have delegated to somebody else in view of his rank, but which he had undertaken nevertheless. When it was all finished and he was installed at his desk, summing up, he was at least able to confirm that during the past week none of the eleven boutiques had sold, rented out or been robbed of a wig similar to the one worn by the killer on the night of the murder at Majorna.

He had expected no other outcome. Why should such an intelligent and cold-blooded person – which is what they seemed to be dealing with, no matter what – have done something so stupid? But everything had to be checked, and now that was done.

The work carried out by the pathologist and the forensic team had failed to produce a breakthrough, either. Meusse's observations had been confirmed down to the smallest detail, and what the forensic boys liked to call their Hoovering operation produced as little in the way of results as if the crime scene had been an operating theatre instead of a ward in a psychiatric hospital.

Nevertheless, the evening brought with it a faint ray of light, even if it had nothing to do with the case. Just as he was about to go to bed, Renate had called and announced that she didn't think it was such a good idea for them to move back together after all. In any case, there was certainly no hurry. There's a time for everything, she had said; and for once he was in full agreement with her. They had concluded their telephone conversation on the best of terms, and she had even persuaded him to promise to pay a visit to their lost son in state prison as soon as he had time.

He drove on through the afternoon, along the narrow, winding roads over the moors and beside the river, as the darkness and the fog grew deeper and denser: and now came the illusory breakthrough he had been hoping for. The very essence of movement, involving a mutual play-off between driving through the countryside and the time that took, stimulating a sense of movement in other respects as well. Thoughts and patterns and deductions flowed through his consciousness, effortlessly and without resistance, accompanied by the unfilled space created by the classical guitar.

But the direction taken by these expanding movements kept pace with the oncoming darkness. There was something about this case, about both these murders, that was constantly forcing everything onto a downward path, and leaving a nasty taste in his mouth. A feeling of disgust and impotence, similar to what he used to experience every time he'd been confronted by a violent murder; when he'd still been a young police officer who believed he could bring about change; before the daily confrontation with a certain kind of behaviour blunted him sufficiently for him to be able to carry out his job properly.

Hand in hand with these suspicions was the fear that he knew more than he understood. That there was a question, a clue, that he ought to be able to pin down and examine in more detail, or some connection that he had overlooked which, when exposed to the light of day, would prove to be the key to the case as a whole.

But this was no more than a vague feeling, perhaps no more than a false hope given the lack of anything else; and whatever the truth, it had not become one jot clearer this afternoon. It had been, and continued to be, a journey into the unknown. What was growing inside him was worry – the worry that everything would take too long, that he would get it all wrong again, that evil would turn out to be much more powerful than he had wanted to acknowledge.

Evil?

That was not a concept he liked to be confronted with.

The woman who opened the door had long, red hair and looked as if she might give birth at any moment.

'Van Veeteren,' he said. 'I phoned yesterday. You must be Mrs Berger?'

'Welcome,' she said with a smile; and as if she had been able to read his thoughts, she added:

'Don't worry about me, there's a whole month to go yet. I always get to look like this.'

She took his coat and ushered him into the house. Introduced two children, a boy aged four to five and a girl aged two to three; it was a long time since he'd been any good at making more precise estimates in that age group.

She shouted upstairs, and a voice announced that he was on his way. Mrs Berger invited Van Veeteren to sit down in a cane armchair, part of a small group in front of an open fire, and excused herself, saying her presence was needed in the kitchen. The boy and girl peered furtively at Van Veeteren, then decided to accompany their mother.

He was left alone for about a minute. It was clear that the Berger household was not exactly suffering from a shortage of money. The house was located securely and well away from the nearest neighbours at the edge of the little town, with uninterrupted views of the countryside. He had not had enough time to form an opinion about the exterior of the house, but the interior and fittings demonstrated good taste and the means to satisfy it.

For a brief moment, he may have regretted accepting the invitation he had been given. Interrogating one's host over dinner was hardly an ideal situation. Not easy to bite the hand that feeds you, he thought; much easier to stare somebody down across a rickety hardboard table in a dirty prison cell.

But no doubt all would be well. It was not the intention to cross-question Andreas Berger, even if it might be difficult to resist the pleasure of doing so. Van Veeteren had come here simply to establish an impression – surely there was no more to it than that? For even if he had every confidence in Münster's judgement, far more so than Münster could ever have imagined, there was always a little chance, a possibility, that Van Veeteren might notice something. Something that might require a special sixth sense to pick up, an advanced sort of intuition or a particular kind of perverted imagination . . .

And, if nothing else, four eyes had to be able to see better than two.

That boy, for instance. Was it possible that he was a little bit on the old side for the circumstances? No doubt it would be an idea to check the dates when he had an opportunity. For if it really was the case that the new Mrs Berger was pregnant before the old Mrs Berger had made her final exit, well . . . That would surely be of some sort of significance?

Andreas Berger looked more or less as Van Veeteren had imagined him. Trim, easy-going, about forty; polo shirt, jacket, corduroy trousers. A somewhat intellectual air.

The prototype of success, Van Veeteren thought. Would fit into any TV ad you care to name. Anything from aftershave and deodorants to dog food and pension insurance. Very pleasant.

Dinner took an hour and a half. Conversation was easy and unexceptional, and after the dessert, the wife and children withdrew. The gentlemen returned to their cane armchairs. Berger offered his guest a range of drinks, but Van Veeteren was content with a whisky and water, and a cigarette.

'I need to be able to find my way back to the hotel,' he said by way of explanation.

'Why not stay the night with us? We've got bags of room.'

'I don't doubt that for a second,' said Van Veeteren. 'But I've already checked in, and I prefer to sleep where my tooth-brush is.'

Berger shrugged.

'I have to get up rather early tomorrow morning as well,' said Van Veeteren. 'Would you have any objection to our com-ing to the point now, Mr Berger?'

'Of course not. Don't be afraid to ask, Chief Inspector. If I can help in any way to throw light on this terrible tragedy, I'd be only too pleased to do so.'

No, Van Veeteren thought. I'm not normally accused of being afraid to ask questions. Let's see if you are afraid of answering them.

'How did you discover that Eva was being unfaithful?' he asked to start with.

It was a shot in the dark, but he saw immediately that he had scored a bullseye. Berger reacted so violently that the ice cube he was in the process of dropping into his glass landed on the floor.

'Oh, bugger,' he said, groping around in the shaggy carpet.

Van Veeteren waited calmly.

'What the hell are you talking about?'

It was so amateurish that Van Veeteren couldn't help smil-ing.

'Did you find out yourself, or did she tell you?'

'I don't know what you're talking about, Inspector.'

'Or did somebody else tip you off?'

Berger hesitated.

'Who has told you about this, Inspector?'

'I'm afraid we shall have to stick to the rules, Mr Berger, even if you have served me a delicious dinner.'

'What rules?'

'I ask the questions, you answer them.'

Berger said nothing. Sipped his drink.

'You really have been most hospitable,' said Van Veeteren, making a vague gesture that incorporated the food, the wine, the whisky, the open fire and all the other things Berger had provided: but your thinking time is now over!'

'All right,' said Berger. 'There was another man. Yes, that's the way it looked.'

'You're not certain?'

'It was never confirmed. Not a hundred per cent.'

'You mean that she didn't confess?'

Berger gave a laugh.

'Confessed? No, she certainly didn't. She denied his existence as if her life depended on it.'

Perhaps it did, Van Veeteren thought.

'Can you tell me about it?'

Berger leaned back and lit a cigarette. Inhaled deeply a few times before answering. It was obvious that he needed a few seconds to plan what he was going to say, before starting to speak. Van Veeteren acceded to his wish.

'I saw them,' Berger said eventually. 'It was the spring of 1986, March to April or thereabouts. I saw them together twice, and I have reason to believe that they carried on meeting occasionally until the middle of May, at least. There was something . . . Well, I could see it in her, of course. She wasn't the kind of woman who could keep a secret, you might say. It was sort of written in her face that something was wrong. Anyway, I suppose you understand what I mean, Inspector?'

Van Veeteren nodded.

'Can you say exactly when it all started?'

'Easter. It was the Thursday before Easter in 1986, I don't know the date. It was one of those cases of sheer coincidence – I've thought a lot about that afterwards. I saw them in a car, during the lunch break. I had to drive through the centre of town in order to meet a researcher in Irgenau, and they were diagonally in front of me, in another car . . .'

'You're sure it was your wife?'

'One hundred per cent.'

'And the man?'

'Do you mean what did he look like?'

'Yes.'

'I don't know. He was driving. Eva was sitting next to him; I could see her in profile when she turned her head to talk to him, but all I could see of him was his shoulders and the back of his neck. They were in the right-hand lane, ready to turn off; I was going straight on. When the lights changed to green, they turned right. I had no chance of following them, even if I'd wanted to. I think . . . I think I was a bit shocked as well.'

'Shocked? How could you know that she was being . . . unfaithful? Wasn't it possible for your wife to be sitting in somebody else's car for some perfectly innocent reason?'

'Of course. That's what I tried to tell myself as well. But her reaction when I asked her about it was quite . . . well, it left no room for doubt.'

'Meaning what?'

'She was extremely upset. Claimed that she had been at home all day, and I was either mistaken or lying and was trying to destroy our relationship. And lots of other things along similar lines.'

'And it's not possible that she might have been right?'

'No. I started to query what I'd seen, naturally . . . But after a few weeks, we were back there again. A colleague of mine saw them together in a cafe. It was most distressing. He mentioned it in passing, as a sort of joke, but I'm afraid I lost my cool.'

'What did Eva have to say this time?'

'The same as before. That was what was so odd. She denied everything, and was just as upset as the previous time, said that my colleague was a liar, claimed she'd never set foot in that cafe. It was so flagrant, the whole thing; I thought it was beneath her dignity to lie, as you might say. And to lie over and over again. I told her it was much more difficult to cope with the lies than with her infidelity. The odd thing was that she seemed to agree with me.'

'What happened next?'

Berger shrugged.

'Our relationship hit the rocks, of course. She became a stranger, you might say. I couldn't stop thinking about it and asking myself questions. Asking her as well, but she refused to discuss it. As soon as I tried to start talking about something, she shut up like a clam. It was sheer hell for a few months. And it got worse. I'd never expected anything of the sort. We'd been married for five years, had known each other for ten, and we'd never had any problems like that before. Are you married, Chief Inspector?'

'Sort of.'

'Hmm . . . Ah, well . . . Before long I suppose I started to think that maybe I'd got hold of the wrong end of the stick after all. It started to feel as if everything was beginning to move in her favour, somehow or other . . . As if I was to blame for everything, because it was me who'd accused her. I recall thinking that the whole business was beginning to look like a real *folie à deux*, if you understand . . .'

'Don't underestimate me.'

'I'm sorry . . .'

'You said you caught her out several more times?'

'Yes, but never in quite the same way. I caught a glimpse . . . I overheard a few telephone calls . . .'

'Did you hear what they were talking about?'

'No. But it was pretty clear even so.'

'I'm with you.'

'I caught her out telling lies several times as well. She claimed she'd been at home, despite the fact that I'd gone home during the lunch break and found the house empty . . . Said she'd been at the cinema with a woman friend of hers. To see a film that had finished its run the week before.'

'What did she have to say about all these things?'

'I never confronted her with them. I didn't know what to do. I suppose I was just waiting for something crucial to happen. The whole situation seemed so unreal, I simply didn't know what to do.'

'Did you speak to anybody about it?'

'No . . . No, unfortunately not. I thought it was something that would blow over, that we'd sort it out between ourselves eventually, somehow.'

Van Veeteren nodded.

'Is that a Vrejsman?' He pointed at the big watercolour over the fireplace.

'Yes, you're right,' said Berger in surprise. 'Don't tell me you're an art expert as well as a detective chief inspector?'

'Of course,' said Van Veeteren. 'I'm familiar with Rembrandt and Vrejsman. Vrejsman is my uncle. Are you absolutely certain, Mr Berger?'

'Excuse me? I don't really understand . . .'

'Certain that she was unfaithful. Could it possibly have been something else?'

'Such as?'

Van Veeteren flung out his arms.

'Don't ask me. But what you discovered wasn't especially compromising. You never found them in bed together, as it were.'

'I didn't think that was necessary.'

'Why didn't you tell us about this last time? When you spoke to Inspector Münster?'

Berger hesitated.

'It . . . It never cropped up, I suppose I didn't think it was important. I still don't, come to that.'

Van Veeteren didn't respond. Berger was rather annoyed now. Van Veeteren almost wished he'd been in a position to have him locked up in a police cell overnight and been able to continue questioning him first thing next morning. That would have made his next move easier. But while he was wondering what to do next, Mrs Berger appeared and informed her husband that he was wanted on the telephone.

The Devil looks after his own, Van Veeteren thought. Berger went to answer the call, and Van Veeteren was able to spend the next ten minutes staring at the embers and the fading blue flames while thinking over his own infidelities.

They were two in number; the most recent one was eighteen years ago, and had been just as catastrophic as the first one. His marriage had been catastrophic as well, but at least it had the advantage of not affecting any innocent party.

Perhaps it wasn't a bad idea to let the same thing apply to the marriage of Andreas Berger and Eva Ringmar as well? He decided to accept another whisky and water while waiting for the next round to commence. He would have to make sure it took up rather less time than the last one. The clock on the mantelpiece was showing half past nine, and even if he generally paid no attention to the requirements of common decency and decorum, there were limits.

He lit a cigarette, and put another four in his breast pocket.

28

'Could you please tell me a bit about the accident, Mr Berger. I promise I shan't trouble you for much longer.'

Berger poked around in the glowing embers. Remained sitting for a while with his arms between his knees, staring into the fire, before he started.

'It was the first of June. A Saturday. We were invited to the Molnars, a colleague of mine: they have a house in the Maarensjöarna lake district. We were going to stay overnight. When it was time to eat, we realized that Willie had disappeared. He was four, had just celebrated his fourth birthday. The Molnars had two children, a few years older. They'd all been playing in the garden. Willie had said he needed to go to the lavatory. We didn't find him until Sunday morning. Some fishermen pulled his body out of an inlet – he'd floated with the current for nearly two miles.'

He fell silent and lit a cigarette.

'How far was it from the house to the lake?'

'Only a hundred yards. We'd been swimming earlier, but Willie knew he wasn't allowed to go there on his own.'

'Was there a thorough investigation?'

'Yes, but there wasn't much to say. Willie had presumably wandered onto the jetty and fallen in the water. He had all his clothes on, so he hadn't gone swimming on his own. Chief

Inspector, do we really have to go through all this? I told the full story to your colleague . . . Münster, was that his name?'

Van Veeteren nodded.

'What about Eva's reaction, could you talk about that? I understand that it's difficult for you, but I'm looking for a murderer, Mr Berger. Somebody killed Eva, somebody killed Janek Mitter, her new husband. There must be a reason why. I'm afraid it's necessary to follow up every clue.'

'I understand. I hope you can understand the trauma caused by the death of a child. We can accept that adults die, even if it happens suddenly and unexpectedly; but when a little boy, only four years old, is snatched away from you . . . Well, it can seem as if everything – and I really do mean every-thing – is meaningless. Any reaction at all has to be regarded as normal.'

'Eva was the one who reacted worst?'

Berger nodded,

'Yes.'

There was a pause. Berger poured himself a small whisky.

'Would you like some?'

Van Veeteren shook his head. Berger dug into the ice cubes with the tongs, but failed to ensnare one. He put the tongs on the table and used his fingers instead. Dropped three or four half-melted ice cubes into his glass and licked his fingers.

Manners, Van Veeteren thought.

'Eva, yes . . .' said Berger. 'She lost control of herself com-pletely, it would be fair to say.'

'How?'

'How? She became hysterical. She seemed out of her mind. It was impossible to make her see reason, or to get a sensible comment out of her. She wanted to kill herself – we had to keep an eye on her all day and night. And fill her with drugs, of course.'

'How long did this last?'

'The whole summer. It was . . . It was sheer hell, Inspector. I didn't get a chance to grieve myself; all my strength was needed to keep Eva alive. As I was the stronger, I had to carry the whole burden. But I suppose that's the way it is . . .'

He laughed.

'1986 is not a year that I would like to live through again, Inspector. Everything happened in 1986; maybe I should have gone to an astrologist and checked the stars. There must have been some terrifying constellations.'

'Was Eva at home or in hospital?'

'Both. At first she was mainly in hospital. She had to be watched over constantly. I was there as well most of the time. As the weeks went by, I took her home more and more, but I didn't dare leave her on her own. I didn't start work again until October.'

'But she got better?'

'Yes. When the summer was over, it was clear to me that she no longer intended to take her own life.'

'Did you discuss the accident?'

'Never. I tried, of course; but it was absolutely impossible to talk about that. We never mentioned Willie, and she insisted that we threw away all his things. I managed to hide some away for myself. But it was as if he'd never existed, as if she wanted to obliterate even his memory.'

'Photographs?'

'The same. I gave a few pictures to a good friend, who kept them safe for me.'

'Didn't you think her reaction was strange?'

'Yes, of course. I spoke to several psychologists and psychiatrists, and it's obvious that Eva's behaviour was psychotic. But even so, it was an improvement compared with the summer. She managed to survive some days with hardly any problems at all.'

'Did she get help?'

'You mean psychiatric help? All the time.'

'When did she start drinking?'

'Around the time I started work again, I think. Possibly a bit earlier. But it was when she was alone at home that it really got out of hand.'

'Why didn't she go to work?'

'We spoke about it. She'd been at home ever since Willie was born. I thought it would make things easier for her if she had something to do during the day. I think she agreed, but we kept putting it off. In any case, she wasn't exactly in the right condition to stand in front of a class of schoolchildren.'

'That doesn't usually seem to be a problem,' said Van Veeteren, and Berger gave a little smile.

'And the drinking got worse?'

'Yes. It went very quickly. Before we knew where we were, she was like a sponge. Every single day she was dead drunk by the time I got home. She was drinking four or five bottles of wine a day, it was awful. In November, about the same time of year as now, in fact, I decided we couldn't go on like that any longer. I called a good friend of mine in Rejmershus, and they took her in right away. I think that was her salvation, they really did manage to help her. She stayed there until May, May 1987. And when she came out, she was in working order again.'

'When did you divorce?'

'In April. It was what Eva wanted. She was absolutely adamant. Right from the very start, when she was at her worst, she was quite definite that she wanted a divorce. Ah well, shit and hellfire.'

His voice suddenly broke, weighed down with bitterness. About time, Van Veeteren thought. He fumbled in his breast pocket for a toothpick, but found a cigarette instead. He lit it, and waited for what Berger was going to say next. But he said nothing.

'You must have had a hell of a time,' Van Veeteren said eventually. 'Your wife is unfaithful, your son dies, your wife goes crazy, you rescue her and bring her back to life. And by way of thanks, she divorces you . . .'

Berger laughed drily.

'Did you love her?'

'What do you think?'

'How long?'

'November, or thereabouts. All the drunkenness and vomiting and humiliation – it became too much.'

'I understand.'

'Maybe I managed to raise some new hope in January or February, when I saw that she was getting better, but there again . . .'

'What?'

'I'd met Leila by then.'

Van Veeteren nodded. Sat there for a while without speaking, thinking things over, then made to stand up. He asked his last questions on his feet, while Berger remained seated, rotating his whisky glass and staring into the fire.

He's suffering, Van Veeteren thought. The whole business is still very much alive and painful as far as he's concerned.

Thank God for that.

'Do you know a psychiatrist by the name of Eduard Caen?'

'Yes, he took care of Eva at Rejmershus. Later on as well, I think.'

'What do you think of him?'

'Very good, as far as I know. But I've only met him very briefly.'

'I see . . . And that man, the one you suspect your wife had an affair with, did he ever turn up again?'

'No . . . No, he didn't.'

'Did you ever speak about him?'

'No.'

'Do you know of any other men who played a part in Eva's life?'

'Before we divorced, or after?'

'Why not both?'

'Afterwards: nothing. Before . . . Well, when we first met she was only twenty-two and almost virginal . . . No, I'm afraid I can't help you there, Chief Inspector. Let's say, I don't think there were many.'

Van Veeteren shrugged.

'Anyway, very many thanks,' he said. 'If you should happen to think of anything, anything at all, no matter how small, that you think might be of significance, please get in touch.'

He handed over his card. Berger put it in his wallet. He stood up, and Van Veeteren noted that he was slightly intoxicated. He was no longer the prototype of success. In Van Veeteren's eyes that was without a shadow of a doubt a distinct improvement.

Out in the hall they shook hands and Berger held on while he tried to control his emotions.

'I hope you get him, Chief Inspector,' he said. 'I hope you nail the bastard who did this and put him behind bars.'

I hope so as well, Van Veeteren thought as he raised his collar in an attempt to protect himself from the damp night air.

29

It was a few minutes past nine when Münster and Reinhart parked in the street outside Bunge High School. Blue-grey dawn light had begun to trickle down the majestic old castle; the school playground was deserted, apart from a janitor pulling a cart laden with broken chairs. Münster suddenly felt distinctly uneasy. It was hard to imagine there being over seven hundred people inside that building. Lights were on in every room, as far as one could see, but the tall, pale-yellow, rectangular windows seemed devoid of any sign of life. Around the high tower and the chimneys on the steeply sloping roof swirled croaking cascades of jackdaws.

'Ugh,' said Reinhart. 'Did you go to this school?'

Münster shook his head.

'Me neither. Thank God – it must be like being buried under a quarry. Day in, day out. Poor devils!'

They stayed in the car for a few minutes, while Reinhart cleaned out his pipe and they put the finishing touches to their strategy. It was always an advantage if the left hand knew what the right hand was doing.

Then they braced themselves to face the wind, and hurried over the playground.

'Have you thought about the fact that there might be a murderer in one of those classrooms just now?' said Reinhart. 'Do you know what we ought to do?'

Münster said nothing.

'We ought to grab a megaphone and shout out that we have the whole place surrounded, and that the murderer should give himself up and come out. Just think how much time that would save.'

Münster nodded.

'Do you have a megaphone with you?'

'No.'

'A pity. We'll have to talk to Suurna instead.'

The headmaster was wearing a dark suit, and it was obvious that he had been expecting them. The tray of coffee and biscuits was already on the table, and every paper clip was in its appointed place on the red oak desk.

'Good morning, Mr Suurna,' said Münster. 'We've met already. This is my colleague, Inspector Reinhart.'

'A terrible business,' said Suurna. 'I must say that I'm deeply shocked. And worried.'

He gestured towards the armchairs, but remained standing himself.

'I thought I would gather all the pupils together in the assembly hall later today, and say a few words. I haven't fixed a time yet, I thought you might want to have a say in that. But it's awful, no matter how you look at it. Extraordinarily horrendous!'

Extraordinarily horrendous? Münster thought. The guy must have difficulty in expressing himself.

'Mr Suurna,' said Reinhart. 'We don't want you to do anything at all in connection with the murders until we have given our approval. You must be clear about the fact that, in all probability, the murderer is somewhere in this building.'

Suurna turned pale.

'We shall ask you to help us to lay down the guidelines now; it will take about half an hour, more or less. We assume you are still willing to cooperate with us . . .'

'Of course – but are you really sure that . . .'

'The discussions we are about to have,' said Münster, interrupting the headmaster, 'are strictly confidential. You must not divulge a single word of what we are about to agree. Not to anybody. Have you any objection to that?'

'No . . . no, of course not, but . . .'

'This investigation depends upon your silence,' said Reinhart.

'We have to be able to rely on you one hundred per cent,' said Münster.

'And to be certain that you will follow our instructions in every detail,' said Reinhart.

Suurna sat down and picked nervously at the crease of his trousers. Münster considered for a moment asking Suurna where he had been last Thursday evening; but that had already been checked, and the headmaster seemed to be sufficiently convinced for that not to be necessary.

'Of course . . . Of course I shall do whatever you want me to,' he said. 'But surely you don't think that . . . that it must be one of our . . . I simply can't believe that . . .'

'OK,' said Münster, 'we're grateful for your cooperation. Can you make sure that we are undisturbed for at least thirty minutes – completely undisturbed?'

'Yes, certainly.'

Suurna stood up again, went to his desk and pressed a button. Münster took off his jacket, and rolled up his shirt sleeves.

'Is there any coffee?' Reinhart wondered.

It was not a bad start.

'How many teachers do you have on your staff, Mr Suurna?'
Münster asked.

'You mean altogether?'

'Every man jack of them,' said Reinhart.

'It depends on how you count them . . . I suppose we have
fifty or more on permanent contracts – full time, more or less
– and fifteen or twenty temporary staff . . . A few part-timers,
mainly for minor languages . . . Swahili, Hindi . . . Finnish . . .'

'We want to interrogate all of them tomorrow,' said Reinhart. 'We'll start at nine, and keep going until . . .'

'Impossible!' exclaimed Suurna. 'How can that be done? I
can't . . .'

'You'll have to,' said Münster. 'We need a list of all
members of staff, and we want to meet them one at a time
tomorrow. What other people are there?'

'I beg your pardon?'

'Other people who work here,' said Reinhart. 'Not teachers, but other categories.'

'Oh, I see. Well, the senior management team, of course:
myself and Eger, the deputy head . . . office staff and arch-
ivists . . . the school doctor and the school nurse . . . school
janitors and caretakers . . . the welfare officer, psychologist,
careers adviser . . .'

'How many altogether?'

'Oh, twenty or so.'

'So somewhere in the region of eighty-five persons in all,'
said Münster. 'There'll be four of us, so it won't be a problem.
Please reserve four separate rooms for us to use, preferably
next to one another.'

'But the lessons . . .?'

'Four lists of names and times. Twenty minutes each, one

hour for lunch. If you can arrange lunch here in the school, so much the better.'

'But the pupils . . .?'

'I suggest you give them the day off,' said Reinhart. 'Working at home, or whatever you call it. I'd have thought it would be difficult to run a teaching timetable, but that's up to you. In any case, I suggest that you call a meeting of all staff as soon as possible . . .'

'And most certainly not a meeting for all the pupils in the assembly hall!' said Münster. 'Any questions?'

'I have to say . . .'

'OK, then,' said Reinhart. 'We'll start at nine o'clock sharp tomorrow morning. Was there anything else, Münster?'

'The post.'

'Ah, yes. Would you please describe to us the postal routines you have here, Mr Suurna.'

'Postal routines?'

'Yes. What time does the post delivery arrive? Who takes charge of it? Who distributes it? And so on . . .'

Suurna closed his eyes, and Münster had the impression he was about to pass out. Small beads of sweat could be seen on his forehead, and he was holding on tight to the arms of his chair, as if he were in a dentist's chair or on a roller-coaster.

'Postal routines?' said Reinhart again after a while.

'Excuse me,' said Suurna, looking up. 'I sometimes get dizzy spells.'

Dizzy spells while sitting down? Münster wondered. Suurna wiped his brow and cleared his throat.

'We have two post deliveries,' he said. 'In the morning and immediately after lunch – one o'clock, half past, or thereabouts. Why do you want to know that?'

'We can't tell you that, for reasons connected with the investigation,' said Münster.

'And we'd like you not to breathe a word about any of this,' said Reinhart. 'Can we rely on you? It's absolutely vital!'

'Yes . . . Of course . . .'

'Who's in charge of the post?'

'Er . . . Miss Bellevue or the caretakers. It varies. We try to be as flexible as possible with regard to specific duties on the administration side . . .'

'Do you have several caretakers?'

'Two.'

'Could you please find out who was in charge of the post on Tuesday last week . . . Who received it, and who distributed it.'

'The morning or the lunch delivery?'

'Both. We'd like to talk to whoever it was as soon as possible.'

Suurna looked confused.

'You mean . . . right now?'

'Yes,' said Reinhart. 'If we could summon the caretakers and Miss . . . er . . .'

'Bellevue.'

'Bellevue, yes. If you could ask them to come here right away, we'll be able to sort this matter out on the spot.'

'I don't understand why . . .' Suurna didn't finish the sentence. Stood up and went to the intercom on his desk.

'Miss Bellevue, would you mind finding Mattisen and Ferger and bringing them to my office as soon as possible? We want to speak to you as well. As soon as possible, please!'

He stood up and looked at Münster and Reinhart, apparently at a loss. Reinhart took out his pipe and started to fill it.

'Perhaps you wouldn't mind leaving us alone for a short while,' he said, brushing a few flakes of tobacco onto the carpet. 'If you'll allow us to use your office as our headquarters . . .'

'Of course . . .'

Suurna fastened the buttons of his jacket and disappeared through the door.

Münster smiled. Reinhart lit his pipe.

30

Rooth met Bendiksen in the Roman section of the Central Bathhouse. It was Bendiksen's suggestion: he always spent a few hours of Monday evening in the bathhouse, and after yet another day spent at Majorna, Rooth had nothing against it.

It transpired that Bendiksen lived a life governed by strictly observed regular activities. Being a bachelor of many years' standing, he adhered to a strictly disciplined regime as befitted a gentleman of good character. He bathed on Mondays, played bridge on Tuesdays and Thursdays, and attended meetings of the local history society on Wednesdays. He went jogging at the weekend, and socialized with friends; the cinema on Fridays, the pub on Saturdays. On Sunday he generally made an excursion, did the cleaning, and finished reading the historical novel he'd taken home the previous Monday from the library, where he'd been working for sixteen years.

He explained all this to Rooth during their first five minutes in the sauna.

When do you manage to fit in a shit? wondered Rooth, who was also a bachelor.

'What did you think of Eva Ringmar?' Rooth asked when they'd progressed as far as the cold bath.

'I know nothing about women,' said Bendiksen. 'But I know quite a lot about Greek and Hellenic culture; and I can do a pretty good interpretation of Culbertson.'

'Good for you,' said Rooth. 'How often did you meet her?'

'Hard to say,' said Bendiksen. 'Three or four times, maybe; but only in passing.'

'In passing?'

'Yes, amidst the madding crowd, as you might say. We bumped into each other in town, at the library once. That was about it, really.'

'I thought you were a close friend of Mitter's?'

'Yes, you could say that. We met at high school, and we've been meeting occasionally ever since. Only now and then, I should say.'

'How?'

'What do you mean by "how", Inspector?'

'What did you do when you met?'

'We sometimes had a glass or two together, and a chat, occasionally something else – I think it's time to start beating each other with birch twigs now, Inspector.'

'What else did you do, Mr Bendiksen?'

'Call me Klaus.'

No fear, Rooth thought.

'We made a few trips together – after Janek's divorce, of course. We did some fishing. What are you getting at?'

The sauna was empty. Empty and scalding hot. Rooth sighed and slumped down on the lowest bench.

'Nothing special,' he said. 'It's just that we're looking for a murderer. Who do you think it was that stabbed Mitter to death?'

'The same person as drowned his wife.'

Rooth nodded.

'That's what we think as well. So you don't have anything to say that could help to put us on the right track?'

Bendiksen scratched away at his armpits.

'You have to understand that I hardly met the man after he started going with Miss Ringmar. We were both at a meeting of old friends down at Freddy's one night in June. Seven or eight of us, but I didn't speak much with Janek. And then we were both at a meeting of the local history club around the beginning of August . . .'

'What was he like then?'

'As ever. But we didn't have much to say. We exchanged a few ideas about megalithic cultures, if I remember rightly. That was the theme for the evening.'

'So you didn't meet very much after Eva Ringmar entered the stage. Why was that?'

'Why? Well, I suppose that's the way it goes.'

'Meaning what?'

'With women. You should have friends, or a woman, according to Pliny. If you don't have any friends, you might as well get married. Don't you think, Inspector?'

'Maybe,' said Rooth. 'But let's get down to some details . . . Am I right in thinking that you'd arranged to go fishing the Sunday after Eva Ringmar's murder?'

'You're right, yes. We always used to drive out to Verhoven's cottage – he's another good friend of ours – one Sunday in October. It's on the banks of Lake Sojmen, on the eastern side. There's lots of perch and grayling, and sometimes, if you're lucky, you can catch the odd Arctic char and whitefish. Anyway, Verhoven and me and Langemaar – the fire-brigade boss, I don't know if you're familiar with him – the three of us went there, but Janek had a few problems that prevented him from joining us, of course. I must say, it's a shithouse of a set-up, Inspector. Do you think you're going to catch him? The murderer I mean, of course.'

'Definitely,' said Rooth. 'Incidentally, what were you doing last Thursday evening?'

'Me? Thursday? Bridge club, of course. Surely you don't imagine for one second that I . . .'

'I don't imagine anything at all,' said Rooth. 'Can't we go and have a beer now?'

'Now?' said Bendiksen. 'Of course not. We have to take a swim now, and then we need to go back into the sauna for a few minutes before having a good sweat. That's when we can indulge ourselves in a beer. Have you never had a sauna before, Inspector?'

Rooth sighed. He had spent two whole days trying to squeeze information out of God knows how many maniacs, catatonics and schizophrenics, and now he had ended up in this sauna with the librarian, Bendiksen.

Why the hell did I become a cop? he asked himself. Why didn't I become a concert pianist, like my mum wanted me to be? Or a priest? Or a fighter pilot?

I shall report sick tomorrow, he decided. It's my day off, but I shall report sick even so.

To be on the safe side.

31

'Sankta Katarina is a school for girls, Chief Inspector. Our teachers are women, our house matrons are women, our school caretakers, our gardener, our kitchen staff – all of them are women. I'm the headmistress and I'm a woman. That's the way it's been since the very start, in 1882: exclusively women. We think it is a strength, Chief Inspector: it's not good for girls if men come into their lives too early. But I assume I'm talking to deaf ears.'

Van Veeteren nodded and tried to sit upright. He had a pain in the small of his back, and what he would really like to do was to lie on the floor with his legs on the seat of the chair, that usually helped. But something told him that Miss Barbara di Barboza didn't like men lying on the floor of her study. It was bad enough having to be visited by a man in the first place. And a police officer at that.

But his back was giving him hell. It was that damned hotel bed, of course. He had felt stiff when he got up that morning, and a two-hour drive hadn't improved matters. Perhaps he would have to call on Hernandez, the chiropractor, when he got back home. It was six months since he'd last been, so it was about time for another visit. The worst thing was the bad-minton, of course. Chasing down Münster's short, angled returns could spell disaster for a bad back, he knew that, but he certainly didn't want to postpone the match planned for Tuesday evening. So he'd have to grin and bear it.

He shifted his weight from right to left. It hurt. He groaned.

'Are you unwell, Chief Inspector?'

'I'm all right, thank you; just a bit of pain in my back.'

'Probably due to the wrong diet. You'd be surprised if I were to tell you the effect various foods have on one's muscles and muscular tension.'

Not surprised, Van Veeteren thought. I'd be bloody furious. I might even be tempted to do things that would make it necessary for me to arrest myself.

'Sounds interesting,' he said, 'but I'm afraid I'm a bit short of time, so we'd better concentrate on what I've come here for.'

'Miss Ringmar?'

'Yes.'

The headmistress took a folder from the shelf behind her and opened it on the desk in front of her.

'Eva Ringmar. Appointed by us on 1 September 1987. Taught French and English. Resigned at her own request on 31 May 1990.'

She closed the folder and returned it to its place.

'What was your impression of her?'

'My impression? Good, of course. I interviewed her personally. There was nothing about her to object to. She lived up to my expectations of her, and carried out her teaching and other duties impeccably.'

'Other duties . . . What do you mean by that?'

'She had certain duties as a class teacher and house matron. We are a boarding school, as you may have noticed. We don't only look after the girls in the classroom, but we take care of the whole of their upbringing. Fostering the whole person is one of our principles. Always has been from the very beginning. That's what has created the good reputation we enjoy.'

'Really?'

'Do you know how many applications we receive at the beginning of each academic year? Over two thousand. For two hundred and forty places.'

Van Veeteren lowered his shoulders and tried to curve his back inwards.

'Did you know Miss Ringmar's background when you appointed her?'

'Of course. She'd had a hard time. We believe in people, Chief Inspector.'

'And are you aware of what has happened, that both she and her husband have been murdered?'

'We are not isolated in this school, don't think that. We read the newspapers and keep abreast of what's happening in the world. More so than many others, I would suggest.'

Van Veeteren wondered if she was well up on the reading habits of police officers, but had no desire to ask her to comment on that. He took out a toothpick instead. Put it into his mouth and made it move slowly from one side to the other. Barboza slid her spectacles to the tip of her nose and observed him critically.

Before long she'll be demanding to see my identity card again, he thought. It's preposterous, the extent to which a bit of a pain in the back restricts your abilities.

'Well, what else do you want to know, Chief Inspector? I don't have all day to spare, either.'

He stood up and walked over to the window. Stretched his back and gazed out at the mist-filled grounds. Several other buildings could be glimpsed through the trees, all of them in the same dark-red brick as the 'refectory', which was where

Barboza held sway, and the head-high wall that surrounded the whole establishment. In Anglo-Saxon style, this barrier was topped by broken glass. It had made him smile as he drove in through the gates – smile and wonder if the symbolic broken glass was meant to deter outsiders from breaking in, or inmates from breaking out.

He certainly did have prejudices against this place. He was full to the brim with prejudices, and he was slightly irritated to find that they had not been reinforced by what he had seen and heard that morning, despite Barboza's willingness to show him round. He had taken lunch in the large dining room in the company of a hundred or so women of various ages, mainly young women, of course; but nowhere had he been able to discern the oppressed sexuality or sexual frustration or whatever it was that he thought he could sense. Perhaps it was just a matter of the good old fear of women, the realization that, despite everything, it was the opposite sex that had the best prospects of coming to grips with life.

At least, that is how his wife would have diagnosed the situation, he didn't doubt that for one second.

If I'd been born a woman, he thought, I'm damned if I wouldn't have turned out more or less like Barboza!

'Well?' said Barboza.

'Well, what?'

'What else do you want to know? I'm starting to run out of time, Chief Inspector.'

'Two things,' he said. 'First of all, do you know if Miss Ringmar had a relationship with a man while she worked here . . . She lived in, I believe, is that the case?'

'She had a room in the Curie Annexe, yes. No, I don't know if she had a relationship. Was that one question or two, Chief Inspector?'

He ignored the correction.

'Can you give me the name of a colleague, somebody who was friendly with her, who might be able to answer some more detailed questions?'

The headmistress slid back her spectacles and thought that one over.

'Kempf,' she said. 'Miss Kempf has the room next to the one Miss Ringmar used to live in. I believe they were good friends as well. In any case, I saw them together occasionally.'

'You don't mix with the other teachers yourself, Miss Barboza?'

'No, I try to keep a certain distance. We respect one another, but we cannot ignore the fact that we have different responsibilities. Our statutes define the role of the headmistress as the person in overall charge of the school, and the responsibilities that entails. It's not up to me to question those statutes.'

She checked the watch that was hanging on a chain round her neck. Van Veeteren remembered something Reinhart had said not so long ago:

'I normally steer well clear of women who wear a watch round their neck.'

Van Veeteren wondered what it meant. Perhaps it contained a kernel of great wisdom, like quite a few things that Reinhart came out with.

In any case, he was relieved to get out into the fresh air. He crossed over the large lawn, despite Barboza's express instructions to stick to the paved paths. He could feel her eyes boring into his back.

Two girls aged about twelve, wearing overalls over their school uniform, were busy painting the trunk of a fruit tree white. He approached them cautiously, and attracted their attention by coughing.

'Excuse me, but does this happen to be the Curie Annexe?'

'Yes. The entrance is over there.'

They both pointed with their paintbrushes, and giggled modestly.

'Why are you painting the tree white?'

They looked at him in surprise.

'Dunno . . . It's what we were told to do.'

Presumably to discourage the male dogs in the neighborhood from peeing on it, he thought as he opened the door.

It was some time before he was able to talk to Miss Kempf. She had three more tests to mark, and it was impossible to break off until the whole damned lot was finished, if he didn't mind.

He didn't. He sat in an armchair behind her back and watched her as she completed her task. A well-built woman in late middle age, more or less as old as he was in fact. He wondered if Barboza had been right to pair her off with Eva Ringmar – there must be at least fifteen years between them?

But it was correct. Eva Kempf put the kettle on for tea, and explained. Friends was probably a bit too strong a word: Miss Ringmar was not the type to open her heart up, but it had seemed that she felt the need for . . . an elder sister? Yes, more or less. Eva and Eva. A big one and a small one. And they lived next door to each other, after all. What did he want to know?

For the hundredth time he asked the same question and received the same answer.

No, she hadn't seen a man around. Miss Kempf was lesbian herself, there was no point in pretending otherwise . . . Or rather, had been: she had now withdrawn for good from the battlefields of love.

And it was a damned good feeling, she could assure the chief inspector.

No, Eva Ringmar hadn't had the slightest lesbian tendencies, you could see that kind of thing right away.

But men?

No. Not that she knew of. But she didn't know everything, of course. Why was he sitting like that? Something wrong with his back? If he lay down on the bed she could massage his muscles for a while.

Presumably he had other things to ask about while she was doing that?

Van Veeteren hesitated. But not for long.

She couldn't make it any worse, surely?

'So there! Fold the waistband of your trousers down a bit so that I can get at you. That's better!'

'Ouch! For Christ's sake! Fire away, Miss Kempf!'

'What about, Chief Inspector?'

'Anything at all. Did she go away sometimes? Did she receive any letters? Mysterious telephone calls in the night . . .?'

She pressed her thumbs into his spine.

'She received letters.'

'From a man?'

'That's possible.'

'How often?'

'Not all that often. She didn't get much post at all.'

'Where were they posted?'

'I've no idea.'

'Domestic or from abroad?'

'I don't know. From abroad, perhaps.'

'But she received a number of letters from the same person?'

'Yes. I think it was a man.'

'Why do you think that? Ouch!'

'You can tell.'

'Travels?'

'Yes. She did a fair bit of travelling. Several times to her mother. Or so she said, at least.'

'But?'

'She might have been lying.'

'So it's possible that she received letters from a man, and it's possible that she occasionally went off to meet this man?'

'Yes.'

'How strong is the possibility?'

'I don't know, Chief Inspector. She was a bit . . . reserved. Secretive. I never pressed her. People have a right to a life of their own – believe you me! I've been lesbian since I was seventeen!'

'Aaagh! Christ Almighty! Be careful . . . that's where it's worst.'

'I can feel that, Chief Inspector. What kind of a bed did you spend last night on? Go on.'

'How often?'

'How often did she go away, do you mean?'

'Yes.'

'Two or three times a term, perhaps. Just for the weekend, a few days.'

'Holiday?'

'I don't know. I'm always away during the holidays. But I don't think she stayed here. She went on a package holiday once. Greece, I think. But she liked travelling, that's for sure.'

'Her husband . . . Andreas Berger?'

'No, it wasn't him, she never mentioned him.'

'Could he have been the letter writer?'

'I suppose so, but I doubt it . . .'

'What about her son? The son who died. Did she tell you about him?'

'Yes, but only once . . . I'll have to stop now, Chief Inspector. My fingers are going to sleep. How does it feel?'

Van Veeteren sat up. Not bad. He moved tentatively . . . bent forward . . . to the right, to the left. It was actually feeling better.

'Excellent! A pity I have to sit behind the wheel again. Many thanks, Miss Kempf. If you ever find yourself in jail, just give me a call and I'll come and get you out.'

She smiled and rubbed her fingers.

'Not necessary, Chief Inspector. I'll find my own way of breaking out. But I have a lesson in ten minutes, so I think we'll have to stop now.'

Van Veeteren nodded.

'I'd like to ask you just one more question. I can see that you are a lady of good sense, Miss Kempf. I'd like you to use that, and refrain from answering if you are doubtful.'

'I understand.'

'OK. Do you think it's possible that all the time you knew her, there was a man in Eva Ringmar's life . . . A man who, for whatever reason, she kept secret?'

Miss Kempf removed her oval glasses. Held them up to the light and examined them. Breathed heavily on the lenses and rubbed them with a corner of her red tunic.

He realized that it was a ritual. A ceremony performed while she formed her conclusions. What a waste, this lesbian love business, he thought.

She replaced her spectacles and met his gaze. Then she answered.

'Yes,' she said. 'I think that's possible.'

'Thank you,' said Van Veeteren.

He left Gimsen at about three, and ran into rain as soon as he reached the A64 trunk road. Darkness was also closing in rapidly, but he didn't put any music on. Devoted his mind to thoughts and guesses instead, and lapped up the monotonous sound of rubber tyres on a wet road.

He tried to conjure up a picture of Eva Ringmar, but he was unable to pin her down – just as nobody else seemed to have managed to do. He regretted not having tried to get more information out of Mitter, but that was water under the bridge now. Perhaps it wouldn't have been possible anyway. Mitter had only known her for six months. He'd married her on some inexplicable impulse, and probably knew no more about her background than Van Veeteren had managed to piece together by this time.

It was in the background, somewhere in the past, that the murderer was hiding. There could be no doubt about that any more. He had been there for a number of years, at the very least since the Thursday before Easter 1986; but there was nothing to exclude the possibility that it had all started much earlier than that.

Or? Surely that must be the case?

But what did he actually know? How much were all these guesses worth, when it came to the crunch?

If Eva Ringmar was a shadowy figure, the murderer's outline was even more blurred. The shadow of a shadow.

Van Veeteren cursed and bit the end off a toothpick. Was there anything at all to suggest that he was on the right track? Wasn't the fact of the matter that he was groping his way through the dark, in far more than one sense of the words?

And what the hell was the motive?

He spat out the splinters of wood and wondered what he should do next. There were several possibilities, each one vaguer than the other. The safest bet, of course, would be to place all his hopes on Münster and Reinhart. With a little bit of luck they ought to be able to tighten the net round Bunge High School to such an extent that one or two ugly customers would be trapped inside it, worth studying in more detail.

Always assuming that they were fishing in the right place . . . Ah well, he would find out soon enough. In any case, there were a few questions they must not overlook. He assumed the interrogations would begin the following day. They could hardly have done any more today than putting headmaster Suurna under the cosh, and drawing up procedures. He checked his watch and guessed that Münster would be back home by now. He also recognized that he himself had no great desire to drive another 250 miles that evening. Another hour, perhaps, then a hotel, a chat on the phone with Münster and a decent dinner. A large lump of meat and something creamy with garlic in, he thought, would fit the bill.

And a full-bodied wine.

He sorted through the cassettes on the seat beside him. Found Vaughan Williams and inserted him into the player.

32

Liz Hennan was scared.

It was only after she had taken a long and thorough shower and lain awake in the darkness for half an hour that she realized what the problem was.

For it was not something that used to afflict her very often. As she lay there, staring at the digital clock spitting forth the red minutes of the night, she tried to recall the feeling.

When had she last been scared? As scared as this?

It must have been a long time ago, that was certain.

Perhaps even when she was a teenager. She had reached the age of thirty-six now, and there had doubtless been many opportunities to be scared. Lots of them. But was it not the very fact of there being so many that had taught her to cope? Chastened and taught her.

That life wasn't all that dangerous. It was no dance on roses, that was for sure – but what the hell? She'd never expected it to be that. Her mother had been able to make her understand that, and good for her.

There were men and there were men. And sometimes you made a mistake. But there was always a way out, that was the point. If you'd demeaned yourself, or landed up with a real shit, all you needed to do was to get out of the mess. Tell him to go to hell, and start all over again.

That's the way things were, and had been all her life. There were good times and there were bad times. That's life, as Ron used to say.

The clock showed 00.24. She had difficulty in settling down tonight, she could feel it . . . Feel it in her stomach and in her breasts. And in her pussy. She ran her fingers over her labia: dry. As dry as rusks. That's not how things usually were when she'd been so close to a man . . .

Scared.

It wasn't Ron she was scared of, even if she wouldn't want to be anywhere near him if he found out about this new man. But why should he find out? She'd been more careful than ever, not breathed a word to anybody, not even to Johanna. No – in fact, it was Ron she was longing to be with just now. Wished that he was lying behind her, snuggled up close, with his strong, protective arm round her . . .

That's how things ought to have been. She'd married Ron three years ago, and they had not been bad years. But now he wasn't at home. This wouldn't be his home for another eighteen months yet, and that was an awfully long time to wait. His next leave wasn't for another three weeks, and he was insisting on spending it to visit that bastard Heinz in Hamburg. Instead of coming home to her, the shit. What right had he to complain about her, if she took another man occasionally?

Yes, she was in fact scared of what Ron would do if he found out about it; but that level of fear was nothing like this other one. He would no doubt give her a good beating, throw her out for a while perhaps; but this other fear was something different. She could feel it.

To tell the truth, she wasn't sure what she felt; it must be something new. She had been convinced that there was nothing new any more, as far as she was concerned, thought she had already experienced every kind of nastiness in existence. But this felt . . . horrendous?

Was fear the wrong word for this? she wondered. Was it too weak? Perhaps there was something stronger?

Terror?

She shuddered. Wrapped the covers more closely around her.

Yes, that's what it was. It was a feeling of terror creeping up on her. This new man filled her with terror.

She reached out and switched the light on. Sat up and lit a cigarette. What the hell was going on? She inhaled deeply several times, and tried to sort out her thoughts.

Tonight had been their third meeting, and they still hadn't been to bed together. That said all there was to be said. Something must be wrong.

The first time, she'd had her period. Looking back now, she realized that he had almost seemed relieved.

The second time, they'd gone to the cinema. There had been no question of anything else.

But this evening ought to have been when it happened. They'd drunk a few glasses of wine, and watched some idiotic programme on the telly. She'd been wearing a thin, flimsy dress and not a stitch underneath, and they'd sat on the sofa. She had caressed the back of his neck, but all he'd done was to stiffen up . . . Stiffen up and place a heavy hand on her knee. Left it lying there like a dead fish, while he attacked the wine even more voraciously.

Then he had apologized for not feeling well, and gone to the bathroom. He'd left soon after eleven.

They were going to meet on Saturday for the fourth time. He would pick her up straight after work. They'd go for a drive, if the weather was anything like reasonable, and then go to his place. He was adamant that he wanted her to stay the night. Only half an hour after leaving her, he'd called and made the arrangements. Apologized again for not feeling on top form. And she had agreed to all the plans, of course. Said she was looking forward to it.

She had second thoughts almost before replacing the receiver. Why hadn't she said that she had a previous engagement? Why had she been so stupid as to say yes to a man she didn't want?

Why could she never learn?

She stubbed out her cigarette in annoyance, and noticed that her fear was giving way to anger. Perhaps that was a sign.

A sign that she was only imagining things. Surely it couldn't be all that dangerous? She'd had so many men in her life, surely she could cope with one more. No doubt she would get this John, as he called himself, where she wanted him.

Satisfied with these conclusions, she switched off the light and rolled over onto her side. It really was time for some sleep now. She would get up at seven, and be in place in the boutique at half past eight, as usual. Just before falling asleep, however, she managed to make two decisions that she promised herself she would remember when she woke up next morning.

Firstly, she would talk to Johanna after all. Impress upon her that she had an obligation of absolute silence, of course; but nevertheless, fill her in on the circumstances.

Secondly, she would meet this man on Saturday, but if the slightest thing went wrong, she would turn heel without more ado, and that would be that.

That's what would happen.

Once this had been decided, Liz Hennan was finally able to drop off to sleep.

Thinking about more down-to-earth matters.

Such as those expensive trainers, for instance: the ones she was intending to buy in order to improve her times and boost the number of calories she could burn off.

Which must have been a bad investment and wishful thinking, of course, in view of the fact that she had only three days left to live.

33

'Where's Reinhart?' wondered Van Veeteren, arranging two used toothpicks in the form of a cross on the desk in front of him.

'Here!' said Reinhart, as he came in through the door. 'I nipped into the book auction for a few minutes. Am I late?'

'Who the hell has time to read books?' said Rooth.

'I do,' said Reinhart, sitting down next to the radiator. 'Shitty weather, by the way! You wonder how people can raise the strength to go out and kill one another.'

'Go out?' said deBries, and sneezed twice. 'Most of the murderers I know kill one another indoors.'

'Yes, but that's because they can't go out to do it,' said Rooth. 'They obviously get on everybody's nerves, just sitting around and gaping at this non-stop rain day after day.'

'It stopped raining in the afternoon the day before yesterday,' said Heinemann.

'Can we get started?' asked Van Veeteren. He counted his flock: Münster, Reinhart, Rooth, deBries, Jung and Heinemann. That made seven, including himself. Seven officers working on the same case. That wasn't something that happened every day.

Mind you, this was only the first week. The newspapers were still dreaming up headlines. Psycho Murderer. Death

High School. And so on. There again, the word count diminished noticeably with every new edition. Presumably he could expect several of his team to be given other assignments from Monday onwards. DeBries, Jung and Heinemann . . . perhaps also Rooth.

But for the time being, they were at full strength. Hiller had committed himself to several pledges, both on TV and in the newspapers. It would soon be time to bid for money for the next financial year. It wouldn't do any harm if they had a murderer under lock and key before Christmas, at the latest.

And the right murderer this time.

Rooth blew his nose. Reinhart looked as if he needed to do the same, but lit his pipe instead. Van Veeteren was being careful with every movement involving the small of his back. The match against Münster on Tuesday had left its mark, no doubt about that. He was in pain, especially when he sat down. He glanced at deBries and Heinemann. They looked distinctly groggy as well. Who knows if that was due to a cold or a lack of sleep? But in any case, his collection of police officers was not a particularly impressive bunch, to be honest.

Not something to line up for a live broadcast, he thought. Let's hope the inside looks a bit better than the shell.

'Can we get started?' he said again.

'Majorna first?'

Van Veeteren nodded, and deBries took a notebook out of his briefcase.

'There's not a lot to say,' he said. 'We've spoken to every living soul out there, apart from those afflicted with mutism and the potted plants. Doctors, staff, patients . . . A total of one hundred and sixteen in all. About a hundred haven't seen a thing, but half of them think they have. Several have had dreams and visions . . . For fuck's sake, four have admitted to the murder.'

He paused and blew his nose into a paper handkerchief.

'Nevertheless, we've pinned down an overall picture that seems to hold water. Ninety-five per cent, in any case. The murderer appeared in the office a few minutes past five. Asked about the patient Janek Mitter. Said she was a colleague of his, and would like to see him. Nothing unusual about that. Mitter had had several visits earlier.'

'Did he use the word "colleague"?' Van Veeteren asked.

'Yes, they're sure about that. There were two people in reception when she turned up.'

'And both of them have forgotten all about her?' said Reinhart. 'Great.'

'Well, it was only one of them who handed over to the night shift later,' said Rooth. 'We asked all sorts of questions about the pitch of this person's voice, of course, and it seems highly likely that it was a man. He found it necessary to ask the way several more times, and everybody had the impression that there was something odd about the voice.'

'OK,' said Van Veeteren. 'We've established that it was a man. Go on!'

'As for where he hid himself,' said deBries, 'we don't really know a thing. There are plenty of possibilities – to be precise, sixteen places that weren't locked: storerooms, lavatories, communal rooms and no end of cupboards.'

'I had the impression that everything was locked up, apart from the patients,' Reinhart said.

'No, that's not true,' said Rooth. 'But whatever, we haven't found any clues at all.'

'I don't think that's very important,' said Van Veeteren. 'What about the letter?'

Rooth thumbed through his notebook.

'We've checked what Mitter was up to that Monday, from the moment he woke up to the time when he handed over the letter to Ingrun.'

'Ingrun?'

'That's the name of the carer. He received the letter at precisely five minutes past two. We tried to discover if Mitter could have checked a telephone directory before he started writing – bearing in mind the address, of course . . .'

'Tell us about the time after lunch,' said Van Veeteren. 'That will suffice.'

'Yes, probably. We have an interesting piece of information regarding the morning, but we can come back to that later. Anyway, there's a telephone kiosk for the use of patients on every floor. And in every kiosk there's a directory for the local district. Mitter finishes his lunch in the dining room at about a quarter past one, then he sits in the smoking room with several other patients and a few carers. Then, according to a couple of witnesses, he goes to the lavatory. Comes out again a few minutes after half past. Then there's a bit of a gap. Some maintain that he goes back to his room for a while, others say that he went straight to the office to collect what he needed to write his letter, and that he had to wait for a few minutes. In any case, Ingrun turns up at the office at a quarter to two. He finds Mitter waiting there, produces a pen, some paper and an envelope, and takes Mitter with him to the day room. He stands outside for the ten minutes it takes Mitter to write the letter; he stays outside because he wants to smoke in peace and quiet. He's just finished his coffee in the staff canteen.'

'Did Mitter have a note with him?' asked Münster.

'No,' said deBries. 'We pressed Ingrun hard on that point. I suppose you could say that he's not the most gifted of all the people we questioned, but we're as sure as you could expect us to be. Mitter had no papers, apart from what he was given by Ingrun.'

'Did this clown notice if Mitter wrote the letter first, or the envelope?' Van Veeteren asked.

'No, unfortunately not,' said Rooth. 'He was too preoccupied with his cigarette. I think you've met him, haven't you?'

'Yes,' said Van Veeteren. 'I agree with your assessment of the creature.'

He paused and contemplated the little pile of chewed-up toothpicks on the desk in front of him.

'Anyway,' he said. 'The question is whether the man wrote to Bunge High School, or to somewhere else. As far as I'm concerned, I shall continue to assume that he wrote to Bunge. You are welcome to reach a different conclusion. What was all that about something that happened during the morning? I think I know what you are referring to, but it would be as well if everybody was informed.'

Rooth sighed.

'Mitter was in the telephone booth for some time in the morning, but evidently not to look for an address. He called somebody.'

'Very interesting,' said Van Veeteren. 'Who did he call, if I might ask?'

'Perhaps you can tell us that yourself, Chief Inspector, if I've understood the situation correctly,' said deBries.

'Mmm,' growled Van Veeteren. 'Klempje has confessed.'

'Confessed what?' asked Reinhart, blowing out a cloud of smoke.

'There was a call from Majorna to the duty officer last Monday. It was Mitter who had something to tell us. He asked for me, but I wasn't in . . . Nobody informed me when I did come in.'

'But that's a bloody scandal!' said Reinhart.

There was a pause for several seconds.

'What happened to Klempje?' asked Jung? 'When did you hear about this, Chief Inspector?'

'Yesterday,' said Van Veeteren. 'Klempje has been temporarily replaced.'

Reinhart nodded. DeBries snorted.

'Anything else from Majorna?' asked Van Veeteren.

Rooth shook his head.

'If we find any more dead bodies out there,' he said, 'I suggest that deBries and I should be spared the job of investigating. It's not a healthy place for fragile police officers to be.'

'Questions?' said Van Veeteren.

'One,' said Reinhart. 'If they managed to forget about that visitor all night, isn't it also possible that he simply cleared off? Left the place without anybody noticing? Much earlier?'

'In principle, yes,' said Rooth. 'But hardly through the main entrance.'

'But he could have left through some other door?'

'Of course,' said deBries.

Reinhart emptied the contents of his pipe into the wastepaper basket.

'Are you sure it's completely extinguished?' asked Rooth.

'No, but if a fire breaks out, we'll probably notice. There are seven coppers sitting around in here, after all.'

Van Veeteren made a note in the pad he had in front of him.

'Damnation!' he said. 'We'd overlooked that possibility. Thank you, Reinhart.'

Reinhart flung out his arms.

'You're welcome,' he said.

'So, let's move on. Bunge! First the letter, please.'

Münster sat up straight.

'Unfortunately, we didn't get anywhere with that,' he said. 'Reinhart and I put both school caretakers and Miss Bellevue through the mangle, but we can't expect them to remember one little letter that arrived a week ago. They receive nearly three hundred items of post every day, about two hundred in the morning and roughly half as many after lunch.'

'Who distributes the post?'

'On that particular day it was Miss Bellevue and one of the caretakers in the morning, and the other one in the afternoon.'

Van Veeteren nodded.

'A pity,' he said. 'Is there anything that doesn't fit in?'

'Possibly,' said Reinhart. 'But you might well think it's nit-picking. I'd prepared three envelopes: I knew for certain that two of them had been in last week's mail to Bunge . . .'

'How the hell could you fix that?' interrupted deBries.

'Don't worry about that,' said Reinhart. 'I have a contact.'

'A Portuguese lady who teaches there part-time,' explained Münster.

'Hmm,' said Reinhart. 'Anyway, all three of them – the two school caretakers and Miss Bellevue – recognized the two I mentioned, but nobody appeared to have seen the letter from Majorna at all.'

'And what conclusion do you draw from that?' asked Van Veeteren.

'The devil only knows,' said Reinhart. 'None at all, I suppose. But perhaps it's worth noting that they recognized those envelopes, even if they didn't remember who they were addressed to, but that they didn't even remember the letter from Mitter.'

'Not much of a point to note,' said deBries.

'I agree,' said Reinhart.

Van Veeteren sighed and looked at the clock.

'How come we haven't got any coffee? Rooth, would you mind . . .?'

'I'll get some,' said Rooth as he vanished through the door.

'Carry on!' said Van Veeteren taking a Danish pastry.

'OK,' said Münster. 'We were hard at it all day Tuesday – Reinhart and I, Jung and Heinemann, and we interrogated eighty-three persons in all. Seven were absent, but Jung paid them a visit yesterday. Two members of staff have been on study leave for three weeks, and I think we can forget them. I met most of these characters in connection with the investigation a month ago, and I can assure you that it wasn't exactly a case of "How nice to see you again!", not for any of the parties concerned.'

'We don't get paid for being liked,' said Van Veeteren. 'Did you find a murderer?'

'No,' said Münster. 'Quite a few who probably ought to be behind bars, but nobody who was a candidate for this murder.'

'Any . . . suspicions?' Van Veeteren wondered.

'Not as far as I'm concerned,' said Münster.

'Same here,' said Heinemann. 'No suspicions at all.'

Jung and Reinhart shook their heads.

'Hardly to be expected anyway,' said Reinhart. 'Any damned idiot can keep a straight face when there are ninety of them to be interviewed!'

'No doubt,' said Van Veeteren. 'Let's concentrate on the main points: the alibis and date of appointment.'

'What has the date of appointment got to do with it?' asked Rooth.

'I think the murderer has been employed by the school for quite a short time,' said Van Veeteren.

'Why?'

'It's just a feeling I have. Nothing rational, nothing that would stand up in court. Anyway, let's get on with it!'

Jung handed the papers he'd had on his knee to Münster.

'All right,' said Münster. 'This is going to be mainly juggling with figures, but if we can exclude eighty-nine out of ninety, all we need to do then is to pick the bastard up, I suppose.'

'Speaking of what will stand up in court . . .' said Rooth.

'Ninety persons, in other words the whole lot of them, maintain that they are innocent,' said Münster.

'You don't say?' ventured deBries.

'Eighty-two say that they have an alibi for that Thursday night when Mitter was murdered, the remaining eight went home immediately after school and were alone all evening and all night.'

Van Veeteren made another note.

'We have checked up on sixty-one of the eighty-two. Checked up and eliminated. Of the twenty-one doubtful cases, we can probably exclude about fifteen. That leaves eight, plus the six who either don't have an alibi or have a particularly ropey one. If we have counted correctly, and we think we have, that leaves fourteen persons, and possibly the odd one more, who might have been able, hypothetically, to murder Mitter.'

Münster paused. Rooth stood up and started serving more coffee. DeBries cleared his throat. Reinhart took his pipe from his mouth and leaned forward. Van Veeteren dug out the remains of a Danish pastry with a pencil.

'Fourteen persons,' he said thoughtfully. 'Do you have a list of them, Munster?'

Jung handed over another sheet of paper.

'Yes,' said Münster.

'Have you checked which of them have an alibi for the first murder?'

'Yes,' said Münster. 'Six of them have watertight alibis for the Ringmar murder.'

'How can there be so many in that category?' interrupted deBries. 'We're talking about half an hour, or forty-five minutes at most, in the middle of the night . . .'

'Conferences,' said Reinhart. 'Four of them were at the same conference three hundred miles away from here.'

'And the other two were in Rome and London,' explained Münster.

'Eight left,' said Van Veeteren. 'How many of them are women?'

'Five,' said Münster.

'Three left. Is that right?'

'Yes,' said Münster. At Bunge High School, there are only three men who don't have an alibi for both murders.'

Rooth took a handkerchief out of his pocket, and sat with it in his hand.

'Good,' said Van Veeteren. 'How many of those have been appointed within the last few years?'

Münster paused for three seconds.

'None,' he said. 'The youngest has been working there for fourteen years.'

'Shit,' said Van Veeteren.

34

'There's something that doesn't add up.'

'Quite a few things, I'd have thought,' said Münster.

Coming from Münster, that was definitely cheek, but Van Veeteren let it pass. He suddenly felt weary . . . An exhausted ox sinking into a swamp.

Where the devil did all these images come from? Something he'd read in a book, presumably. He stared listlessly at his notes. What the hell was it that was wrong?

Perhaps everything, as Münster had implied?

Or was it just a detail?

Münster sighed and looked at the clock.

'What shall we do now?' he asked. 'Check the alibis more carefully?'

'No,' said Van Veeteren. 'It's obvious that we could smash one or two of them, but we're not allowed to keep pestering the Bunge crowd: specific orders from above. The Parents' Association has threatened to keep the children at home if we turn up any more. Suurna has phoned Hiller seventeen times.'

'Hmm,' said Münster. 'In that case, I don't see what . . .'

'Go and fetch Rooth again,' said Van Veeteren.

Münster stood up.

'But leave me alone for half an hour before the pair of you turn up.'

Münster opened his mouth and intended to say something, but the chief inspector swivelled round on his chair and turned his back on him.

In nineteen cases he was sure. In the twentieth . . .

Underneath all the broken and chewed-up toothpicks was his diary, and it was not long before that had engaged his attention.

Twenty-six days to Christmas Eve, he worked out.

Nineteen sweet young ladies

Aspired to be his wife . . .

How much overtime could he turn into holiday time?

Number twenty killed him . . . no, *spurned him . . .*

Presumably enough for him to take the rest of the year off?

The next one took his life.

What the hell was he doing? What was it, whizzing round so helplessly in his ancient, sluggish brain? Was he thinking of giving up? Was he thinking . . .

There was no point. The thought had struck home right away, he wasn't going to be able to banish it . . . He might as well admit it. An easy chair on a terrace in . . . Casablanca. He'd be able to sit back there in just a few days from now! A warm breeze, a book and a glass of white wine. Why continue to kid himself that this pretentious guessing game served any purpose at all?

But there again, should he not . . .? Didn't he owe it to Mitter, at least, to crack this case? Incidentally, what was the average temperature in North Africa in December? Not much to shout about, presumably. Cold winds from the Sahara, and all the rest of it . . .

The next one he got wrong!

Wouldn't the chances of success be better if somebody else took over completely?

Australia! That was it! What was it Caen had said?

Twenty-five degrees . . . Lemon blossom? Australia . . .

He dialled Hiller's number.

'I'm thinking of handing this case over to Münster. I've got stuck.'

'The hell you will,' said Hiller.

'I'm old and tired,' said Van Veeteren.

'Crap!'

'I've got back pain.'

'You're supposed to work with your head, not your back. For Christ's sake, you have six men under you!'

'I was thinking of going to Australia.'

There was silence for a while.

'All right,' said Hiller. 'Why not? Put this bastard behind bars, and you can have a month's holiday. Shall we say you have six days in which to crack it? I've promised on television that we'll clear up this case within two weeks. There's a direct flight to Sydney every Thursday.'

Van Veeteren thought it over. Put down the receiver and studied his diary again.

'Are you still there?'

'Yes, dammit!' said Van Veeteren.

'Well?'

'OK, let's say that,' said Van Veeteren with a sigh. 'But if I haven't cracked it by Wednesday, you'll receive my letter of resignation. This time it's serious. I shall buy a ticket tomorrow.'

He hung up before Hiller had chance to get the last word in. Looked through his notes one more time. Then he tore them out of the pad and threw them into the waste-paper basket.

Six days to go, he thought.

Didn't the last one in the rhyme get away with it, by the way?

Rooth sat down on the chair he had vacated half an hour earlier.

'What did you do before going to Majorna?' Van Veeteren asked.

'Bendiksen.'

'A possible murderer?'

'No way.'

'Had he received a letter?'

'No.'

'What else?'

'Former wife. The children. No letters . . .'

'Tips?'

'No. The ex-wife seemed shocked.'

'Out of the question as the murderer, I take it. Any more?'

'Marcus Greijer and Uwe Borgmann.'

'Brother-in-law and . . . neighbour?'

'Correct. Nothing.'

'Alibis?'

'Watertight.'

'How long have they been living in Maardam?'

'Greijer for about ten years, Borgmann all his life.'

'OK, anything else?'

Rooth shook his head. Van Veeteren dug a sheet of paper out of a desk drawer.

'I have a list here of twenty-eight names. It's Mitter's suggestion for people who might have killed Eva Ringmar. I think we've investigated most of them, but not all.'

He handed the paper to Rooth.

'I want you and deBries to take a look at them.'

'What exactly are we after?'

'Alibis, of course. And their past. The interesting ones are those who've only moved to Maardam recently. And . . . well, use your imagination, for Christ's sake!'

Rooth blew his nose loudly.

'When are we supposed to do this by?'

Van Veeteren looked at his diary.

'Let's say Monday. But if you find the murderer before then, do feel free to let us know.'

'With the greatest of pleasure,' said Rooth. 'Have a nice weekend!'

He folded the sheet of paper and put it in his inside pocket. Stood up and added:

'We'll find him, no doubt, never fear.'

'Clear off,' said Van Veeteren.

'And what do we do, then?' asked Münster when they were alone again.

Van Veeteren tore up a few more notes while he thought the matter over.

'You and Reinhart can do what the devil you like,' he said eventually. 'Whoever solves the case gets a bottle of cognac.'

'Five-star?' asked Münster.

'Four,' said Van Veeteren. 'Can I give you a few tips?'

Münster nodded.

'Concentrate on newly appointed staff at Bunge. I'll wager that's where we'll find him, in any case. But for God's sake don't actually go there!'

'We've got their names,' said Münster. 'All the ones appointed after Eva Ringmar.'

'How many of them are there?'

Münster took out his notebook and leafed through it.

'Men?'

'Yes, only the men, of course.'

'Eleven.'

'So many?'

'Yes, there is a certain amount of turnover, after all. That's probably not so odd, come to that.'

'How many have an alibi for the first murder?'

'Only the first one?'

'Yes.'

Münster checked.

'One,' he said.

'Only one?'

'Yes.'

'That leaves ten. Are any of those on Mitter's list as well?'

'You gave that to Rooth.'

Van Veeteren produced another sheet of paper from his desk drawer.

'Have you ever heard of photocopying, Inspector?'

Münster took the list and started comparing. Van Veeteren stood up and walked over to the window. Stood with his hands behind his back, staring out at the rain.

'Two,' said Münster. 'Tom Weiss and Erich Volker.'

'Is Weiss as new as that?'

'Yes. He arrived at more or less the same time as Eva Ringmar.'

'I see . . . I see. This Erich Volker, who the devil's he?'

'Temporary teacher of chemistry and physics,' said Münster. 'Appointed September '91.'

'Interesting,' said Van Veeteren. 'If I were you, I'd squeeze him a bit extra. Come down hard on them all, of course. And Weiss. Can I see the list of the new staff?'

Münster handed it over. Van Veeteren studied it for half a minute, rocking back and forth on his heels and muttering.

'Hmm,' he said. 'Maybe . . . But maybe not. You never know.'

Münster waited for clarification, but it never came.

'Any other tips?' he asked after a while.

'The Thursday before Easter 1986. If the person under consideration was in Karpatz in a car at lunchtime, then he's the one. Together with Eva Ringmar, that is.'

Münster looked as if he'd eaten something unpleasant. Then he nodded and made a note. He'd been through this kind of thing before.

'Anything else?' he asked.

'The whole of April and May '86,' said Van Veeteren. 'In Karpatz, of course. But for Christ's sake don't ask him outright. If he has the slightest suspicion, he'll wriggle out of it.'

Münster made another note.

'Is that all?'

Van Veeteren nodded. Münster put his notebook into his jacket pocket.

'Monday?'

'Monday,' said Van Veeteren.

'What are you intending to do yourself?' Münster asked as he stood in the doorway.

Van Veeteren shrugged.

'We'll see,' he said. 'Beate Lingen to begin with.'

Münster closed the door behind him.

Who the hell is Beate Lingen? he wondered. Ah well, no badminton for the next few days, at least. If he worked all day Friday, he might even have a weekend off.

When he got back to his office, the phone rang.

'Another thing,' said Van Veeteren, 'while we're at it. The first of June is also a good date – 1986, that is. Saturday afternoon, somewhere among the lakes at Maarensjöarna. But it's only a hunch, and you'll need to be extremely careful. Have you understood?'

'No,' said Munster.

'Good,' said Van Veeteren, and hung up.

35

He stayed at home on Friday.

Woke up at about nine and plugged the telephone in again.

Looked up the travel agents in the Yellow Pages and, before getting out of bed, he had booked his ticket. An Australian Airways flight on Thursday 5 December, departure time 07.30. Open return.

Then he unplugged the telephone again and got up to have breakfast.

Sat at the kitchen table. Listened to the rain. Chewed at a justifiably thick sandwich of wholemeal bread with cheese and cucumber. The morning paper was spread out in front of him, and suddenly, he had that feeling.

A feeling of well-being. He tried to suppress it, but it was there all the time, warm and persistent and totally unambiguous. A feeling of gratitude for the infinite riches of life.

No matter what happened, seven days from now he would be having breakfast on the balcony of his hotel room in Sydney. Thumbing absent-mindedly through a guide to the Great Barrier Reef. Lighting a cigarette and turning his face up to the sun.

By then he would either have captured a murderer, or resigned his job.

It was a game with only winners. A morning dripping with

freedom. No dog throwing up in front of the refrigerator. No wife thinking of moving back in with him. The door locked. The telephone unplugged.

He recalled Ferrati and the frilly knickers. Dammit all, life was a symphony.

Then he thought about Mitter. And Eva Ringmar, whom he had never met while she was still breathing. She was the one it was all about.

And he realized that the symphony was in a minor key.

He had finished reading the newspaper by eleven. He ran a foam bath, put on Bach's cello suite at high volume, lit a candle on the lavatory seat and slid down into the water.

After twenty minutes he hadn't moved a fin, but a thought had floated up to the surface of his brain.

A thought had been born, thanks to a mixture of the water's warmth, the candle's flame and the harsh tone of the cello.

It was a terrible thought. A possibility he would prefer to dismiss. Drown. Blow out. Switch off. It was the image of a murderer.

No, he hadn't cornered him yet. But there was a way.

An accessible path that he merely needed to follow to its end. Keep going for as long as possible, and see what lay concealed at the destination.

In the afternoon he lay down on the sofa and listened to more Bach. Slept for a while and woke up in darkness.

Got up, switched off the tape recorder and plugged the telephone back in.

Two calls.

The first was to Beate Lingen. She remembered him – she said she did, and he could hear it in her voice. Nevertheless, he managed to get himself invited to tea on Saturday afternoon. She had an hour, would that be enough?

That would be fine, he said. She was only an intermediate stop, after all.

The other was to Andreas Berger. Once again, he was in luck. Berger answered the call. Leila was out with the children. He could speak uninhibitedly, and that was a requirement.

'I have a question that is very personal. I have a question that I think could be the key to this whole tragedy. You don't need to answer if you don't want to.'

'I understand.'

Van Veeteren paused. Searched for the right words.

'Was Eva . . . a good lover?'

Silence. But the answer was audible in the silence.

'Will you . . . Will you use whatever I say in some way or other? I mean . . .'

'No,' said Van Veeteren. 'You have my word.'

Berger cleared his throat.

'She was . . .' he began hesitantly. '. . . Eva made love like no other woman in existence. I haven't had many, but I think I can say that even so. She was . . . I don't know, words seem so inadequate . . . She was angel and whore . . . woman and mother . . . and friend. She satisfied everything. Yes, everything.'

'Thank you. That explains a lot. I shall not use what you have said in any improper way.'

Saturday brought with it a pale-blue sky and thin, scudding clouds. A sun that seemed cold and distant, and a wind from the sea. He spent the morning walking by the canals, and noticed to his surprise that he could breathe. The air weighed little; there was a whiff of winter in it.

At about two he took the tram to Leimaar. Beate Lingen lived in one of the newly built houses on top of the ridge. High up, on the sixth floor, with a view over the whole town. Over the plain, and the river as it meandered its way to the coast.

She had a glazed balcony with infra-red heating and tomato plants, and they sat out there all the time, drinking her Russian tea and eating thin Kremmen biscuits with jam.

'I spend most of my time out here when I'm at home,' she said. 'If there was room, I think I'd move my bed out here as well.'

Van Veeteren nodded. It was a remarkable place. Like sitting in a warm glass cage, hovering untramelled above the world. With a view of everything, yet completely divorced from everything.

I'd like to write my memoirs in a place like this, he thought.

'What do you want to know, Chief Inspector?'

He reluctantly allowed himself to be returned to reality.

'Miss Lingen, if I remember rightly, you knew Eva Ringmar at school. This time, that's the period I'm most interested in. Let me see, it was . . .'

'Mühlboden. The local high school.'

'And you were in the same class?'

'Yes. Between 1970 and 1973. We took the school leaving exam in May.'

'Were you born in Mühlboden?'

'In a little village just outside. I was bussed in.'

'And Eva Ringmar?'

'The same. She lived out at Leuwen. I don't know if you are familiar with the place?'

'I've been there.'

'Yes, quite a lot of us lived outside the town: it's a big school. Serves a very large district, I believe.'

'How well did you know her?'

'Not at all, really. We didn't go around together. We were never in the same gang – you know how it is. You're all in the same class, sit in the same room every day, but you know nothing at all about most of your classmates.'

'Do you know if she . . . If Eva had a boyfriend around that time, somebody she was pretty steady with?'

What an awful expression, he thought.

'I've been thinking about that,' said Beate Lingen. 'I remember there was an incident in class three – the final year, that is, in the autumn – when a boy had an accident. It wasn't a lad from our class, I think he was a year older in fact; but I have the impression that Eva was mixed up with it somehow or other.'

'How?'

'I don't really know. I think it was something to do with a party of some kind. Some of the girls from our class were there in any case, and there was an accident.'

'What sort of an accident?'

'This boy died. He fell over a cliff. They were in a holiday cottage at Kerran – there are quite a few escarpments out there, a geological fault I think they say – I seem to remember they found his body the next morning. I assume strong drink played a part as well . . .'

'But are you quite sure that Eva was present?'

'Yes, she must have been there. They tried to hush it all up, I seem to recall. Nobody wanted to talk about what had happened. It was as if . . . as if there was something shameful, in fact.'

'And it was an accident?'

'I beg your pardon? Er, yes . . . Of course.'

'There were never any, er, suspicions?'

'Suspicions? No. What kind of suspicions?'

'Never mind,' said Van Veeteren. 'Miss Lingen, have you ever spoken to Eva Ringmar about what happened? Later, I mean. In Karpatz, or when you used to see each other here in Maardam.'

'No, never. We didn't really spend time with each other in Karpatz. We just met occasionally, as you do when you're in the same class. It was more of an obligation, I think, almost . . . She had her own circle of friends, and so did I, come to that.'

'But then in Maardam. Did you use to talk about your schooldays?'

'No, not really. We might have mentioned a teacher, but you could say that we moved in different circles. There wasn't a lot to talk about.'

'Did you have the impression that Eva Ringmar was reluctant to talk about the past?'

She hesitated.

'Yes . . .' she said eventually, 'I suppose you could say that.'

Van Veeteren said nothing for several seconds.

'Miss Lingen,' he said eventually, 'I'm very keen to hear about certain matters from that period – the high-school years in Mühlboden. Do you think you could give me the name of somebody who was close to Eva Ringmar at that time . . . Somebody who knows more about her than you do? Preferably several.'

Beate Lingen thought about that.

'Grete Wojdat,' she said after a while. Yes . . . Grete Wojdat and Ulrike deMaas. They were great pals, I know that. Ulrike was from the same place, I think: Leuwen. They came to school on the same bus, at any rate.'

Van Veeteren made a note of the name.

'Have you any idea of where they are now?' he wondered. 'If they've got married and changed their name, for instance?'

Beate Lingen thought that over again.

'I know nothing at all about Grete Wojdat,' she said. 'But Ulrike . . . Ulrike deMaas, I met her a few years ago in fact. She was living in Friesen . . . she was then in any case . . . married, but I think she kept her maiden name.'

'Ulrike deMaas,' said Van Veeteren, underscoring the name. 'Friesen . . . Do you think it's worth a visit?'

'How on earth would I know, Inspector?' She looked at him in surprise. 'I don't even have the slightest idea about what you're trying to find out!'

I think you ought to be grateful for that, Miss Lingen, Van Veeteren thought.

When he left it was dark, and the wind was blowing stronger. When he came to the tram stop he found that it was in possession of a gang of football hooligans shrieking and yelling, in their red and white scarves and woolly hats. Van Veeteren decided to walk instead.

As he passed through the Deijkstraat district he crossed over Pampas, the low-lying area just to the south of the municipal forest, where, once upon a time, he had set out on his chequered career as a police officer. When he came to the corner of Burgerlaan and Zwille, he paused and contemplated the dilapidated property next to the Ritmeeters brewery.

It looked exactly as he remembered it. The facade cracked and disintegrating, the plaster flaking away. Even the obscene graffiti at street level seemed to be from another age.

There was no light in either of the two windows on the third floor, just as had been the case that mild and fragrant summer evening twenty-nine years ago when Van Veeteren and Inspector Munck had broken into the flat after an hysterical telephone call. Munck had gone in first and taken the volley of shots from Mr Ocker in his stomach. Van Veeteren had sat on the hall floor, holding Munck's head while the man bled to death. Mr Ocker was lying on the floor three yards further into the flat, shot through the throat by Van Veeteren.

Mrs Ocker and their four-year-old daughter were found by the ambulance team: strangled and stuffed into a wardrobe in the bedroom.

He tried to recall when he had last heard anything from Elisabeth Munck. It must have been many years ago; despite the fact that he had very nearly become her lover, in a desperate attempt to make amends and build bridges and come to terms with his own distorted guilt feelings.

He continued strolling over the Alexander Bridge, while asking himself why he had chosen this particular route. For Christ's sake, there were plenty of memories to keep the Burgerlaan 35 story alive: it wasn't necessary to dig up anything new.

It was several minutes after half past five when he entered his office on the fourth floor, and a mere fifteen minutes later he had established contact with Ulrike deMaas. Spoken to her on the telephone, and arranged a meeting for the following day.

Then he phoned the police garage and ordered the same car as he'd had the previous Sunday. When that was sorted out, he switched off the light and remained seated in the darkness with his hands clasped behind his head.

Strange how everything fell into place.

It's as if somebody were pulling the strings, he thought.

It wasn't a new thought, and as usual he cast it aside.

36

The body of Elizabeth Karen Hennan was found near the edge of Leisner Park in Maardam by an early riser taking his dog for a walk. It was naked and had been thrown into a hawthorn thicket only a few yards from the path for cyclists and horse riders that cut across the whole park, and there was good reason to suspect that the murderer had taken her there in a car or some other vehicle.

No attempt had been made to conceal the body. Mr Moussère saw it even before his German shepherd had reached the thicket, although his attempt to prevent the dog from following its natural instincts had been in vain.

The police were called from a nearby telephone kiosk, and the call was logged at 06.52. First on the scene, after only a few minutes, was patrol car No. 26; Constables Rodin and Markovic immediately cordoned off the area and carried out the first interrogation of Mr Moussère.

At 07.25, Inspector Reinhart arrived, accompanied by Inspector Heinemann and two crime-scene technicians. The medical team arrived twenty minutes later, and the first journalist, Aaron Cohen from the *Allgemejne*, failed to put in an appearance until about half past eight. Evidently whoever was supposed to be listening in to the police radio had fallen asleep, but Cohen insisted that he was not to blame.

Almost everything was clear by then, and for once Reinhart was able to make a fairly considered and appropriately doctored summary of the situation.

The body appeared to be that of a certain Elizabeth K. Hennan, aged thirty-six, resident in Maardam and employed as an assistant at the souvenir boutique Gloss in Karlstorget. Although the body had been naked when discovered, identification had been easy as the victim's belongings had been found a little further into the same thicket. The police had recovered her clothes, apart from her knickers, and her purse containing money, keys and identification documents.

The time of death had not yet been established, but the police pathologist, Meusse, had been able to make an estimate. Judging by the temperature of the corpse and the degree of rigor mortis, it would seem to have ceased to live at some time between one o'clock and three o'clock in the morning.

There was no doubt about the cause of death. Elizabeth Hennan had been strangled, probably at a different location from the place where the body was found. There was no sign of the victim having offered any resistance to her attacker, which could be explained by the apparent fact that she had first been rendered unconscious by a blow to the temple with a blunt instrument.

Among the details omitted from Reinhart's summary was the fact that the body had been subjected to a degree of sexual violence, probably before as well as after the moment of death.

Chief of police Edmund Hiller was informed of the murder at about ten o'clock that same morning, while partaking of a cup of coffee at home, and he immediately ordered Detective Inspector Reinhart to take charge of the investigation. He also withdrew Inspectors Rooth and Heinemann from the so-called teacher murder, and put them at Reinhart's disposal.

At this point neither Hiller nor anybody else had reason to suspect a connection between the two cases.

When Chief Inspector Van Veeteren collected his red Toyota from the police pool that same morning, he was totally unaware of the night's events; but of course there is no reason to think that his knowing about what had happened would have altered the subsequent course of events in any significant way.

III

Sunday, 1 December–
Thursday, 5 December

III

37

The town of Friesen seemed not to have bothered to get out of bed, this grey, misty December Sunday. On the stroke of half past two he parked outside the railway station, and it only took him a couple of minutes to find the restaurant Poseidon, which was in a basement on the north side of the market square.

The premises were barren and deserted, but even so he was careful to choose an enclosed booth in a far corner. Sat down and ordered a beer. The waiter was chubby and completely bald, and reminded Van Veeteren of a film gangster he had seen many years ago.

In a whole series of films, no doubt; but his name escaped him. Both the name of the character and of the actor.

And as he sat there, waiting for Ulrike deMaas, a new feeling started to creep up on him: that this was the right place, the very place.

That this is where he ought to have come a long time ago, for a conversation with this old friend of Eva's. He could feel it in the atmosphere, in the damp emptiness. As if this restaurant and this Sunday afternoon had been waiting for him. If this had been a film, what was lying in store for him would have been the inevitable key scene; the one that could have been edited and used over and over again. Showing short flashbacks, each one lasting only a second or two, from the whole story so far . . . It was all very clear now, the whole thing; but this was also the kind of knowledge that he would usually prefer not to be aware of. This intuition that seemed to affect only himself, and could almost persuade him to imagine that he was some kind of a vehicle for a higher level of justice; a tool that was never wrong, not even in the twenty-first case . . .

However, it was nothing to brag about. He recalled how he had once found a rapist by locking himself up in his office and playing patience for half an hour. That wasn't something to include in lectures addressed to new recruits.

He sipped his beer slowly, and waited. Sat like an imperturbable godfather in the dirty yellow light shining down onto the table. Baldy had been to light a candle in order to indicate that this booth had been claimed, but apart from that it remained in the shadows, waiting, like Van Veeteren, for Ulrike deMaas.

She arrived shortly after three, exactly as she had promised. A slim, dark woman in a duffel coat and a rust-red shawl. She had finished work at the museum at three o'clock; that was located on the other side of the square, and it didn't take long to turn off the lights and lock up. Van Veeteren assumed that the number of visitors was similar to that at Poseidon; it was Sunday, and the first Sunday in Advent at that: people no doubt had better things to do than visiting local museums and restaurants.

'Chief Inspector Veeteren?'

'Van Veeteren. Please sit down. You are Ulrike deMaas, I take it?'

She nodded, took off her duffel coat and hung it over her chair.

'Please excuse me for suggesting that we should meet here rather than in my home, but things are a bit hectic just at the moment, and you said you wanted to talk in peace and quiet . . .'

She smiled timidly.

'I couldn't imagine a better place than this,' said Van Veeteren. 'What would you like?'

Baldy had slunk out from the shadows.

'To eat?' she wondered.

'Of course,' said Van Veeteren. 'I've been driving for two hours, and will have to spend another two hours driving back home. A stew in the autumnal darkness is the very least I require. Choose whatever you like. The state is paying.'

She smiled again, a little more sure of herself now. Removed a band from her hair and released a shower of chestnut. Van Veeteren reminded himself that he was an ancient cop with only ten years left before retirement.

She lit a cigarette.

'You know, Chief Inspector, when I read about her death, it was as if . . . well, not quite as if I'd expected it, but I wasn't shocked or dismayed, or whatever it is one ought to have been. Isn't that strange?'

'Perhaps. Could you explain in more detail?'

She hesitated.

'Eva was . . . She was that sort of person, in a way – she lived a high-risk life. Well, maybe that's overstating it, but there was something . . . something dramatic about her.'

'Did you know her well?'

'As well as anybody, I think. In those days, I mean. We never met later. We were in the same class for six years – the last three years at our junior school in Leuwen, and three years at high school in Mühlboden. We saw quite a lot of each other at high school; there were four or five of us in the same group. We used to call it our gang.'

'Girls?'

'Yes, a gang of girls. There were generally only two or three of us when we did something together. The others would be preoccupied with boys at the time, but who was doing what kept changing.'

'I'm with you. Did Eva have many boyfriends in those days?'

'No, she was probably the most careful of all of us. Yes, I'd say that was beyond doubt, but . . .'

'But what?'

'In some strange way she had more reason than the rest of us to be careful. That sounds odd, but she always used to jump into things with both feet, as it were, and she had to keep herself on a tight rein to make sure she wasn't injured . . . or hurt, perhaps I should say. She was strong and fragile at the same time, if you see what I mean.'

'Not really, no,' Van Veeteren admitted.

'She changed quite a lot when we were at high school as well. I barely knew her when we were at school in Leuwen. She and her brother Rolf – they were twins – were more or less inseparable. Their father died at some point around that time, I think that was good from her point of view. He was a heavy drinker. I wouldn't be surprised if he beat them, her mother as well, I suspect.'

'How did Eva change at high school?'

'She became more open, sort of. Made some good friends. Started to live, you might say.'

'Thanks to her father's death?'

'Yes, I think so. The close link with Rolf seemed to become

looser as well, I think they'd probably needed each other mostly as a sort of protection against their father.'

'Rolf moved away later on, is that right?'

'Yes, he also went to high school, in a parallel class, but he soon left. Went to sea instead . . . Eventually settled down in America, I seem to recall.'

Van Veeteren nodded.

'Do you remember the names of any boys Eva went with?'

'Hmm, I've been thinking about that since you called, but the only two I can remember, ones she had a close relationship with, if you see what I mean, were Rickard Antoni, who was in the same class as us – that was right at the end, just before we left school. I think it only lasted for a few weeks; in any case, she'd left him when she started at university in the autumn. He was with another girl by then, Kristine Reger, a friend of mine. They got married eventually.'

'And who was the other one?'

'The other one?'

'Yes, you said you remembered two boys that Eva had a relationship with.'

'Paul Bejsen, of course. The one who died.'

'Can you tell me about it?'

She sighed deeply. Lit another cigarette and sat quite still for a while, her head resting on one hand.

She's pausing in order to brace herself, he thought. To overcome her reluctance.

'It was the All Saints Day holiday in our last year,' she began. 'One of the boys in our class, Erwin Lange his name was, had a holiday cottage – or rather, his parents had a holiday cottage – not far from Kerran. It's lovely, dramatic countryside out there, with moors and crags and ravines. I don't know if you've ever been there?'

Van Veeteren shook his head.

'Anyway, we had a party. I think there was about twenty of us, most of them from our class, but some others as well. Eva had been with this Paul Bejsen for a few months. He was a bit older, he'd already passed his school leaving exam. But they were having a real relationship, I know that.'

'Was he her first lover?'

Ulrike deMaas hesitated.

'Well, I don't know who else her first could have been . . . And yet . . .'

'Go on.'

'And yet you couldn't help feeling she'd been through it all before, that she was quite experienced, in fact.'

'Why did you have that feeling?'

'I don't know. It's just something you notice. We girls, we women if you like, notice it anyway. You can tell if a girl's been to bed with a boy before.'

Van Veeteren nodded. She might be right.

'What happened that evening?'

'There was quite a lot of strong drink on the go, a fair amount of hash and stuff, but nobody went off the rails, you might say. We had great fun, in fact. We were gathered round a big bonfire in the garden all night, we grilled a pig, we drank and we sang, and . . . Well, you get the picture. Couples would get together and wander off now and then, into the house or behind a bush. I know at least two girls who lost their virginity that night.'

She paused briefly.

'I was one of them.'

Van Veeteren exchanged his toothpick for a cigarette.

'I was eighteen years of age, for Christ's sake! It was about time. Anyway, the next morning we found out what had happened, and it was one hell of a bloody awful morning, as you can no doubt imagine. We were all woken up by the police. I think it couldn't have been any later than about half past seven. Twenty young people with hangovers and only a couple of hours' sleep in their bodies. The police came with a neighbour. He'd found a dead body at the bottom of a precipice. I think . . . I think that was the morning quite a few of us grew up.'

She said nothing for a few seconds.

'I certainly did, at least. I lost my virginity and a good friend that same night.'

'Were you a very good friend of Paul Bejsen's?'

'Well, perhaps not; but I knew him quite well. He was a nice lad, likeable and gifted. Everybody liked him. I expect several girls were in love with him.'

'You as well?'

'No. Not then. Had been, perhaps.'

'What had happened?'

Ulrike deMaas raised her shoulders, as if she suddenly felt cold.

'They'd been out on the moor, him and Eva. She'd told him it was over between them, for some reason or other. Left him out there. I don't know, he must have been pretty drunk, I suppose, but that was one of the things that were hushed up, of course. In any case, he'd done away with himself. Thrown himself over a precipice. Strangely enough, he'd picked the right place. Macabre, it was. According to local folklore, Vejme Klint used to be the suicide precipice – you know, the place where old people used to go many years ago when they began to feel that their life was coming to an end. So that they didn't become a burden to their families . . .'

She shook her head.

'It was a terrible business, Chief Inspector. And there's never been a heavier lid placed over anything boiling as much as that. His parents were very religious, Reformerde Kirk, and he was an only child . . . Well, I'm sure you understand the circumstances. Mühlboden is not a very big place.'

Van Veeteren nodded.

'What about the police investigation? You must all have been interrogated?'

'Yes, we all had to turn up at the police station and tell our version of what happened . . . Separately, at different times. That took several days, and we were excused lessons. But there wasn't much we could say, of course.'

'He didn't leave a letter?'

'No.'

'How did Eva Ringmar take it?'

'Hard. Really hard, I think. If I remember rightly, she stayed at home for the rest of the term . . . Or most of it, at least. Yes, she was there for the end-of-term ceremonies, I remember now. We were in the choir, both of us; she hadn't practised anything, of course, but that didn't matter. It was just the usual songs . . .'

She paused again.

'It's the first Sunday in Advent today. It's twenty years since it happened. I hadn't thought about that. May I . . . May I ask you a question, Chief Inspector?'

'Of course.'

'Why are you raking over this old business – surely you don't think it has anything to do with, with . . .'

'With what, Miss deMaas? Or is it Mrs?'

'Somewhere in between, I suppose . . . With what has happened now, of course. The murders of Eva and her husband. Surely you don't think there's a connection?'

'Miss deMaas,' Van Veeteren decided, 'if there's anything I've learned in this job, it's that there are more connections in the world than there are particles in the universe.'

He paused and allowed her green eyes to observe him.

'The hard bit is finding the right ones,' he added eventually.

'Have you managed to do that?' she'd asked, just before they'd said their goodbyes in the square. 'Found the right connections, I mean?'

'I think so,' he'd said. 'I just need to study the components a little more carefully in order to be sure.'

He had not been quite clear about what he meant when he said that . . . Her eyes had been so big and serious, and it didn't sound so silly . . . Besides, why was it essential to think before speaking? Had he not learned over the years that it could just as well be vice versa?

Let the words come out, they always conceal something, as Reinhart kept saying.

She had given him a hug and thanked him for the meal, and it occurred to him that she was the second woman in this investigation that he could have fallen for.

If he had been at an appropriate age, that is. And the type to fall.

It took half an hour of driving to shake off these unbidden emotions, but that still left him with plenty of time to think over what he had been told, and to plan his next step.

There was not far to go now, he could feel it. One, possibly two more interviews. A few specific questions to the right person, and the whole background ought to be clear.

Then all that remained would be to pin down the key player in the drama. The person playing the leading role . . .

The murderer.

He sighed, and felt his disgust rising.

The weariness and hopelessness.

How many were they, when it came to the crunch? How many people had lost their lives because of this compulsive, this perverted . . .?

He wasn't sure.

Two . . . quite certainly.

Three . . . most probably.

Four . . . possibly

Even more?

He considered that to be not unlikely. After all the years he had spent on the shady side of society, there was not a lot that he considered to be unlikely.

But nevertheless. What if he didn't confess?

What if he had become so hardened that he denied everything when confronted by Van Veeteren?

That was not very likely, but it was possible, of course. In that case they would have to dig out proof for the whole cartload of shit!

He cursed out loud and increased speed . . . But then he remembered the circumstances.

Proof?

That wasn't his problem. That was something the rest of them could sort out – Münster and Reinhart and Rooth while he sat back under the palm trees in Brisbane.

Were there palm trees in Brisbane?

He put Handel on, and increased speed even more.

38

Münster contemplated his lists. Then he contemplated Jung, who was sitting half asleep under the portrait of the Minister of Justice.

Master and slave, Münster thought. The eagle-eyed minister was standing stiffly erect, portrayed full length against a pale-blue background, flanked by the flag and the lion on one side, and his desk with a statute book and a judge's hammer on the other.

Jung, on the other hand, looked more like a professional criminal. Hunched, wearing grubby corduroy trousers and a coffee-stained shirt, unshaven and with several days' work collected in black bags under his eyes.

'Well,' said Münster, clearing his throat, 'as far as I can see, we've finished.'

'Hmm?' said Jung.

'There's one left. So it must be him.'

'What the hell are you saying?' said Jung, rubbing his eyes with his fists. 'Is there any more coffee?'

Münster poured out two mugs.

'Sit down here and check what I'm doing while I run through them one more time.'

Jung left the minister and sat down by the desk.

'Here we have the names of those who don't have an alibi

for the Eva murder,' said Münster, handing over a sheet of paper. 'There are quite a lot of them, of course.'

'Does this cover the whole population of the world, or just Europe?' Jung wondered.

'Bunge staff plus a few other acquaintances,' said Münster.

Jung nodded and took a sip of coffee.

'Here are the ones who have lived in Maardam for no more than two years,' said Münster, passing him another sheet of paper. 'And here are those who don't have a cast-iron alibi for the Mitter murder.'

'The ones who might have been able to call in on him for a while,' said Jung.

'And then gone back in,' said Münster, 'and battered him to death.'

'Then run for it,' said Jung.

'Run him through,' said Münster. 'Incidentally, I've just received a report from deBries. It seems pretty likely – those were his words, pretty likely – that somebody climbed up or down the drainpipe more than once.'

'How can he have worked that out?'

Münster smiled.

'He and Moss have been out there, climbing. Or rather, Moss did the climbing and deBries made notes. They tried eight different drainpipes, between the ground and the third floor. All of them survived being climbed down with flying colours, but only three of them held for four attempts.'

'How much does Moss weigh?' asked Jung.

'About eleven stone, I should think,' said Münster. 'He's considering leaving the force, according to deBries; but both the patients and the doctors seem to have had a most enjoyable day . . . Anyway, look closely at the names and compare the lists. How many can you find on all three?'

Jung examined the sheets of paper for a few moments.

'One,' he said.

'Exactly,' said Münster. 'We've got him. There's another thing that indicates him – can you see it?'

'The letter?' said Jung.

'Yes,' said Münster 'If it is him, that confirms the letter theory as well. Shall we go?'

Jung looked at his watch.

'Go where?' he wondered.

'Home, of course,' said Münster. 'I'll phone Van Veeteren tomorrow morning.'

'I say, Münster,' said Jung as they were on the way down in the lift. 'What's behind it all? The motive, I mean?'

'I haven't a clue,' said Münster.

'Reinhart here,' said Reinhart.

'What the devil . . .' said Van Veeteren. 'Do you know what time it is?'

'Half past four,' said Reinhart. 'Were you asleep?'

'Go to hell!' said Van Veeteren. 'What do you want?'

'Did you hear about the woman in Leisner Park?'

'Yes, I heard a bit. What about it? Has she woken up?'

'I think there's a link.'

'A link?'

'Yes. A connection.'

'With what?'

'With your murderer, of course. I thought I had the pleasure of talking to the astute Detective Chief Inspector Van Veeteren . . .?'

'No, this is the trustee of his estate,' said Van Veeteren. 'For Christ's sake tell me what you want, Inspector, or there'll be another case for us to solve.'

'I've interrogated several people . . .'

'I should hope so.'

'Among others, a friend of the deceased, Johanna Goertz. Apparently this Liz Hennan confided a few things in her.'

'Hennan? Is that the victim?'

'Yes, Liz Hennan. She told Johanna Goertz, last Tuesday, that she'd met a new man. She was going to meet him again on Saturday – last Saturday, that is – and that she felt a bit scared. She told Goertz a bit about him as well, not all that much because she didn't know much. Not even his name. He called himself John, but she didn't think that was his real name. Are you with me?'

'Yes,' said Van Veeteren. 'Get to the point, Reinhart.'

'Any moment now,' said Reinhart. 'Anyway, he'd apparently told Liz Hennan something odd, just in passing, or however you might want to see it . . . He'd told her that he came across the welfare officer with a pupil one day.'

'Eh?'

'Yes. In flagrante. The welfare officer with a pupil. What do you think that suggests?'

Van Veeteren sat in silence for a few seconds.

'School,' he said.

'I agree,' said Reinhart. 'But I'm a bit on the tired side now . . . I think I'll go to bed and disconnect the telephone. You can ring me at nine.'

'Hang on a minute,' said Van Veeteren. But it was too late.

He wrote the sixth name down at the very end of the book.

He contemplated the list for a few moments. Three women and three men. There was a sort of balance, no matter what – even if one of the men had only been a child.

He noted down the date as well. Tried to find some kind of harmony there as well, but that was harder. The specific dates were spread out over years, and months: the only trend was that the gap between them grew shorter. Eight years . . . six years . . . six years again . . . seven weeks . . . ten days . . .

He closed the book and put it in the outside pocket of his bag. Checked his watch. A few minutes past five. It was still pitch-dark outside. His suitcases were all packed and lying ready on the bed. No point in waiting any longer. Best to get going right away.

Leave everything behind now, yet again.

Exhaustion felt like needles sticking into him, and he resolved not to drive too far. Two or three hundred miles, perhaps. Then a hotel and a bed.

The most important thing was to get away from here. Vamoose.

As long as he got some sleep, he would be ready to face up to life again tomorrow morning. From the beginning, this time.

Without all the old stuff. That was in the past now. He understood that it was all over and done with, at last.

Tomorrow. In a new place.

39

'What the hell are you doing here?' said Suurna.

'I've come to say hello to my old school,' said Van
Veeteren. 'When did you start swearing, Headmaster?'

'We're here to pick up a murderer,' said Reinhart.

Suurna opened and shut his mouth a few times, but no
words emerged. He grasped hold of his desk, and once again
Münster had the impression he was about to faint.

'Do sit down, Headmaster,' he said. 'There, that's it.'

'We're looking for Carl Ferger,' said Van Veeteren. 'Do you
know where he is right now?'

'The school caretaker?' said Suurna. 'Are you really sure
that . . .?'

'Absolutely certain,' said Reinhart. 'Can you find out where
he is, please?'

'Er . . . Yes, of course,' said Suurna. 'I can ask Miss Bellevue . . .'

He pressed the intercom.

'Ask her to come here,' said Van Veeteren. 'We don't want
to warn him.'

Half a minute later Miss Bellevue appeared, with wide eyes
and dangling earrings.

'These gentlemen are looking for Ferger,' said Suurna. 'Do
you know where he is?'

'He hasn't arrived yet,' said Miss Bellevue, dangling her earrings.

'Hasn't arrived?' said Suurna. 'Why . . .'

'What time is he supposed to start work?' interrupted Van Veeteren.

'Half past seven,' said Miss Bellevue. 'He hasn't reported sick. I don't know what's happened. Mattisen has been asking for him several times – they were supposed to be moving the grand piano today.'

'Shit!' said Van Veeteren.

'Has anybody phoned him?' Reinhart asked.

'Mattisen has called, but there was no answer. Perhaps his car has broken down, or something of the sort.'

'And it's taken two hours?' said Suurna. 'He only lives a ten-minute walk from here, doesn't he?'

'Shit!' said Van Veeteren again. 'Hand over his address, Headmaster. You and I are going to pay a call, Münster! Reinhart, you take care of the welfare officer!'

'With pleasure,' said Reinhart.

He knocked and walked in.

The welfare officer was in his forties. Beard, sandals and a ring in his ear.

'Hey, hold on a minute, what the . . .' he began.

'I'm a bit short of time,' said Reinhart. 'Might I suggest that you take care of this lad a bit later.'

The youth on the sofa stood up reluctantly.

'Would you mind waiting outside for a few moments,' said the welfare officer. 'What the hell do you mean by bursting into here and . . .'

Reinhart waited until the boy had closed the door behind him.

'To tell you the truth, I'm in *one hell of a hurry*. That's why I'm going to give you a chance to save your skin.'

'I don't know what you're talking about. Who are you, to start with?'

'Police,' said Reinhart. 'If you confess right away, I promise not to take it any further, not this time. If you mess me about . . . well, I find it hard to see how the hell you'll be able to keep your job.'

The welfare officer said nothing. Sat down carefully on the edge of his desk.

'Have you, or have you not, had an affair with a pupil during this last year? Even screwed her here in school . . .'

No answer. The welfare officer swallowed and held onto his beard.

'It's not you I'm after, for fuck's sake!' said Reinhart. 'I'm on the tail of an even bigger shit. You have ten seconds, then I'm taking you to the police station!'

The welfare officer let go of his beard and tried to look Reinhart in the eye.

'Yes,' he said. 'It . . .'

'Thank you,' said Reinhart. 'That's enough.'

He went out and slammed the door so that the noise echoed down the corridor.

'Knock the door down!' ordered Van Veeteren.

'We have people who can pick locks,' said Münster.

'No time,' said Van Veeteren.

'There's usually a caretaker,' said Münster.

'Knock the door down, I said! Do I have to do it myself?'

Münster sized it up. The door was ideally located, no doubt about that. Furthest away from the staircase. He'd have a run-up of a good eight yards. Van Veeteren stepped to one side.

'Give it all you've got!'

Münster barged into the door, shoulder first. There was a loud creaking noise, from both the door and Münster, but that was all.

'One more time!' said Van Veeteren.

Münster charged again, with just as little result.

'Fetch the caretaker!' said Van Veeteren. 'I'll wait here.'

After ten minutes Münster returned with a thin man wearing an overall and a flat cap.

'Mr Gobowsky,' explained Münster.

A circle of discarded toothpicks had formed round Van Veeteren's feet, and Mr Gobowsky eyed it critically. Then he asked to see Van Veeteren's ID.

The bastard had been to the cinema, it seemed.

The flat comprised two small rooms and an even smaller kitchen, and it took them about five seconds to establish that the tenant had flown. Van Veeteren slumped down into an artificial leather chair.

'He's done a runner,' he said. 'We'll have to set off a nationwide alert. This guy is going to bankrupt the police force. Münster, you stay here and root around! I'll send somebody to help you.'

Münster nodded. The chief inspector turned to the caretaker, who was loitering in the hall, eager to know what was going on.

'Did he have a car?' Van Veeteren asked.

'A blue Fiat,' said Mr Gobowsky. 'A 326, I think.'

'Where did he usually park it?'

'In the car park outside.'

Mr Gobowsky nodded in the direction of the courtyard.

'Come with me, please, and see if it's still there,' said Van Veeteren. 'We'll leave the inspector here.'

'Wait!' shouted Münster, just as they were passing through the door. 'Look at this!'

He held out a little photograph in a frame. Van Veeteren took it and examined it.

'Eva Ringmar,' he said. 'A few years younger, but it's her, sure as hell.'

'No more doubts, then?' said Münster.

'Have I ever had any doubts?' said Van Veeteren, leaving Münster to his fate.

'Carl Ferger, yes,' said Reinhart. 'Came here in 1986, presumably, possibly a year or so earlier. Send the faxes immediately! And tell them we need answers PDQ, if not sooner, the moment they find him! Stick on red flags and express labels and Interpol and whatever else you have in that line! And make sure you inform me, or one of the others, the moment you get an answer! Is that understood?'

Widmar Krause nodded.

'One to the Immigration Office, and one to the other side, OK?' Reinhart repeated. 'Let them fight to see who wins!'

Krause left the room. Reinhart looked at the clock. A quarter past twelve. Looked at Van Veeteren, who was slumped over the desk.

He looks like a half-finished stuffed animal, Reinhart thought.

'Where do you think he is?' he said.

'Probably lying low and dossing down in a hotel somewhere,' said Van Veeteren. 'Not a bad idea, in fact. Do you know that some shit-heap woke me up at four-thirty this morning? Let's go and have lunch.'

'By all means,' said Reinhart. 'But not the canteen.'

'No, Christ no,' said Van Veeteren. 'If we have nothing else to do but sit and wait, we might as well go somewhere a bit classier.'

'Good,' said Reinhart. 'Let's go to La Canaille and leave the number with the switchboard. But what if it's Klempje on duty?'

'No chance,' said Van Veeteren. 'He's still in exile.'

40

The turnaround came with the twelve o'clock news.

He'd slept for three hours in a car park. Curled up under a blanket on the back seat, and woken up because he felt cold. Before driving off he'd switched on the radio, caught the middle of the news and heard that he was wanted by the police.

Nationwide alert. Carl Ferger. Suspected of three murders. Travelling in a blue Fiat, registration number . . .

He switched off. For a few seconds, time and the world stood still. Blood was pounding hard in his temples. His hands grasped the steering wheel so tightly that his knuckles turned white.

He'd been rumbled. Was wanted by the police.

Hunted.

He was on the run.

It took a while for it to sink in.

Three murders?

He couldn't help laughing.

Which ones, he could ask them. Yes, he'd try to remember to ask them that, if they caught up with him. Excuse me, you fucking police bastard, he'd say. I've committed six murders. Which three am I suspected of?

The windows had misted over from his breath. He wiped them clean with his handkerchief. Opened the driver's window slightly, looked round. The car park was empty, apart from one long-distance lorry some fifty yards ahead of him.

A blue Fiat . . . Oh, fuck! Why had he turned off the radio? He switched on again, but there was only music.

What else did they know?

Where did they think he was?

Nationwide alert. What did that mean? Road blocks?

Hardly. He'd driven almost 200 miles since leaving Maardam. If they knew roughly when he'd left, they must realize that he could be more or less anywhere by now.

But how?

How the hell had they found him out?

He started the car. Drove slowly past the lorry and onto the main road.

It must have been Liz. That fucking whore. Something had gone wrong, but he didn't understand how they could link her with the others. The bitch! If only he'd listened to his inner voice from the start . . . The voice that had warned him, told him to steer well clear of her, of that tart. That fucking bitch.

Nothing more than a fucking bitch.

He would never repeat that mistake, at least. And let's face it, it was only reasonable for the police to agree that he'd performed a public service in ridding society of the likes of Liz Hennan? He'd nothing to reproach himself with in her case. The others were not so good. They'd been driven by a different kind of necessity. But now wasn't the time to sit back and take stock.

Action was called for now. Something had clicked – he'd sensed it coming, hadn't he? His intuition had saved him yet again – why else would he have run away? It was just the same as it had been with Ellen . . .

Ellen. That was twelve years ago now. She'd also been a

tart, no doubt about that. A disgusting little tart, just like Liz. He could see them both in his mind's eye, just as randy, just as desperate for it . . .

He stepped on the accelerator. Saw from the gauge that he'd soon need to fill up. Why did he keep seeing them? Their naked bodies, their quivering pussies . . . He had no time to waste on them now. He must get a grip of essentials, not dilly-dally with these disgusting images. He must be ready. Must be on his toes, do the right thing, and it was urgent now.

Wanted by the police.

He checked his watch. Only a quarter past twelve. Was that message he'd heard the first one, or had there been several more, earlier? Better keep the radio on, so that he didn't miss anything.

He switched on, and lit a cigarette. Hardly any of those left, either.

Fill up and buy cigarettes, that was the most urgent thing. Then?

The radio? he thought. What about the television? Newspapers? Had they published a photo of him?

Would he be as easily recognized as the president the moment he entered the petrol-station kiosk?

The telly wasn't such a problem, he thought. Nobody sat gaping at the box in the mornings. The newspapers were worse. But the morning papers hadn't carried anything – not the one he'd bought earlier on, at least. They'd reported the murder, of course; but not a word about Carl Ferger in a blue Fiat.

It would be in the evening papers, naturally. A photo on the billboards, perhaps. Like when a government minister had been murdered a few years ago.

He couldn't help smiling. When did the first edition generally hit the streets?

Two? Half past?

Before then he needed to have become somebody else.

It was as easy as that. He must get to a decent-sized town as soon as possible, and fix some kind of disguise. A pity that he'd dumped the wig – although they'd know about that, no doubt. What else?

The car.

Get rid of it and hire another?

He didn't like that idea. It would involve obvious risks. He decided to risk it anyway and carry on in the Fiat. As long as he was careful to park somewhere out of the way, he should be OK. Spread a lot of shit over the number plates, perhaps. There must be thousands of blue Fiats all over the country.

But then what?

The question grabbed hold of him, and kept him trapped in its iron grip for several seconds. Threatened to choke him. What the hell should he do after that?

This evening? Tonight? Tomorrow?

He swallowed and stepped even harder on the accelerator. Suppressed the question. He needed to take things one at a time. First his appearance, then he could make decisions as things developed. That was his strength, after all. His instinctive ability to make the right decision at the critical moment. Money, for instance. He'd emptied his account as early as the previous Saturday. They'd have frozen it by now, of course, but so what? He had enough to last him for a few weeks, at least.

Don't do anything rash. Everything was under control. They wouldn't catch him this time either, the bastards. The thought of lounging around in some obscure little hotel for a few days made him smile again. Reading about the hunt in the newspapers, sitting in the communal television room every evening, hearing about how the hunt for him was going . . .

Next exit Malbork, 1,000 yards, he read on the signs. Excellent.

He signalled he was about to turn off, and drummed his fingers on the steering wheel.

41

'What's the time?' growled Van Veeteren. 'What the hell is that great detective the general public playing about at? Why haven't they found him?'

'Half past eight,' said Münster. 'I expect he's gone into hiding.'

'You don't say?'

'He can hardly have avoided discovering that the police are after him. There'll be another appeal on the TV at nine, incidentally.'

'I'm not an idiot,' said Van Veeteren. 'But why has nobody replied to our faxes? Could you kindly explain that as well, Inspector?'

'The Immigration Office's computers have been down, but they were running again this morning. The other lot are in a different time zone, of course. Their reply could come as late as midnight, even one in the morning.'

Van Veeteren contemplated his toothpick.

'Can I ask you something?' Münster ventured.

'Fire away,' said Van Veeteren. 'But I don't promise to answer it.'

'Who exactly is this Carl Ferger?'

'Haven't you caught on yet, Münster?'

Münster blushed and cleared his throat.

'How could I when I'm not given all the information?' he asked. 'To be honest, I can't see the point of you withholding important details, sir. Information vital to the case, that is.'

He blushed again, this time at his own audacity. But the chief inspector didn't react. Merely sat motionless on his desk chair, resting his chin on his hands. Narrowed his eyes to form two slits as he stared at Münster. Making no attempt to respond quickly.

'Münster,' he said eventually. 'Your sense of timing is hopeless. If you listen to me, I shall explain a few things for your benefit. I don't suppose you'll understand much of what I'm talking about, but even so, I'm prepared to spare you a couple of minutes.'

'Thank you,' said Münster. 'That's very kind of you.'

'You must understand, Münster, that things are interlinked. There are certain laws that apply, and certain patterns. We are swimming around inside those patterns, we move about, we think, we live in accordance with those rules. It boils down to the subtleties – they are not easy to identify, but we have to listen out for them, look for them, we have to be wide awake and keep our eyes skinned for the right turnings. Do you know what the determinant is?'

'The determinant?'

'Yes.'

'No idea,' said Münster.

'Nor have I,' said Van Veeteren. 'But I'm on its heels. That's what is telling us where to go, Münster; that's what is pointing out the path we have to follow, what to do next, which turnings to take. I take it you agree that there has to be a plot in a novel?'

'Yes, of course.'

'That there has to be a story, or at the very least a sort of connecting thread that runs through a film or a play and links all the episodes together?'

'Yes . . .'

'A novel, a film, or a play, Münster – they are nothing but stuffed life. Life that has been captured and stuffed like a taxidermist stuffs a dead animal. They are created so that we can reasonably easily examine it. Clamber out of current reality and look at it from a distance. Are you with me?'

'Yes,' said Münster. 'I think so . . .'

'Anyway, if there have to be plots and connecting threads ensuring that stuffed life, the artificial version, hangs together, then of course the same thing must apply to the genuine article, to real life. That's the point.'

'The point?'

'Yes, the point. Obviously, you can choose to live a pointless life if you want to – watch the film backwards, for Christ's sake, or hold the book upside down as you read it. But don't kid yourself that, if you do, you've understood anything. You see, there's not just one, but thousands of points, whole series of points . . . patterns . . . rules . . . determinants. I'm off to Australia on Thursday, Münster, and I can sure as hell assure you that it's not mere chance. It's exactly the right thing to do. Don't you think so?'

Just for a moment Münster had visions of his own ideal lagoon . . . Synn and the children and two weeks by the blue sea . . .

'If we were a film, you and me,' said Van Veeteren, snapping a toothpick, 'or a book, then of course it would be unforgivable of me to tell you certain things at this point in time. It would be a kick in the teeth for cinema-goers, an insult to the genre as such. Perhaps also an underestimate of your talents, Münster. Are you with me?'

'No,' said Münster.

'A crime against the determinant,' said Van Veeteren, looking just for a second as if he might smile. 'If we don't have a religion, the least we can do is to try to live as if we were a book or a film. These are the only hints you are going to get, Münster.'

What the hell's going on? Münster wondered. Is he really sitting there and saying this, or am I dreaming?

'That's why I'm annoyed,' said Van Veeteren. 'They ought to find him tonight. I want him here tomorrow, and I want to confront him with the answers we've had to our faxes. And with another person. What we are dealing with is a mass murderer, Münster, are you clear about that? It doesn't often happen.'

I am dreaming, Münster decided.

There was a knock on the door, and Constable Beygens looked in.

'Excuse me, Chief Inspector, but we've just received a fax from abroad.'

'Excellent,' said Van Veeteren. 'Hand it over!'

42

'You're a real pal!' said Ulich.

Tomas Heckel wasn't supposed to start his shift until ten, but this evening they had a special agreement. If Heckel started at a quarter to nine instead, Ulich would have time to get to the boxing gala where his son was due to take part in a light-heavyweight bout with a black Englishman by the name of Whitecock.

It wasn't the main event, of course, just one of the supporting fights. But like his dad in the old days, young Ulrich packed a formidable punch. And a marked ability to take punishment.

Heckel, who was a second-year medicine student, was well aware of the risks boxers took when they allowed other people to bash them around the head for money. but his job as night porter was too important for him to get into an argument about the rights and wrongs of it. Nor did he want to deprive the father of the opportunity to sit at the ringside as his son's brain cells hit the canvas. As well as sandwiches and coffee, his rucksack contained three fat anatomy books. He intended to stay awake all night, swotting. Time is money, and there were only six days to go before his exam.

'You're a real pal,' said Ulich again as he eased his gigantic body out of the porter's booth. 'There'll be a bottle of the hard stuff for you if the lad wins!'

'I wouldn't dream of accepting it,' said Heckel. 'Is there anything I need to know?'

Ulich thought for a moment.

'There's a handball team from Copenhagen on the third floor,' he said. 'You'd better keep an eye on them. Oh yes, there's somebody who has to move his car. He's parked in such a way that the rubbish van won't be able to get at the bins tomorrow morning. Prawitz called in to tell me, there's a note by the telephone. I think it's that Czerpinski character in number twenty-six. I rang his room, but he wasn't there.'

'OK,' said Heckel. 'Have a good time. I hope he does well.'

'He'll skin the guy alive, dammit!' said Ulich, shadow-boxing his way out through the swing doors.

Heckel sat down and leafed through the log book. Thirty of the thirty-six rooms occupied – not bad for a Monday in December. He switched on Ulich's little television set: it might be an idea to watch the news before devoting himself to his anatomy studies. Besides, he usually found it difficult to settle down and read before midnight.

A few minutes still to go. Some ridiculous programme called *A Question of Sport* hadn't finished yet. What had Ulich said?

A wrongly parked car?

He found the note. Scrutinized it and memorized the car registration number while calling room twenty-six. No answer. He hung up, but taped the note to the telephone, so that he wouldn't forget about it.

The news programme was starting. The lead item was that murder hunt, of course. He'd heard about it several times during the course of the afternoon. There was something about it in the newspapers lying on the counter as well, he noticed. Carl Ferger . . . At least three murders . . . Blue Fiat, registration number . . .

He stared at the plate on the television screen.

Stared at the telephone.

Switched off the TV and grabbed one of the newspapers. He snatched at the note he had just taped to the telephone and started comparing, letter for letter, number for number. As if he could barely read. Or was standing there with a lottery ticket in his hand, one that had just won over a million and he couldn't really believe it was true . . .

An absurd but irritating thought buzzed around inside his head: he wasn't going to get much anatomy revision done that night.

Then he pulled himself together and phoned the police.

The first call came just after half past nine. Münster took it, as Van Veeteren happened to be in the bathroom.

'Excellent,' said Münster. 'Yes, I see. He'll get back to you in five minutes. What's your number?'

He made a note of it, then settled down again with the evening paper. Van Veeteren returned. Münster waited for a few seconds.

'They've got him, up in Schaabe,' he said, in the calmest tone of voice he could manage.

'They've what?' Van Veeteren exclaimed. 'About bloody time.'

'Well, nearly got him,' Münster added. 'You'd better ring back. It was a Detective Chief Inspector Frank. Do you know him?'

Van Veeteren nodded and dialled the number.

'Frank? Van Veeteren here. I'm delighted to hear that a blind chicken can still find a grain of corn . . . What did you say?'

Münster observed his boss over the top of his newspaper.

Van Veeteren was hunched over the telephone and looked as if he were trying to squeeze the murderer out of the receiver. All the time he was chewing away at two toothpicks, and listening.

'I see . . . Make sure you grab him when he comes back, or I'll have you skinned alive. I'm flying to Australia on Thursday, and I need him before then.'

Frank said something, and Van Veeteren nodded slowly.

'All right,' he said. 'I'll stay here. Ring the moment you've got him.'

He hung up.

'You can go home now,' he said to Münster. 'They'll pick him up as soon as he shows at the hotel. He's shaved off all his hair, started wearing glasses and made himself up, it seems. An ingenious bastard. Booked into the Palace Hotel for four nights, a congress for artificial-limb salesmen . . . Have you ever heard anything like it, Münster? Artificial-limb salesmen!'

'How did they find him?'

'Parking offence,' said Van Veeteren with a shrug. 'The deadly sin of our time, no doubt about it.'

When Münster emerged into the raw night air, he realized to his surprise that he wasn't dying to get home: he would have happily stayed up there with the chief inspector and waited. Sat reading his newspaper for a while longer, until the next call came . . .

The last verse.

The signal to indicate that the hunt was over.

Case closed. Murderer captured.

Time for the wheels of justice to start grinding . . .

There were still a few loose ends, it seemed; but even so, the basic facts appeared to be clear. The fax had explained everything, there was no longer scope for alternative theories and solutions. Van Veeteren had been right. As usual. Carl Ferger was their man.

And it was, as somebody had remarked a few weeks ago, a shitty business.

As he drove to the suburb where he lived, Münster thought over what Van Veeteren had said about the determinant. He couldn't quite work out if the chief inspector was being serious or not. However, it couldn't be denied that there was some truth in it, and maybe it was yet again the same old story: the only way of catching the big and most evil players was by trawling with a wide-meshed net aimed at capturing both the serious and the frivolous.

He was momentarily surprised by the wording of that thought, but then it dawned on him that it must be something Reinhart had said.

A wide-meshed net . . .

In any case, he made up his mind to look up 'determinant' in his new and as yet incomplete twenty-four-volume encyclopedia when he got home.

Van Veeteren didn't have to wait for as long as he'd feared. The call from Frank came as early as half past ten.

Ferger had been arrested.

He had strolled into the hotel without a care in the world, and immediately been overpowered by twelve armed police officers.

'Twelve?' wondered Van Veeteren.

'Twelve,' said Frank.

'Has he confessed?'

'No. He's playing silly buggers.'

'OK,' said Van Veeteren. 'Put him in a prison van and shunt him up here tonight. I fancy him for breakfast.'

'Your word is my command,' said Frank. 'How's your

backhand nowadays? I seem to recall that you had a few problems with it when we were in Frigge . . .'

'Lethal,' said Van Veeteren. 'Next time you're in these parts, call in and I'll give you a demonstration.'

43

Münster would never have recognized him.

To be honest, he didn't have a clear recollection of him from the interviews at Bunge, but this shrunken specimen of humanity bore virtually no resemblance to the picture of Ferger that had been broadcast on television and promulgated in the press.

In a way, he looked younger. His totally bald and rounded head gave a dubious impression of innocence. Of naivety. Or perhaps something quite different: advanced senility.

A combination of the two?

He was sitting next to the wall, his hands clasped in front of him on the rickety table. His gaze was lowered. He was probably closing his eyes now and then.

Reinhart and Münster were sitting in front of the opposite wall in the oblong-shaped room. On either side of the door. The chief inspector's chair appeared to have been placed meticulously in the geometrical centre. All Münster could see of him was his back: he was as static as a sphinx for the whole of the interrogation. His questions were spat out as tonelessly as they were contemptuous, as if he knew all the answers in advance, and as if he had no interest at all in the proceedings.

'Do you know why you're here?'

'No.'

'I didn't ask if you were guilty. I asked if you knew why you're here. An appeal for information about you has been featured on radio and television, and in sixty-eight different newspapers, together with your name and a picture. And despite that, you claim that you don't know why you are here. Are you thinking of pleading that you are an idiot, or that you can't read?'

'No. I know why I'm here.'

The voice was faint, but with no trace of unsteadiness.

'Let me make it clear from the very beginning that I have nothing but contempt for you, Mr Ferger. The sight of you arouses no reaction in me but utter disgust. In different circumstances, in a less civilized society than the one we live in, I would have no hesitation in executing you on the spot. Have you understood?'

Ferger swallowed.

'I'm convinced that my feelings are shared not only by my colleagues, but also by more or less everybody who knows what you have done.'

'I'm innocent.'

'Shut up, Mr Ferger. You are sitting here because you are a murderer. You will be charged with the murder of Eva Ringmar on 5 October, of Janek Mitter on 22 November and of Elizabeth Hennan on 30 November. You also killed a four-year-old child on 1 June 1986, but we haven't yet finished accumulating the necessary proof for that murder.'

'It's not true.'

That was a whisper, so faint that Münster could barely hear it. Van Veeteren ignored it.

'If you think that the answers you give will make the slightest difference, let me relieve you of that illusion. You will be found guilty, and you will spend the rest of your life in prison.

I must warn you that there is a possibility that you will be executed . . .'

'What the hell are you saying?'

He was still talking to the table rather than to Van Veeteren.

'– Not as a result of due process of law, of course, but by one of your fellow prisoners. There is a deep-seated contempt for scum like you even inside our prisons. Some very nasty things can happen. I want you to be aware of that, so that you can take whatever precautions might be necessary.'

Ferger squirmed on his chair.

'Nobody will lift a finger to help you. Why don't you want a lawyer?'

'That's my business.'

'There are no volunteers to defend you, of course; but even so, you have a legal right to a lawyer if you want one. The law applies even to the likes of you, Mr Ferger. Why did you kill Liz Hennan?'

'I've never set eyes on her.'

'Was it because you couldn't satisfy her?'

'I've never set eyes on her.'

'Was it because she mocked you for being such an inadequate lover?'

No response.

'Are you frightened of women? Do you think Liz Hennan was a tart?'

Ferger muttered something.

'Was that a "yes"?'

'I've never set eyes on her.'

'Why did she have a photograph of you, then?'

'I've never given her a photograph.'

'But you had a photograph of her.'

'No . . . It . . . You're lying.'

'I'm sorry. I meant to say that you had a photograph of Eva Ringmar. Is that true?'

'Maybe . . . I don't remember.'

'We found it in your flat. Did you have a relationship with Eva Ringmar?'

No response.

'Was Eva Ringmar a tart as well?'

'No. I've no desire to answer any more questions.'

'I've no desire to ask you any, either. Why did you go to the home of Janek Mitter and Eva Ringmar on 4 October?'

No response.

'You went there in the evening, but you went back in the early hours of the morning and murdered Eva Ringmar by drowning her in the bath.'

No response.

'Do you think we don't know who you are?'

'I don't know what you're talking about.'

'What's your alibi for the murder of Janek Mitter?'

'I was at a pizzeria . . .'

'Between eleven and twelve o'clock, yes. But Mitter was murdered after that, in the early hours of the morning. Don't you have a better alibi than that?'

'I returned home and went to sleep. I thought . . .'

'What did you think?'

'Nothing. I'm not going to answer any more of your questions.'

'Why do you think Eva preferred Mitter to you?'

Ferger lowered his head even further and stared down at the table.

'Why did she prefer Andreas Berger?'

He waited for a few seconds.

'Even if you are a shit, Mr Ferger, surely there's no reason for you to be such a stupid shit? You claim that you are innocent, and that you had nothing to do with the murders of Eva Ringmar, Janek Mitter and Liz Hennan. Is that correct?'

'Yes.'

'Then why did you shave off all your hair, make yourself up and go into hiding if you are innocent?'

'I hid myself away because I gathered the police were looking for me.'

'The first Wanted message wasn't broadcast until noon yesterday. You'd already gone into hiding several hours before then.'

'No, I had problems with the car. I'd gone away for the weekend, but I couldn't get back.'

'Where were you?'

'Up north.'

'Where did you spend the night?'

'In a hotel.'

'Name and location.'

'I can't remember.'

'Why didn't you let school know?'

'I tried to ring, but I couldn't get through.'

'If you can't produce better answers than that, Mr Ferger, I suggest that you'd be better off holding your tongue. You're making a fool of yourself.'

Van Veeteren paused.

'Would you like a cigarette?'

'Yes, please.'

Van Veeteren took a pack out of his pocket and shook out a cigarette. Stuck it into his mouth and lit it.

'You're not going to get a cigarette. I've had enough of you.'

He stood up and turned his back on Ferger. Ferger looked up for the first time. It was only for a brief moment, but even so, Münster had time to register the expression in his eyes. He was scared. Completely and absolutely scared stiff.

'Just one more thing,' said Van Veeteren, turning to look at Ferger again. 'What does it feel like, drowning a child? He must have put up a bit of resistance. How long did it take? What do you imagine he was thinking while it happened?'

Ferger was clasping his hands tightly now, and his head was shaking slightly. He said nothing, but Münster wouldn't have been surprised if he'd broken down at that very moment. Flung himself on the floor, or overturned the table, or simply bellowed and howled.

'He's in your hands now,' said Van Veeteren. 'I'll be away for three hours. He mustn't leave this room, he's not to have anything to eat or drink. He's not allowed to smoke. Ask him questions if you like. It's up to you.'

Then he nodded at Reinhart and Münster, and left the room.

The closer he came, the slower he drove.

With only a couple of miles to go, he stopped in a car park. Got out of the car. Stood with his back to the squally wind and smoked a cigarette. He'd almost got used to it now, smoking. He couldn't recall any other case that had induced him to smoke so many cigarettes. Not in recent years, at least.

No doubt there were reasons. But it was all over now, more or less. Just this final dotting of the i. The final pitch-black brush stroke to complete this repulsive painting.

He wondered about how necessary it was. He'd been wondering ever since he set off. Tried to think of ways of getting round it, of avoiding this final step.

Sparing both himself and her this final degradation.

Maybe him as well?

Yes, perhaps even him as well.

But it was all in vain, of course. It was no more than the

usual, familiar reluctance that he was always forced to deal with when he rang the bell and had to inform the wife that unfortunately, her husband . . . Yes, sad to say, he had no choice, he would have to tell her . . .

There was no escape.

No extenuating circumstances.

No way of easing the pain.

He tossed his cigarette into a pool of water and clambered back into the car.

She opened the door almost immediately. She'd been expecting him.

'Good morning,' he said. 'Well, here I am.'

She nodded.

'I take it you've been following the news these last few days?'

'Yes.'

She looked round, as if to check that she hadn't forgotten anything: watering the flowers, or switching off the cooker.

'Are you ready to come with me?'

'Yes, I'm ready.'

Her voice was just as he remembered it. Firm and clear, but flat.

'Can I ask you something?' he said. 'Did you know what the real situation was? Did you know about it, even then?'

'Perhaps we should leave now, Chief Inspector?'

She took her overcoat from the coat hanger, and he helped her on with it. She wrapped a silk shawl round her head, picked up her handbag and gloves from the basket chair and turned to face him.

'I'm ready,' she said.

The journey back was much faster. All the time she sat erect and immobile in the front passenger seat beside him. Hands crossed over her handbag. Staring straight ahead.

She didn't say a word, nor did he. As everything was absolutely clear now, all done and dusted, there was nothing more to say. He understood this, and the silence was never awkward.

Even so, he might have preferred to ask her a question, make an accusation, but he recognized that it would have been impossible.

Don't you see, he'd have liked to ask her, don't you see, that if only you'd told me everything that first time, we could have saved a life? Possibly two.

But he couldn't ask that of her.

Not that she would answer him now, anyway.

Nor that she should have done so then.

When they entered the room, nothing had changed.

Reinhart and Münster were sitting on their chairs, either side of the door. The murderer was hunched over his table in front of the opposite wall. The air felt heavy, possibly slightly sweet: Van Veeteren wondered if a single word had been exchanged here, either.

She took three strides towards him. Stopped behind the chief inspector's chair and rested her hands on the back.

He looked up. His lower jaw started to tremble.

'Rolf?' she said.

There was a trace of happy surprise in her voice, but it was crushed immediately and brutally by the facts of the situation.

Rolf Ringmar collapsed slowly over the table.

44

'I'll be damned if this whole affair isn't a genuine Greek tragedy,' said Van Veeteren, closing the car door. 'There's an inevitability about it from the very beginning. As you know, incest was regarded as one of the worst sins you can possibly commit. Nothing less than a crime against the gods.'

Münster nodded. Backed out of the car park.

'Just imagine it,' said Van Veeteren. 'You're thirteen, fourteen years old. The early stages of puberty. You're sensitive and as vulnerable as an open wound. A boy on the way to becoming a man. The first tentative steps. What's the first thing you identify with?'

'Your father,' said Münster. He's been through this himself, he thought.

'Right. And what does your father do? He drinks like a fish and demeans himself. He hits you. He really beats you up, not just once, but night after night, perhaps. He tortures you, he insults you. Your mother is too weak to intervene. She's as scared of him as you are. You pretend it isn't happening. You keep quiet and let it carry on, keeping it inside the family. You are defenceless. You have no rights: he's your parent and he's fully within his rights. You've nowhere to turn to, nowhere to find consolation – apart from one person. There's only one person who can comfort you . . .'

'Your sister.'

'Who also gets beaten sometimes, but not nearly so often. She is there, she's a bit stronger than you are, a little less wounded. She's there in the room you share when you finally get away from him. Let's say you're fourteen years old, both of you. You lie in bed together, and she consoles you. You snuggle up to her and she protects you. She places her healing hands on your body . . . you're fourteen years old . . . you hold tightly onto each other, you feel safe in each other's arms, and you can hear him ranting and raving. He sets on your mother instead, demands his conjugal rights . . . Hell and damnation, Münster!'

Münster coughed tentatively.

'It's night now and you are naked. You're fourteen, you're brother and sister. There's nothing wrong in what you do, Münster – who the hell is going to blame them for it? Who apart from the gods has the right to condemn these two children for the way things turn out? For becoming lovers? Who, Münster? Who?'

'I don't know,' said Münster.

'Can you understand what she gave him?' said Van Veeteren, taking a deep breath. 'To be able to come to a woman when you are beaten and degraded and worthless . . . To a woman who is your lover, your mother and your sister. All at the same time. Is there any love that could be stronger than that, Münster? Just imagine being in love for the first time, and everything is perfect from the very start . . . That love, that relationship is so strong that it must be more durable than anything else you will ever experience in the rest of your life . . . Hell and damnation, Münster, what chance did he have?'

'How long did that go on for?' Münster asked.

'Two or three years, I'd have thought. He seems to be a bit

vague about exactly when it began. Most likely it was just as strong on both sides for quite a long time. I think Eva eventually managed to escape from it – not because she really wanted to, but because she knew it was wrong. Forbidden. Impossible to keep going.'

'But for him it was just as impossible to stop,' said Münster.

Van Veeteren lit a cigarette.

'Yes, but she rejected him. What went on in that household, both while the father was still alive and afterwards . . . well, I'd rather not think about it, Münster.'

'And then there was Paul Bejsen,' said Munster.

'Yes. Perhaps it was no more than an attempt from her side, I don't think she was really in love with him. She probably took him to demonstrate that what had been was now over and done with, beyond recall. And Rolf, well, he . . .'

'Bided his time,' said Münster.

'You could say that, yes,' said Van Veeteren. 'He waited for an opportunity to show how serious he was. And when that party took place, he saw his chance.'

'He waited out there on the moor,' said Münster.

'Exactly. Wandered around in the darkness hoping for an opportunity. Like a werewolf, almost.'

'Did he tell you all this as well?'

Van Veeteren nodded.

'Yes. Telegram-style, mind you. That was twenty years ago. The statutory limitation time is twenty-one years – in this country it's not possible to charge anybody with a crime twenty-one years or more after it was committed. So we'd be able to prosecute him for that murder as well – if anybody thought there was any point in doing so.'

'And Eva forced him to go away?'

'Yes. She gave him an ultimatum. Either he disappeared or she would turn him in. Put yourself in his situation, Münster.

He has committed murder, not only because he was jealous, but also to demonstrate how strong his love was. And she rejected him. I think he came close to committing suicide during those months, he hinted as much. And during the early part of his exile as well. Perhaps . . .'

'. . . it would have been just as well,' said Münster, finishing the sentence for him.

'Have we any right to think that?' Van Veeteren asked. 'Have we?'

Münster made no reply. Glanced at his watch. A quarter to six.

'What time does the plane leave? Half past seven?'

Van Veeteren nodded.

'I have to check in an hour in advance.'

'We'll be there in twenty minutes.'

Neither of them spoke for a few seconds, but Münster could sense that they needed to go through everything.

'What about this Ellen Caine?' he said.

'Ah, yes,' said Van Veeteren. 'He got by for eight years – pretty remarkable, that, to say the least, but he got a grip of himself. Settled down in Toronto, drifted from one job to another, but kept himself afloat. Until he met a woman. He claims she was the one who went running after him, rather than the other way round, and that's probably right. In any case, she was unable to give him a fraction of what he received from Eva. God only knows what goes through his mind when it comes to sex and women, Münster. But he demands the impossible, because he has experienced the impossible. Then he killed Ellen Caine because she let him down. I don't know if she left him, he didn't want to speak about that. Perhaps he couldn't cope with being a lover, perhaps there was an element of good old honest jealousy involved. Anyway, he killed her. Threw her off a viaduct in the path of a long-distance lorry. It never occurred to anybody that it was anything but an accident, or possibly suicide. Nobody knew he was anywhere in the vicinity.'

'Why did he change his name?'

'I think he'd started to think about coming back to Europe with a new identity. As early as that, after the Ellen business. 1980 or thereabouts. He moved to New York in any case, became an American citizen after a few years and changed his name to Carl Ferger. He seems to have led a more or less normal life. Superficially, at least. But nevertheless, it's a riddle, Münster. What made him come back here in January 1986? Not even he can give an explanation.'

'The determinant, perhaps?' said Münster with a faint smile.

'What?' exclaimed Van Veeteren in surprise. 'God almighty, I do believe Inspector Münster has begun to catch on to a few things! Whatever, he came back here, tracked down Eva, and started pestering her. In every possible way, no doubt. Presumably the very fact of suddenly being in her vicinity became more or less unbearable for him. That's what he says, at least. Naturally, he was extremely jealous of Berger; but the worst thing was the child. The fact that she'd had a child with somebody else. Ah well, everything is in a hell of a mess now, Münster.'

'So he kills the child in order to punish her?'

'Yes, I think so. His concept of his ego seems to oscillate between an all-powerful god of retribution, and a desperate young boy trying to cope with puberty and a lack of identity.'

'What about after that murder?'

'Eva protected him again, despite the fact that she was starting to go out of her mind herself. I think this is the point when she gave up on her life, when she realized that nothing could ever be normal. Maybe she also recognized that the bond between her and Rolf was stronger than she had imagined. Sexually as well. They resumed their forbidden relationship several times over those years. He lived in France – she didn't want to have him too close – but she occasionally paid him a visit. That's what he says, at least. Perhaps he imagined that everything would turn out as he wanted in the end, perhaps she breathed life back into his hopes.'

'But instead, she discarded him again.'

Van Veeteren nodded.

'She moved here. A new beginning. Maybe she didn't tell him where she'd gone, but he tracked her down, of course. He even managed to get a job at the same school eventually. It must have been a nasty shock for her when the headmaster introduced the new school caretaker.'

'Was that this year?'

'Yes, in January. The beginning of term after the Christmas holidays.'

'And so she married Mitter just to show him the way things stood?'

Van Veeteren sighed.

'Yes, could be. Perhaps she was just as mad as he was. I had the impression from Mitter that their relationship was something that exceeded his comprehension. That their love-making was a matter of life or death all the time. Well, something along those lines, I think.'

'Why did he kill her instead of Mitter?'

'I think it was an impulse, something he did on the spur of the moment. Possibly an attempt to get rid of the awful circumstances once and for all. Whatever, it was all a series of accidents, pure chance. The fact that Mitter was so drunk that he lost his memory was not something Ferger had anticipated, of course. He'd expected Mitter to say that Ferger had been with them earlier that evening, but was confident that there was nothing to indicate that he'd returned later and murdered her. He must have wondered why on earth he heard nothing from the police.'

Van Veeteren shook his head.

'Six murders,' he said. 'I thought there were four, or possibly five. But there were six.'

He paused, and gazed out of the window into the darkness.

'What do you think it is,' he asked, 'that makes his mother want to keep on living? Why the hell doesn't she take her own life? Or just lie down and die?'

Münster thought for a moment.

'Hamlet? Too scared?'

'No. You've met her.'

'Is she religious?'

Van Veeteren couldn't help laughing.

'What sort of a god would allow your husband to mistreat and degrade you, your children to indulge in incest, your son to murder your daughter . . .'

Münster hesitated.

'I don't know. Perhaps she is punishing herself – by carrying on living, I mean.'

Van Veeteren turned to look at Münster.

'Excellent,' he said in surprise. 'Well done, Münster! I shall have to remember not to underestimate you in future.'

'Thank you,' said Münster. 'We're nearly at the airport. There was just one more thing.'

'Well?'

'I'd be grateful if you could send a card, sir. For the sake of the stamp. My boy has started collecting stamps . . .'

'Of course,' said Van Veeteren.

Münster parked the car and took out the bags.

'So, I'll see you in January,' said Van Veeteren.

'The end of January,' said Münster. 'I'm taking two weeks holiday after New Year.'

'Good for you, Münster! Where are you going?'

'The Maldives,' said Münster, smiling modestly.

'Excellent, Münster,' said Van Veeteren, shaking his hand. 'But keep in form. I'm not going to be easy to handle when I get back.'

'I know,' said Münster.

45

The woman grabbed him by the arm.

'What now, for Christ's sake?' Ingrun thought. He had just sat down and lit a cigarette. Why could they never leave him in peace?

'What do you want?' he said, trying to shake his arm free. Her nails were digging into him.

'Luke, chapter 15, verse 11!' she hissed.

'Eh?'

'Luke, 15:11! I was going to read the Bible, and found that somebody's been scribbling in it!'

He saw that she was holding a Bible in her other hand. Brandishing it, with a bony index finger stuck inside it.

'Let me see!'

She let go of his arm. Opened the Bible and handed it to him. Right across one of the pages was written in large, bold letters:

Carl Ferger.

'God will never forgive that!' she cried in anguish, wringing her hands.

Ingrun hesitated for a moment. Then he tore out the page and threw it into the waste-paper basket.

'Read something else!' he said, closing the Bible.

Håkan Nesser's next novel,

Woman with Birthmark,

will be available in Macmillan
hardback in May 2009.

For an exclusive sneak peek, read on . . .

7

He could have sworn that he'd disconnected the phone before going to bed, but what was the point of swearing? The telephone – that invention of the devil – was ensconced on his bedside table and was intent on etching its blood-soaked sound waves onto his cerebral cortex.

Or however you might prefer to express it.

He opened one reluctant eye and glared at the confounded contraption in a vain attempt to shut it up. It kept on ringing even so. Ring after ring carved its way through his dawn-grey bedroom.

He opened another eye. The clock on the aforementioned table indicated 07.55. Who in hell's name had the cheek to wake him up on a Saturday morning when he wasn't on duty, he wondered. Who?

In January.

If there was a month he hated, it was January – it went on and on for ever and ever with rain or snow all day long, and a grand total of half an hour's sunshine.

There was only one sane way of occupying oneself at this lugubrious time of year: sleeping. Full stop.

He stretched out his left hand and lifted the receiver.

'Van Veeteren.'

'Good morning, Chief Inspector.'

It was Reinhart.

'Why the flaming hell are you ringing to wake me up at half past five on a Saturday morning? Are you out of your mind?'

But Reinhart sounded just as incorruptible as a traffic warden.

'It's eight o'clock. If you don't want to be contacted, and refuse to buy an answering machine, you can always pull out the plug. If you'd like to listen, Chief Inspector, I can explain how you . . .'

'Shut up, Inspector! Come to the point instead!'

'By all means,' said Reinhart. 'Dead body in Leufwens Allé. Stinks of murder. One Ryszard Malik. The briefing's at three o'clock.'

'Three?'

'Yes, three o'clock. What do you mean?'

'I can get from here to the police station in twenty minutes. You could have phoned me at twelve.'

Reinhart yawned.

'I was thinking of going to bed for a bit. I've just left there. Been at it since half past one . . . I thought you might like to go there and have a look for yourself?'

Van Veeteren leant on his elbow and raised himself to a half-sitting position. Tried to see out through the window.

'What's the weather like?'

'Pouring down, and windy. Fifteen metres a second, or thereabouts.'

'Excellent. I'll stay at home. I suppose I might turn up at three, unless my horoscope advises me not to . . . Who's in charge now?'

'Heinemann and Jung. But Jung hasn't slept for two nights, so he'll probably need a bit of rest soon.'

'Any clues?'

'No.'

'How did it happen?'

'Shot. But the briefing is at three o'clock, not now. I think it's a pretty peculiar set-up. That's why I rang. The address is Leufwens Allé 14, in case you change your mind.'

'Fat chance,' said Van Veeteren, and hung up.

Needless to say it was impossible to go back to sleep. He gave up at a quarter to nine and went to lie down in the bath instead. Lay there in the half-light and thought back to the previous evening he'd spent at the Mephisto restaurant with Renate and Erich.

The former wife and the lost son. (Who had still not returned and didn't seem to have any intention of doing so either.) It had been one of Renate's recurrent attempts to rehabilitate her guilty conscience and the family that had never existed, and the result was just as unsuccessful as one might have expected. The conversation had been like walking on thin ice over dark waters. Erich had left them half-way through the dessert, giving as an excuse an important meeting with a lady. Then they had sat there, ex-husband and ex-wife, over a cheeseboard of doubtful quality, going through agonies as they tried to avoid hurting each other any more than necessary. He had seen her into a taxi shortly after midnight and walked all the way home in the pious hope that the biting wind would whip his brain free from all the murky thoughts lurking inside it.

That had failed completely. When he got home he slumped into an armchair and listened to Monteverdi for an hour, drank three beers and had not gone to bed until nearly half past one.

A wasted evening, in other words. But typical, that was for

sure. Very typical. Mind you, it was January. What else could he have expected?

He got out of the bath. Did a couple of tentative back exercises in front of the bedroom mirror. Dressed, and made breakfast.

Sat down at the kitchen table with the morning paper spread out in front of him. Not a word about the murder. Naturally enough. It must have happened as the presses were rolling . . . Or whatever the presses did nowadays. What was the name of the victim? Malik?

What had Reinhart said? Leufwens Allé? He had a good mind to phone the inspector and ask a few questions, but pricks of conscience from his better self, or whatever it might have been, got the upper hand, and he desisted. He would find out all he needed to know soon enough. No need to hurry. Better to make the most of the hours remaining before the whole thing got under way, perhaps. There hadn't been a murder since the beginning of December, despite all the holidays, and if it really was as Reinhart said, an awkward-looking case, no doubt they would have their hands full for some time to come. Reinhart generally knew what he was talking about. More than most of them.

He poured himself another cup of coffee, and started studying the week's chess problem. Mate in three moves, which would presumably involve a few complications.

'All right,' said Reinhart, putting down his pipe. 'The facts of the case. At six minutes past one this morning, an ambulance driver, Felix Hald, reported that there was a dead body at Leufwens Allé 14. They'd gone there because the woman of the house, Ilse Malik, had phoned for an ambulance. She was extremely confused, and had failed to contact the police even though her husband was as dead as a statue . . . Four bullet wounds, two in his chest, two under the belt.'

'Under the belt?' wondered Inspector Rooth, his mouth full of sandwich.

'Under the belt,' said Reinhart. 'Through his willy, if you prefer that. She'd come home from the theatre, it seems, at round about midnight or shortly before, and found him lying in the hall. Just inside the door. The weapon seems to be a Berenger-75, all four bullets have been recovered. It seems reasonable to suspect that a silencer was used, since nobody heard anything. The victim is fifty-two years old, one Ryszard Malik. Part owner of a firm selling equipment for industrial kitchens and restaurants, or something of the sort. Not in our records, unknown to us, no shady dealing as far as we are aware. Nothing at all. Hmm, is that it, Heinemann, more or less?'

Inspector Heinemann took off his glasses and started rubbing them on his tie.

'Nobody noticed a thing,' he said. 'We've spoken to the neighbours, but the house is pretty well protected. Hedges, big gardens, that sort of thing. It looks as if somebody simply walked up to the door, rang the bell, and shot him when he opened up. There's no sign of a struggle or anything. Malik was alone at home, solving a crossword and sipping a glass of whisky while his wife was at the theatre. And then, it seems the murderer just closed the door and strolled off. Quite straightforward, if you want to look at it from that point of view.'

'Sound method,' said Rooth.

'That's for sure,' said Van Veeteren. 'What does his wife have to say?'

Heinemann sighed. Nodded towards Jung, who gave every sign of finding it difficult to stay awake.

'Not a lot,' Jung said. 'It's almost impossible to get through to her. One of the ambulance men gave her an injection, and that was probably just as well. She woke up briefly this morning. Went on about Ibsen – I gather that's a writer. She'd been to the theatre, we managed to get that confirmed by a woman she'd been with . . . A Bernadette Kooning. In any case, she can't seem to grasp that her husband is dead.'

'You don't seem to be quite with it either,' said Van Veeteren. 'How long have you been awake?'

Jung counted on his fingers.

'A few days, I suppose.'

'Go home and go to bed,' said Reinhart.

Jung stood up.

'Is it OK if I take a taxi? I can't tell the difference between right and left.'

'Of course,' said Reinhart. 'Take two if you need them. Or ask one of the duty officers to drive you.'

'Two?' said Jung as he staggered to the door. 'No, one will do.'

Nobody spoke for a while. Heinemann tried to smooth down the creases in his tie. Reinhart contemplated his pipe. Van Veeteren inserted a toothpick between his lower front teeth and gazed up at the ceiling.

'Hmm,' he said eventually. 'Quite a story, one has to say. Has Hiller been informed?'

'He's away by the seaside,' said Reinhart.

'In January?'

'I don't think he intends to go swimming. I've left a message for him in any case. There'll be a press conference at five o'clock; I think it would be best if you take it.'

'Thank you,' said Van Veeteren. 'I'll only need thirty seconds.'

He looked round.

'Not much point in allocating much in the way of resources yet,' he decided. 'When do they say his wife is likely to come round? Where is she, incidentally?'

'The New Rumford hospital,' said Heinemann. 'She should be able to talk this afternoon. Moreno's there, waiting.'

'Good,' said Van Veeteren. 'What about family and friends?'

'A son at university in Munich,' said Reinhart. 'He's on his way here. That's about all. Malik has no brothers or sisters, and his parents are dead. Ilse Malik has a sister. She's also waiting at the Rumford.'

'Waiting for what, you might ask?' said Rooth.

'Very true,' said Van Veeteren. 'May I ask another question, gentlemen?'

'Please do,' said Reinhart.

'Why?' said Van Veeteren, taking out the toothpick.

'I've also been thinking about that,' said Reinhart. 'I'll get back to you when I've finished.'

'We can always hope that somebody will turn himself in,' said Rooth.

'Hope lives eternal,' said Reinhart.

Van Veeteren yawned. It was sixteen minutes past three on Saturday, 20 January. The first run-through of the Ryszard Malik case was over.

Münster parked outside the New Rumford hospital and jogged through the rain to the entrance. A woman in reception dragged herself away from her crochet work and sent him up to the fourth floor, ward 42; after explaining why he was there and producing his ID, he was escorted to a small, dirt-yellow waiting room with plastic furniture and eye-catching travel posters on the walls. It was evidently the intention to give people the opportunity of dreaming that they were somewhere else. Not a bad idea, Münster thought.

There were two women sitting in the room. The younger one, and by a large margin the more attractive of the two, with a mop of chestnut-brown hair and a book in her lap, was Detective Inspector Ewa Moreno. She welcomed him with a nod and an encouraging smile. The other one, a thin and slightly hunchbacked woman in her fifties, wearing glasses that concealed half her face, was fumbling nervously inside her black handbag. He deduced that she must be Marlene Winther, the sister of the woman who had just been widowed. He went up to her and introduced himself.

'Münster, Detective Inspector.'

She shook his hand without standing up.

'I realize that this must be difficult for you. Please understand that we are obliged to intrude upon your grief and ask some questions.'

'The lady has already explained.'

She glanced in the direction of Moreno. Münster nodded.

'Has she come round yet?'

Moreno cleared her throat and put down her book.

'She's conscious, but the doctor wants a bit of time with her first. Perhaps we should . . . ?'

Münster nodded again: they both went out into the corridor, leaving Mrs Winther on her own.

'In deep shock, it seems,' Moreno explained when they had found a discreet corner. 'They're even worried about her mental state. She's had trouble with her nerves before, and all this hasn't helped, of course. She's been undergoing treatment for various problems.'

'Have you interviewed her sister?'

Moreno nodded.

'Yes, of course. She doesn't seem all that strong either. We're going to have to tiptoe through the tulips.'

'Hostile?'

'No, not really. Just a touch of the big sister syndrome. She's used to looking after little sister, it seems. And she's evidently allowed to.'

'But you haven't spoken to her yet? Mrs Malik, I mean.'

'No. Jung and Heinemann had a go this morning, but they didn't seem to get anywhere.'

Münster thought for a moment.

'Perhaps she doesn't have all that much to tell?'

'No, presumably not. Would you like me to take her on? We'll be allowed in shortly in any case.'

Münster was only too pleased to agree.

'No doubt it would be best for her to talk to a woman. I'll stay in the wings for the time being.'

Forty-five minutes later they left the hospital together. Sat down in Münster's car, where Moreno took out her notebook and started going through the rather meagre results of her meeting with Ilse Malik. Münster had spoken to Dr Hübner – an old, white-haired doctor who seemed to have seen more or less everything – and understood that it would probably be several days before the patient could be allowed to undergo more vigorous questioning. Always assuming that would be necessary, that is.

Hübner had called it a state of deep shock. Very strong medicines to begin with, then a gradual reduction. Unable to accept what had happened. Encapsulation.

Not surprising in the circumstances, Münster thought.

'What did she actually say?' he asked.

'Not a lot,' said Moreno with a sigh. 'A happy marriage,

she claimed. Malik stayed at home yesterday evening while she went to see *A Doll's House* at the Little Theatre. Left home at about half past six, drank a glass of wine with that friend of hers afterwards. Took a taxi home. Then she starts rambling. Her husband had been shot and lay in the hall, she says. She tried to help him but could see that it was serious, so she called an ambulance. She must have delayed that for getting on for an hour, if I understand the situation rightly. Fell asleep and managed to injure herself as well. She thinks her husband is in this same hospital and wonders why she's not allowed to see him . . . It's a bit hard to know how to handle her: the nurse tried to indicate what had happened, but she didn't want to know. Started speaking about something else instead.'

'What?'

'Anything and everything. The play – a fantastic production, it seems. Her son. He hasn't time to come because of his studies, she says. He's training to be a banking lawyer, or something of the sort.'

'He's supposed to be arriving about an hour from now,' said Münster. 'Poor bastard. I suppose the doc had better take a look at him as well.'

Moreno nodded.

'He'll be staying with his aunt for the time being. We can talk to him tomorrow.'

Münster thought for a moment.

'Did you get any indications of a threat, or enemies, or that kind of thing?'

'No. I tried to discuss such matters, but I didn't get anywhere. I asked her sister, but she had no suspicions at all. Doesn't seem to hiding anything either. Well, what do we do next, then?'

Münster shrugged.

'I suppose we'd better discuss it on Monday with the others. It's a damned horrific business, no matter which way you look at it. Can I drive you anywhere?'

'Home, please,' said Ewa Moreno. 'I've been hanging around here for seven hours now. It's time to spend a bit of time thinking about something else.'

'Not a bad idea,' Münster agreed, and started the engine.

Mauritz Wolff opted to be interviewed at home, a flat in the canal district with views over Langgraacht and Megsje Bois and deserving the description 'gigantic'. The rooms were teeming with children of all ages, and Reinhart assumed he must have married late in life – several times, perhaps – as he must surely be well into his fifties. A large and somewhat red-faced man, in any case, with a natural smile that found it difficult not to illuminate his face, even in a situation like this one.

'You're very welcome,' he said. 'What an awful catastrophe. I'm really shocked, I have to say. I can't take it in.'

He shooed away a little girl clinging on to his trouser leg. Reinhart looked round. Wondered if a woman ought to put in an appearance from somewhere or other before long.

'Not a bad flat you have here,' he said. 'Is there anywhere we can talk in peace and quiet?'

'Follow me,' said Wolff, clearing a way through a corridor to a room that evidently served as a library and study. He closed the door and locked it. Invited Reinhart to sit down on one of the two armchairs by a low smoking table, and sat down heavily in the other one.

'Too awful,' he said again. 'Have you any idea about who might have done it?'

Reinhart shook his head.

'Have you?'

'Not the remotest.'

'Did you know him well?'

'Inside out,' said Wolff, holding out a pack of cigarettes. Reinhart took one. 'Would you like anything to drink, by the way?'

'No thank you. Go on!'

'Well, what can I say? We've worked together for sixteen years. Ever since we started the firm. And we knew each other before that.'

'Did you mix privately as well?'

'Do you mean families and so on?'

'Yes.'

'Well, not really. Not since I met Mette, my new wife, at least. It must be absolutely awful for Ilse. How is she? I've tried to call her . . .'

'Shocked,' said Reinhart. 'She's still in hospital.'

'I understand,' said Wolff, and tried to look diplomatic. Reinhart waited.

'She can be a bit nervy,' Wolff explained.

'I've heard it said, yes,' said Reinhart. 'How's the firm going?'

'So-so. We're keeping going. A good niche, even if it went better in the eighties. But what the hell didn't?'

He started laughing, then checked himself.

'Can it have something to do with work?' Reinhart asked. 'The firm, I mean?'

The question was badly formulated, and Wolff didn't understand it.

'Can the murder of Malik have some connection with your business?' Reinhart spelled it out.

Wolff shook his head uncomprehendingly.

'With us? No, how could that have been?'

'What do you think it could be, then? Did he have a mistress? Any dodgy business deals? You knew him better than anybody else.'

Wolff scratched the back of his head.

'No,' he said after a while. 'Neither of those things. If Malik had been seeing other women I'd have known about it. And I can't imagine him being involved in anything illegal.'

'So he's a model of virtue then,' Reinhart established. 'How long have you known him, did you say?'

Wolff tried to work it out.

'We met for the first time about twenty-five years ago . . . that was through work as well. We were both with Gündler and Wein, and eventually we pulled out and started up on our own. There were three of us to start with, but one left after six months.'

'What was his name?'

'Merrinck. Jan Merrinck.'

Reinhart made a note.

'Can you remember if anything unusual has happened recently? If Malik behaved oddly in some way or other?'

Wolff thought it over.

'No. No, there hasn't been anything as far as I can recall. I'm sorry, but there doesn't seem to be all that much I can help you with.'

Reinhart changed track.

'What was his marriage like?'

'Malik's?'

'Yes.'

Wolff shrugged.

'Not all that good. But he hung in there. My first was worse, I reckon. Malik was strong. A confident and reliable man. A bit dry, perhaps. My God, I can't understand who could have done this, Inspector. It must be a madman, don't you think? Some lunatic? Have you got a suspect?'

Reinhart ignored the question.

'What time did he leave the office yesterday?'

'A quarter to five,' answered Wolff without hesitation. 'A bit earlier than usual as he had to collect his car from a repair workshop. I stayed there on my own until half past five.'

'And he didn't behave unusually in any way?'

'No. I've said that already.'

'This Rachel deWijs who works for you. What have you to say about her?'

'Rachel? A treasure. Pure gold, through and through. Without her we wouldn't survive for more than six months . . .' He bit his lip and drew at his cigarette. 'But everything has changed now, of course. Bloody hell.'

'So Malik didn't have anything going with her, then?'

'Malik and Rachel? No, you can bet your life that he didn't.'

'Really?' said Reinhart. 'OK, I'll take you at your word. What about you yourself? Did you have any reason to want him out of the way?'

Wolff's jaw dropped.

'That was the most fucking . . .'

'There, there, don't get over-excited. You must realize that I have to ask that question. Malik has been murdered, and the fact is that most victims are killed by somebody they know. And you are the person who knew him best; I thought we'd agreed on that already?'

'He was my business partner, for Christ's sake. One of my best friends . . .'

'I know. But if you had a motive even so, it's better for you to tell us what it is yourself rather than leaving us to find out about it later.'

Wolff sat in silence for a while, thinking about that one.

'No,' he said eventually. 'Why the hell should I want to kill Malik? His share in the firm goes to Ilse and Jacob, and all that will do is to make a mess of everything. You must understand that his death is a shock for me as well, Inspector. I know I sometimes sound a bit brusque, but I'm grieving over his death. I'm missing him as a close friend.'

Reinhart nodded.

'I understand,' he said. 'I think we'll leave it at that for today, but you'll have to reckon with us turning up again before long. We are very keen to catch whoever did this.'

Wolff stood up and flung out his arms.

'Of course. If there's anything I can do to help . . . I'm at your disposal at any time.'

'Good,' said Reinhart. 'If anything occurs to you, let us know. Go back to the kids now. How many have you got, incidentally?'

'Six,' said Wolff. 'Three from before and three new ones.'

'Go forth and multiply, and replenish the earth,' said Reinhart. 'Isn't it a bit of a strain? Er, looking after them all, I mean.'

Wolff smiled and shook his head.

'Not at all. The tipping point is four. After that, it makes no difference if you have seven or seventeen.'

Reinhart nodded, and resolved to bear that in mind.

8

In their eagerness to sell a few extra copies to casual readers with nothing better to do at the weekend, the Sunday papers made a meal of the Ryszard Malik murder. Bold-print headlines on billboards and front pages, pictures of the victim (while still alive, smiling) and his house, and a double-page spread in both *Neuwe Blatt* and *Telegraaf*. Detailed and non-committal, but needless to say it was pitched about right – what the hell did people have to keep them occupied on a damp and windy day in January apart from sitting indoors and lapping up the story of somebody who had suffered even more than they were doing?

Van Veeteren had a subscription to both papers and had no need to stick his nose outside the door in order to buy one. Instead he stayed in all day, reading selected chapters of Rimley's *Famous Chess Games* and listening to Bach. He had paid a brief visit to Leufwens Allé on the Saturday evening and established that there was nothing useful for him to do there. The technicians and crime-scene boys had run a fine-toothed comb over both house and garden, and for him to imagine he would be able to find something they'd missed would be to overestimate his abilities. Although it had happened before.

And in any case, it was not even certain that he would need to bother about it. Hiller would no doubt decide when he emerged from the sea on Monday morning; perhaps he would judge it best for Reinhart and Münster to continue pulling the strings. That would be good, he had to admit. A blessing devoutly to be wished, he thought – if he'd been able to choose a month in which to hibernate or to spend in a deep-freeze, he would have gone for January without hesitation.

If he could pick two, he would take February as well.

On Monday his car refused to start. Something to do with damp somewhere or other, no doubt. He was forced to walk four blocks before he was able to scramble into a taxi, soaking wet through, at Rejmer Plejn; and he was ten minutes late for the run-through.

Reinhart, who was in charge, arrived a minute later, and the whole meeting was not exactly productive.

The forensic side was done and dusted, and had uncovered nothing they didn't know already. Or thought they knew. Ryszard Malik had been shot at some time between half past seven and half past nine on the Friday evening, with a 7.65 millimetre Berenger. As none of the neighbours had heard a shot, it could be assumed that the killer had used a silencer.

'How many Berengers are floating around town?' asked Münster.

'Le Houde guesses about fifty,' said Rooth. 'Anybody can get one in about half an hour if he has a bit of local knowledge. There's no point in starting to look, in any case.'

Van Veeteren sneezed and Reinhart carried on describing the wounds, the angles and similar melancholy details. The murderer had probably fired his gun at a distance of between one and one and a half metres, which could suggest that he hadn't even bothered to step inside first. The door opened inwards, and in all probability he'd have been standing ready to shoot the moment Malik opened it. Two shots in the chest, then, each of them would have been fatal, one through the left lung and the other through the aorta – hence the unusually large amount of blood.

And then two under the belt. From a bit closer.

'Why?' asked Van Veeteren.

'Well, what do you think?' said Reinhart, looking round the table.

Nobody spoke. Heinemann looked down at his crotch.

'A professional job?' asked Münster.

'Eh?' said Reinhart. 'Oh, you mean the fatal shots . . . No, not necessarily. A ten-year-old can shoot accurately with a Berenger from one metre away. Assuming you're ready for a bit of a recoil, that is. It could be anybody. But the shots under the belt ought to tell us something, or what do you think?'

'Yes, sure,' said Rooth.

Nobody spoke for a few seconds.

'Don't feel embarrassed on my account,' said Moreno.

'Could be a coincidence,' said Münster.

'There's no such thing as coincidence,' said Reinhart. 'Only a lack of knowledge.'

'So the shots in the chest came first, is that right?' Heinemann asked, frowning.

'Yes, yes,' sighed Reinhart. 'The other two were fired when he was already lying on the floor – we've explained that already. Weren't you listening?'

'I just wanted to check,' said Heinemann.

'It doesn't seem to make much sense, shooting somebody's balls off after you've already killed him,' said Rooth. 'Seems a bit mad, I'd say. Sick, in a way.'

Reinhart nodded and Van Veeteren sneezed again.

'Are you cold, Chief Inspector?' Reinhart wondered. 'Shall we ring for a blanket?'

'I'd prefer a hot toddy,' grunted Van Veeteren. 'Is the forensic stuff all finished? I take it they didn't find any fingerprints or dropped cigarette butts?'

'Not even a grain of dandruff,' said Reinhart. 'Shall we run through the interviews instead? Starting with the widow?'

'No, starting with the victim,' said Van Veeteren. 'Even though I assume he didn't have much to say for himself.'

'I beg your pardon,' said Reinhart, producing a loose sheet of paper from his notebook. 'Let's see now . . . Ryszard Malik was fifty-two years of age. Born in Chadów, but has lived in Maardam since 1960 or thereabouts. Studied at the School of Commerce. Got a job with Gündler and Wein in 1966. In 1979 he started his own firm together with Mauritz Wolff and Jan Merrinck, who jumped ship quite early on – Merrinck, that is. Aluvit F/B, and for God's sake don't ask me what that means. Malik married Ilse, née Moener, in 1968. One son, Jacob, born 1972. He's been reading jurisprudence and economics in Munich for several years now. Anyway, that's about it . . .'

He put the sheet of paper back where it came from.

'Anything off the record?' Rooth wondered.

'Not a dickie bird,' said Reinhart. 'So far, at least. He seems to have been a bit of a bore, as far as I can see. Boring marriage, boring job, boring life. Goes on holiday to Blankenbirge or Rhodes. No known interests apart from crossword puzzles and detective novels, preferably bad ones . . . God only knows why anybody should want to kill him, but apart from that I don't think there are any unanswered questions.'

'Excellent,' said Van Veeteren. 'What about the widow? Surely there's a bit more substance to her, at least?'

Münster shrugged.

'We haven't been able to get much out of her,' he said. 'She's still confused and doesn't want to accept what's happened.'

'She might be hiding something, though,' said Heinemann. 'It's not exactly anything new to pretend to be mad. I recall a Danish prince—'

'I don't think she is,' interrupted Münster. 'Neither do the doctors. We know quite a lot about her from her sister and her son, but it doesn't seem to have anything much to do with the murder. A bit pitiful, that's all. Bad nerves. Prescribed drugs on and off. Taken in for therapy once or twice. Finds it hard to get on with people, it seems. Stopped working at Konger's Palace for that reason, although nobody has said that in so many words . . . As far as we can see Malik's firm produces enough cash to keep the family going. Or has done until now, I should say.'

Van Veeteren bit off the end of a toothpick.

'All this is more miserable than the weather,' he said, spitting out a few fragments. 'Has Moreno anything to add?'

Ewa Moreno smiled slightly.

'The son is rather charming, actually,' she said. 'In view of the circumstances, that is. He flew the nest early, it seems. Left home as soon as he'd finished secondary school and he doesn't have much contact with his parents, especially his mother. Only when he needs some money, or something similar. He admits that openly. Do you want to know about the sister as well?'

'Is there anything for us to get our teeth into?' asked Reinhart with a sigh.

'No,' said Moreno. 'Not really. She also has a stable but rather boring marriage. Works part-time in an old people's home. Her husband's a businessman. They both have alibis for the night of the murder, and it seems pretty unlikely that either of them could be involved – completely unthinkable, in fact.'

All was quiet for a while. Rooth produced a bar of chocolate from his jacket pocket and Heinemann tried to scrape a stain off the table with his thumbnail. Van Veeteren had closed his eyes, and it was more or less impossible to make out if he was awake or asleep.

'OK,' said Reinhart eventually. 'There's just one thing I want to know. Who the hell did it?'

'A madman,' said Rooth. 'Somebody who wanted to test his Berenger and noticed that the lights were on in the house.'

'I reckon you've hit the nail on the head,' said Heinemann.

'No,' said Van Veeteren without opening his eyes.

'Oh, really?' said Reinhart. 'How do you know that?'

'By the prickings of my thumb,' said Van Veeteren.

'Eh?' said Heinemann. 'What the hell does that mean?'

'Shall we go and get some coffee?' suggested Rooth.

Van Veeteren opened his eyes.

'Preferably a hot toddy, as I said before.'

Reinhart checked the time.

'It's only eleven,' he said. 'But I'm all for it. This case stinks like a shit heap.'

On the way home from the police station that gloomy Monday, Reinhart stopped off at the Merckx shopping centre out at Bossingen. It was really against his principles to buy anything in such a temple of commerce, but he decided to turn a blind eye to the crassness of it all today. He simply didn't feel up to running around from one little shop to the next in the centre of town, after rooting about in the unsavoury details of Ryszard Malik's background.

Half an hour later he had acquired a lobster, two bottles of wine and eleven roses. Plus a few other goodies. That would have to do. He left the inferno and a quarter of an hour later went through the front door of his flat in Zuyderstraat. Put away his purchases in their appointed places, then made a phone call.

'Hi. I've got a lobster, some wine and some roses. You can have them all if you get yourself here within the next hour.'

'But it's Monday today,' said the woman at the other end.

'If we don't do anything about it, it'll be Monday for the rest of our lives,' said Reinhart.

'OK,' said the woman. 'I'll be there.'

Winnifred Lynch was a quarter Aboriginal, born in Perth, Australia, but grew up in England. After a degree in English language and literature at Cambridge and a failed and childless marriage, she'd landed a post as guest lecturer at Maardam University. When she met Reinhart at the Vox jazz club in the middle of November, she'd just celebrated her thirty-ninth birthday. Reinhart was forty-nine. He went home with her, and they made love (with the occasional pause) for the next four days and nights – but unusually (to the surprise of both of them, given their previous experience) it didn't end there. They carried on meeting. All over the place: at concerts, restaurants, cinemas and above all, of course, in bed. As soon as the beginning of December it was clear to Reinhart that there was something special about this slightly brown-skinned, intelligent woman, and when she went back to England for the Christmas holiday he felt withdrawal symptoms, the like of which he hadn't experienced for nearly thirty years. A sudden reminder of what it was like to miss somebody. Of the fact that somebody actually meant something to him.

The feeling scared him stiff, no doubt about that; it was a warning, but when she came back after three weeks he couldn't help but go to meet her at the airport. Stood waiting with a bunch of roses and a warm embrace, and of course it started all over again.

This Monday was the fifth – or was it the sixth? – occasion since then, and when he thought about it he realized that it could hardly have been more than ten days since the last time.

So you could bet your life that he'd got something special going.

'Why did you become a policeman?' she asked as they lay back in bed afterwards. 'You promised you'd tell me one day.'

'A trauma,' he said after a moment's thought.

'I'm human, you know,' she said.

'What do you mean by that?'

She didn't answer, but after a while he imagined that he understood.

'All right,' he said. 'It was a woman. Or a girl. Twenty years old.'

'What happened?'

He hesitated, and inhaled deeply twice on his cigarette before answering.

'I was twenty-one. Reading philosophy and anthropology at the university, as you know. We'd been together for two years. We were going to get married. She was reading languages. One night she was going home after a lecture and was stabbed by a lunatic in Wollerim's Park. She died in hospital before I got there. It took the police six months to find her killer. I was one of them by that time.'

If she has the good sense to say nothing, I want to spend the rest of my life with her, he thought out of the blue.

Winnifred Lynch put her hand on his chest. Stroked him gently for a few seconds, then got up and went to the bathroom.

That does it then, Reinhart acknowledged in surprise.

Later on, when they'd made love again and then recovered, he couldn't resist asking her a question.

'What do you have to say about a murderer who fired two shots under the belt of a victim who's already lying dead?'

She thought for a moment.

'The victim's a man, I take it?'

'Yes.'

'Then I think the murderer is a woman.'

Well, I'll be damned, Reinhart thought.